FONDUE
OR
DIE

A Cheese Shop Mystery

BY

KORINA MOSS

St. Martin's Paperbacks

First published in the United States by St. Martin's Paperbacks, an imprint of St. Martin's Publishing Group.

FONDUE OR DIE

Copyright © 2024 by Korina Moss.

For information, address St. Martin's Publishing Group, 120 Broadway, New York, NY 10271.

www.stmartins.com

ISBN: 978-1-250-89391-8

Our books may be purchased in bulk for promotional, educational, or business use. Please contact your local bookseller or the Macmillan Corporate and Premium Sales Department at 1-800-221-7945, ext. 5442, or by email at MacmillanSpecialMarkets@macmillan.com.

Printed in the United States of America

St. Martin's Paperbacks edition / November 2024

10 9 8 7 6 5 4 3 2 1

In memory of my father,
who always read my books twice

ACKNOWLEDGMENTS

I must always start by thanking the people who've made this series possible—my incredible editor Madeline Houpt and the rest of my extraordinary team at St. Martin's, which includes copy editor John Simko; executive managing editor John Rounds; Alan Ayers and Danielle Christopher, who are responsible for my gorgeous covers; and the best cheerleaders a girl could ask for, publicist Sara LaCotti and marketer Allison Ziegler. Thank you all for your diligence and support. And a special thanks to all who participated in the company cheese title contest when I was out of punny title ideas. The title *Fondue or Die* is the genius of Kim Ludlam, Creative Services Director, and senior editor Hannah O'Grady. Teamwork makes the dream work, and I'm very proud to be a St. Martin's author.

I'll be forever thankful to my fantastic agent, Jill Marsal; my first reader, Caitlin Lonning; my cheese-monger extraordinaire, Nina Newton of Fairfield Greenwich Cheese Company; and Spread Cheese Co. owners Jamie Tomassetti and Lindsey Eberle.

To those people who are first in my heart—my son, my family, and my friends, who aren't reserved in their show of support and pride—I appreciate you.

Thanks to reader Rachel Marlatt Donner, whose clever name for the thrift shop in town—Bea's Hive of Thrifted Finds—was chosen from hundreds of entries to be used in my series. My sincere appreciation goes to all my readers, including the bloggers, booktubers, and bookstagrammers, who share their excitement about my series with their followers and with me. #TeamCheese!

No matter the question, cheese is the answer.

—Willa Bauer

CHAPTER 1

"Harbison!" Archie, my cheesemonger-in-training, called out in triumph.

"That's the one," I replied from the opposite side of our Dairy Days festival booth. Archie and I were holding the Curds & Whey sign in place, while my neighbor and best friend, Baz, hammered it into the front of the plywood booth. I was quizzing Archie on the themed grazing boxes we'd be selling at the three-day festival as we readied our cheese shop booth before Dairy Days began tomorrow. Harbison, the Best in Show winner at the American Cheese Society's 2018 competition, was one of the cheeses we included in our All-American grazing box. "It's a pocket-sized wheel and it's wrapped in a pretty white and brown outer layer made of strips of spruce tree bark harvested from the woods of Jasper Hill Farm—"

"In Greensboro, Vermont," he finished proudly. On the cusp of turning twenty-one, Archie was enthusiastic about almost everything, including learning about cheese.

I smiled, recalling how I'd soaked up as much knowledge as I could from my first mentor after I'd stumbled upon her cheese shop in France and begun working there during my semester abroad more than a decade ago. I'd come from a cheese background, having grown up on a dairy farm with a small creamery, but Archie's first introduction to artisan cheese didn't occur until last year when I'd hired him to work at my newly opened cheese shop. He deserved to feel proud.

"That's why it tastes woodsy and sweet, with the hints of lemon and mustard balancing the earthy flavor," I said. "The best part about it is that even without heating, it's almost fondue-like. You just remove the top and dig into the creamy interior like a dip." We'd also filled the box's compartments with slices of another award winner, Pleasant Ridge Reserve from Wisconsin, and a third cheese, the velvety Appalachian from Virginia, as well as flatbread crackers. Slices of tart green apples would go in fresh tomorrow morning.

My other essential Curds & Whey crew member and friend, Mrs. Schultz—who was "smack dab" in her sixties, as she liked to say—stared at the booth from several feet away. Her head of curly blonde hair was slightly cocked to the side as she squinted at the sign's placement. She stuck her hands just below the waist of her floral fit and flare dress and tapped the toe of one of her ballet flats. We'd been at it for more minutes than was probably necessary, but that's what we got for asking a retired high school drama teacher to give us direction, even if it was just to ensure the sign was level.

"A little higher on your side, Willa," she directed over the buzz of other vendors prepping their own festival booths.

The district-wide Dairy Days festival took place annually in Lockwood, the town adjacent to Yarrow Glen where my friends and I lived and where my shop was located. Dairy Days had grown over the past forty-nine years from a farmer's market celebrating the local Sonoma Valley family dairy farms to a very popular festival with total attendance in the thousands. By tomorrow, the grounds would be teeming with festival-goers flitting from booth to booth amid activities like butter churning contests, milking competitions (with fake udders, of course), and the popular cow parade. I could practically hear the giggles of children on the kiddie rides and smell the aroma of food truck offerings that would be wafting through the air.

I stood on my tiptoes to raise the sign, as I was quite a bit shorter than lanky Archie. "Is this enough?" I asked, straining to keep it in place.

Mrs. Schultz held her hands in front of either side of her face, as if framing the booth for a movie shot.

"It's going to have to be," Baz said, driving home the final nail.

"Perfect!" she declared.

The rest of us stepped back to look at it.

"That looks great," I concurred. "Thanks, everybody. And thanks for making the sign at the last minute, Baz. I don't know whatever happened to last year's. You're a lifesaver."

"Sometimes literally," he said, raising his eyebrows so they hid behind his overgrown brownish-blond bangs.

He was referring to a scary situation I'd gotten into while we were investigating the death of an old friend of mine last spring. Team Cheese, the name we'd given our motley group whenever we had a mystery to solve, comprised the four of us—Baz, Archie, Mrs. Schultz, and me. We'd gotten involved in police investigations a time or two . . . or four. It happened more often than one would think—enough for us to give our sleuthing group a name.

"That's true," I replied. "And since you're bringing it up again, I'm guessing you're getting low on cheese curds?"

He grabbed his toolbox from the ground and exchanged the hammer for a mostly eaten snack bag of curds. "My last one."

I chuckled. "I got you covered."

Baz and I started most mornings chatting over coffee on our adjoining decks before work and plenty of evenings grabbing dinner together at our local pub. I knew him well enough to know when free cheese curds were his motive.

"We should get to the stage. It's fifteen minutes until the first dress rehearsal," Archie said, checking his phone for the time.

The Labor Day weekend festival culminated in the Miss Dairy pageant Monday afternoon and, spurred on by Mrs. Schultz, Archie had volunteered to be one of the dancers in the opening number.

"Is it that late? That means Beatrice must be there by now. We'd better go," Mrs. Schultz said, putting a pep in our step. Beatrice was a fellow shop owner originally from Lockwood, who continued her role as head of wardrobe for the Miss Dairy pageant. Mrs. Schultz had been volunteering as her wardrobe assistant for the pageant ever since Beatrice had moved to Yarrow Glen to open her thrift shop five years ago.

The sun was slowly creeping near the distant mountains that surrounded the valley, adding a shimmery kiss to the leaves that had already turned golden. I rubbed my arms, wishing I'd thought to bring something to wear over my T-shirt, which read "I can't help it, I'm too fondue of cheese." It was easy to forget how quickly it cooled down late in the day this time of year.

"We better take my truck. I've got work to do there too. I heard Nadine's not happy with the ramp they put in to access the stage after she broke her foot," Baz said.

"Nadine, the pageant director?" I asked as we walked to the vendor lot. I recalled Archie and Mrs. Schultz mentioning her name a few times in recent weeks.

Mrs. Schultz nodded. "She had a bad fall last week, but she's soldiering on with a cast. Nothing's going to keep her from directing the pageant. She runs the historical society museum, but she's been directing the pageant for over twenty-five years."

Archie and I rode in the cramped back seat of the extended cab pickup. Even though Archie's knees almost came up to his chin, he insisted Mrs. Schultz ride shotgun, as he'd done on the way to the festival grounds earlier.

Within minutes of leaving the vendor's gate, Baz was pulling into the visitor's lot for the Lockwood Historical Society Museum. Instead of parking in one of the handful of spaces, he continued onto the unpaved path, past the carriage house that served as the Lockwood chief of police's temporary headquarters during Dairy Days. A little farther along, we bumped past the museum's 1800s Queen Anne–style ranch house, which sat by itself, separated from the festival grounds by a tall row of cypress trees. Beyond the trees, a line of red plastic fencing indicated the border of the festival grounds where cars were parked in uneven rows.

We easily spotted Beatrice's bright purple van sten-
ciled with the name of her shop, Bea's Hive of Thrifted
Finds, across the side. Baz parked on an available patch
of grass.

He went to the bed of the pickup to retrieve his toolbox, and Archie, Mrs. Schultz, and I walked toward the
van. There was a buzz of activity on the other side of
the plastic fence where at least two dozen teenage girls
and their mothers chattered near a large canvas tent.

Beatrice appeared from the other side of the van
and opened her arms in greeting when she saw us approach. "Hello, my helpers!"

Talk about being on brand—I always saw her dressed
in clothes that were either vintage or made to appear
vintage with accoutrements she'd sew on herself. I was
told she'd dressed like that long before she had her
thrift shop, as she was an excellent seamstress. Today
she wore a cotton patchwork wide-legged jumpsuit in
shades of blue. Her blue-framed glasses hung around
her neck from a bejeweled chain. Her long silver hair was
pulled back on either side with blue gemstone combs and
left to flow down to the middle of her back. I could to-
tally imagine her as a Woodstock-attending, peace-
and-love hippie teenager of the early seventies. Although
now it might be peace, love, and gossip—Beatrice liked
to know what was going on with others.

"This is quite the setup," I commented, admiring
the ten-by-ten canvas-wall tent, which had been erected
behind a large, partially covered stage away from the
main festival hub of booths, rides, and games. Since
this was only my second Dairy Days festival, I'd never
been to this area of the grounds. I expected the stage
to look more like the small platform where I'd seen

different local bands play at last year's festival. This looked like professional stuff.

"It's all Nadine's doing. Ever since she got Spotted Cow Dairy to sponsor the fifteen-thousand-dollar college scholarship for the Miss Dairy winner, she's leveraged it into beefing up the pageant, like securing money for the tent rental for wardrobe changes for the girls and getting big-name guest judges," Mrs. Schultz replied.

I was really excited to see one of those big names— Food Network's Nancy Fuller was slated to be the pageant's guest judge this year. I was a big fan of hers and secretly hoped to get to meet her at the pageant on Monday.

"The Miss Dairy pageant might not be Miss America, but nobody better tell that to Nadine," Beatrice added with a wink. She turned to Archie. "Thanks for assisting us old broads with the costumes."

"Speak for yourself, Beatrice," Mrs. Schultz said, half joking. By my estimation, Beatrice was probably only a few years older than Mrs. Schultz.

As soon as Beatrice slid open the side door of the van, the group of sixteen- and seventeen-year-old girls, along with their mothers, funneled through the fence's opening and descended upon us. Archie hightailed it away from the oncoming mob of women.

"Girls! Girls!" I heard the voice before I attached who it belonged to. A thin, middle-aged woman in a long denim skirt and plain T-shirt whirred over in a three-wheeled electric mobility scooter. Her right lower leg, including her foot, was encased in a plastic orthopedic boot, with only her toes peeking out. The cumbersome boot extended over one side of the rust-colored scooter.

She wore a thick copper-colored headband similar to the shade of her thatch of hair. It was Nadine. "Everyone, away from the van!" she called out.

I didn't think she meant me, but her command was enough to make me step away too. I waited by the fence with Archie and Baz, who'd also stayed out of the fray.

"Girls, wait for the clothes to go on the racks," she yelled as she headed toward us at an alarming speed. With one hand holding a large zipper binder and the other on one of the handlebars, she stopped the scooter abruptly behind the plastic fencing, causing her upper body to jostle forward from its seat. She scowled at the scooter before turning her attention to Beatrice, who'd also extracted herself from the commotion. "There are empty wardrobe racks set up beside the tent. Did you label the clothes?" Nadine asked.

"Of course. I think I know the drill after sixteen pageants," Beatrice replied.

"When you've been doing this as long as I have, *then* you can be snarky." Nadine turned her attention back to the clamor by the van. "Girls! Hands off!"

This time the contestants backed away from the van, although their mothers were still reaching inside, pawing through the costumes.

One mother, whose blonde feathered hair framed her face in layers, marched away from the van in a huff and approached Nadine. She wore a cute sundress and wedge sandals and reminded me of Beach House Barbie.

"Nadine, my Annabelle shouldn't have to wear the oldest dairy dress just because she's statuesque. It's going to reflect poorly on her," the woman, obviously Annabelle's mother, said.

Nadine sighed. "We discussed this the other day at

Beatrice's. It's the only one that fits her, and they only wear the dresses for the opening number. She'll change into her own clothes before the judging begins."

"First impressions count, Nadine!" she bit back before stomping away toward the tent.

Nadine didn't seem to give it a second thought, as her voice projected again. "Beatrice! Are those costumes out of the van yet?"

"We could use some help," Beatrice called.

"Stagehands! Help with the costumes!" Then in a lowered voice, "You people are useless anyway. That ramp is entirely too steep."

Baz crumpled his now empty bag of cheese curds and tossed it in a trash bin before ambling over to Nadine with a toolbox and a grin. "That's why I'm here."

She looked him up and down. "You were helping a few weeks ago, weren't you? What's your name again?" She squinted at him as if it might appear on his forehead.

"Baz Tooney. I'm a handyman and carpenter from Yarrow Glen. I fixed the stage floor after your accident last week."

"One capable soul," she said with a single nod. "My scooter stalls getting up the ramp. It's too steep."

"Do you want the ramp fixed or more power in your scooter?" Baz joked.

Snickering passed through the line of volunteers trickling toward the van to help, which made Nadine appreciate the joke even less. "Let's see what you can do with the ramp. The rest of you, help Beatrice with wardrobe. But no dirty hands! All costumes go directly on the racks until Beatrice or Mrs. Schultz has signed off," she said to the contestants who were still eagerly awaiting access to the clothes. "And nothing is to be

taken home at the end of dress rehearsal! Let's not dilly-
dally. As soon as you're all dressed and at the stage, I
have an important announcement to make." Nadine's
fervor seemed to vanish in those final words.

Curious looks passed through the group as the bus-
tling to and from the van paused. Nadine's glance slowly
swept those gathered in sudden quiet, as if taking it all
in. It seemed like she might say whatever it was right
then with everyone assembled.

Instead, the beeping of the scooter sounded as she
backed it up precipitously and made a wide loop, heading toward the stage.

CHAPTER 2

The whirl of activity picked up where it had left off, kicking up dust where the grass had been chewed by the increased influx of parked cars. We were in our third week of a drought, so the glittery dairy farm costumes being pulled from Beatrice's van were likely to look a little more realistic than intended.

Archie, Mrs. Schultz, and I each grabbed an armful of clothes and made our way toward the tent along with the stream of volunteers.

"Is tonight your last rehearsal before Monday?" I asked Archie.

"I don't know. At the last rehearsal, Nadine told us to recruit our friends because there weren't enough guys for the opening dance."

"Nadine holds rehearsals right up until Monday's pageant, but that could just be for the contestants," Mrs. Schultz added. "We've never included others in the show, so this is all new to me."

I knew we wouldn't have Mrs. Schultz's help at our booth, but I couldn't afford to give up Archie for the entire festival.

We hung the clothes on one of the racks and made another trip. When we went back a third time, there were only a few costumes left—the volunteers had made short work of it. Once we scooped up the last of the clothes, Archie slid the van door shut. He bent down beside it and came up holding a crushed and soiled envelope that had been almost hidden by the van. It had obviously been tromped on, unnoticed. He shook the dirt off it and turned the opened envelope over, revealing the word "Private" handwritten on it.

Mrs. Schultz and I took a closer look at it.

"That could be Nadine's writing," she said, looking inside the opened envelope. "There's a note inside. Yup, probably Nadine—she's forever handing notes to everyone. Not usually private ones, though." Her brows wrinkled in thought. "I'll give this to her just in case it's important." She slid it in one of her enviable dress pockets.

We brought the last of the costumes to the racks. Mrs. Schultz began to help Beatrice put them in some kind of order as the girls and their mothers surrounded us like bees to a hive.

"Just give me a couple minutes and I'll find your costume, Archie," Mrs. Schultz said.

"We'll come back," Archie replied as we extracted ourselves from the pageant fray. "We have to get the schedule from Nadine anyway," he said to me.

We left to find Nadine, who was near the stage in conversation with another woman who was dressed as if she was Nadine's understudy in a similar baggy T-shirt and maxi skirt. Unlike Nadine, however, her hair was straight and fell to her elbows. They didn't take notice of us, even as we approached.

"Mary Ann, check on Beatrice and make sure each girl takes the right outfit. We're starting with the milkmaid dresses for the opening number," Nadine said.

She pulled out a pen hidden under her fabric headband, opened her binder, and quickly wrote something on a notebook inside it. She tore off the note and handed it to Mary Ann.

I recalled Mrs. Schultz telling me at one point that Mary Ann was Nadine's cousin. Besides dressing similarly, I could see a slight resemblance—she was thin like Nadine with pointy facial features, but looked about a decade younger, which would put her in her early forties.

Mary Ann read aloud the note Nadine had handed her: "Milkmaid buckets."

"Give that to Beatrice to make sure they have their props," Nadine said.

"I could just tell her."

"You know how I feel about communication with no excuses. If you get held up, you've got it in your hand. You won't forget and neither will she. Oh, and keep an eye on Annabelle's mother, in particular," Nadine said. "You know what? On second thought, keep the mothers out of the tent altogether. The girls are plenty old enough to dress themselves. Beatrice and Mrs. Schultz can help them if they need it."

"Okay, Deeni." Mary Ann left her for the tent, note in hand.

Still sitting on her scooter, Nadine withdrew a pair of reading glasses that were nestled next to her headband. That headband was like Mary Poppins' bag— what else would she pull out from under there? She stuck her glasses on the bridge of her nose, then concentrated on the notebook in her binder.

Archie moved himself into her line of vision. "Hi. I'm Archie Driscoll. I'm one of the dancers."

She looked him up and down. "Huh. You're early. That doesn't happen much around here." She went back to looking at her notebook as she continued with her directions. "The guys aren't joining rehearsal for another forty-five minutes. Get your costume from Beatrice and stay out of the tent or you'll be banned from the festival." Now she looked straight at him again. "I don't care how badly I need men in this number. We don't abide Peeping Toms."

Archie stood with his mouth agape.

I stepped protectively beside him. "Excuse me, Archie would never be a Peeping Tom, and we don't appreciate the insinuation!" I snapped.

"Oh great, now I have non-pageant mothers to contend with too?" She shook her head and studied the papers in her binder again.

I was only fourteen years older than Archie. Sure, the bangs of my black hair had a few premature gray strands I plucked regularly, but anyone would peg me for mid-thirties, which I was.

"I'm not his mother. I'm his employer, Willa Bauer," I informed her.

She took a second, longer look at me and lifted her glasses off her nose. "Sorry, I've been dealing with pageant mothers for months now, so I assumed. These things are only good for reading." She stuck them back on her head and looked around. "Mary Ann? Mary Ann?" she called before sighing heavily in frustration. "Where is she? Don't ever employ a relative. They'll try to get away with murder."

"You just sent her to the tent," I said.

"Yes, but she should've first told the dancers, including your employee, where to go and what to do, so they wouldn't be coming to me. I either have to hand-hold or do everything myself. Fine. Off to the tent!" Nadine started up her scooter.

Archie and I jumped out of the way as the scooter lurched forward and buzzed past us toward the changing tent. We followed, still needing the rehearsal schedule.

"I'm starting to regret this," Archie said. "I only said yes to being a dancer because Mrs. Schultz asked. I hope it doesn't take too much time away from our booth this weekend."

"It's okay. We'll get this figured out." I patted his shoulder, but I was secretly regretting it too.

We waited behind the group of contestants, as each got their correct milkmaid costume and funneled to the tent.

I lost sight of Nadine, but saw Mary Ann at the tent's opening, keeping the mothers from entering with their daughters. "I'm going to talk to Mary Ann and see what the deal is," I told him.

Just as I reached Mary Ann, a mother and her teenage daughter strode between us to enter the tent. The girl had striking cornflower blue eyes and copper-colored curls that flowed down her back. Mary Ann stepped in front of them to keep them from going in.

"Sorry. Just contestants, please," she said, apologetically.

"There's no reason I can't go in with Tabitha," the mother said. Unlike the Barbie mother who'd argued with Nadine earlier, this mom appeared a bit disheveled. She was lightly made up and her buttoned shirt hung to her hips over stretch pants. Her hair was pulled up in a messy bun.

"There's not enough room in the tent for mothers, Lynette. It's already pretty crowded in there," Mary Ann explained.

"Mom, I'll be fine," her daughter, Tabitha, said

through gritted teeth. The girl stepped around Mary Ann, but her mother grabbed her daughter's arm.

"Tabby, you come right back out as soon as you're done getting changed. I'll be waiting right here." She spoke to her as if she were a six-year-old using a public restroom by herself. I cringed overhearing it.

"Mo-om," her daughter said in a hushed voice. She furtively glanced around, likely hoping none of the other girls were listening, before walking into the tent alone.

Tabitha's mother continued to quarrel with Mary Ann about being denied entry until a horn from inside the tent cut through their argument. Mary Ann tensed and pulled back the tent's flap, exposing Nadine and her scooter waiting to exit.

"There you are," Nadine said to Mary Ann. "It's bedlam in there. Oh, and this woman has questions." She nodded in my direction, then gunned the throttle, sending the scooter forward. Mary Ann and I jumped out of the way, saving our toes. Lynette used the opening to sneak into the tent.

Tension lines, already evident on Mary Ann's forehead, deepened. "Sorry. If it's about a costume, you'll have to talk to Beatrice." She disappeared inside the tent.

I sighed. I'd never been amid so many people with so few answers. I met up with Archie and Beatrice, who were finally alone.

"Is it always this chaotic?" I asked her.

"First dress rehearsal? Kind of, but this one's worse than usual on account of Nadine's broken foot. She was gone for four days, which seems to have put everyone in a tailspin," Beatrice said. "Speaking of, I'd better get to the tent. Oh, here's your costume."

She handed Archie a pair of shiny black pants and a blinged-out button-down shirt.

"I thought I'd be getting overalls or something," Archie said, looking horrified at the outfit.

"This is a pageant. We're not about realism. Do you think milkmaids wore glittery ribbons?"

Resigned, Archie took the costume. "Do you know where I'm supposed to change?"

Beatrice placed her hand on one of her slim hips and looked at the tent. "Hmm, good question. We were supposed to have a second tent for the guys, but like I said, with Nadine gone, it somehow slipped through the cracks. The girls will be practicing their intros before they rehearse the dance, so you might be able to use the tent after they're all on stage. Best to check with Nadine. I don't want to get you in trouble."

"Beatrice, her costume is too short!" one of the mothers called from outside the tent.

"Gotta run." Beatrice trotted over to the tent to do some troubleshooting.

Archie and I sighed in unison—foiled again.

"After the Peeping Tom remark, I'm not chancing the tent. These pants might fit over my shorts. I'm going behind one of the trees to change." Archie walked toward a scarce patch of shade trees.

I saw Baz with Nadine by the stage ramp. I'd give it one last shot to talk to her about the schedule.

Nadine was sitting on the scooter with her foot propped up, watching over Baz's shoulder as he worked on the ramp. Baz noticed me first and said "hey" at the same time an angry woman in a power-red blazer and jeans strode toward us.

"Nadine! You're trying to eliminate me from the pageant?" the woman bellowed, immediately getting our attention. The woman looked about Nadine's age—maybe fifty—entirely too old to compete for Miss Dairy. Her blazer had a logo of two capital Bs where a breast pocket would've been.

Nadine shushed her. "Not here, Fiona!" She started up her scooter and veered it away from me and Baz. In her fury, the woman ran ahead of Nadine and stood in front of her scooter, taking her life in her hands, as far as I was concerned—I'd seen the way Nadine drove that machine. Luckily, Nadine stopped the scooter in time.

The woman continued her tirade. "The judging table has been the same for the last seventeen years. I'm one of the faces of this pageant. You can't eliminate me!"

"Uh-oh," Baz said under his breath.

Looks like I was getting a front-row seat again to another confrontation. I had no idea festival pageants were such hotbeds of drama. I should've brought some cheese to calm everyone down.

"Don't get it twisted, Fiona—*I'm* the only face of this pageant," Nadine shot back. "You're replaceable. We get a new guest judge every year, so filling one more judge's spot isn't the worst thing in the world."

"But I'm Lockwood's local celebrity!"

"Selling Becky's Bakeware doesn't make you a local celebrity, Fiona."

"I'm the number-one seller of Becky's Bakeware in the Sonoma Valley. Everyone knows me! I'm the number-one Becky."

"Forgive me if I don't think anyone's going to notice your absence with Nancy Fuller here."

"You can't get rid of me!" Fiona snapped.

Nadine paused, ending the shouting match. "You know I didn't want to, but you've left me no choice."

She lowered her voice even more, but I still caught the words that followed. "And you know exactly why."

Fiona's gaze left Nadine and darted to the pageant mothers congregated by the tent and the stagehands putting last-minute touches on the set decorations. When her gaze landed on us, Baz and I quickly looked away and took interest in the ramp's construction. A handful of seconds later, we couldn't help but return to eavesdropping.

Fiona leaned into Nadine on the scooter and said something to her, but this time I couldn't make it out. I caught the angry tone of Nadine's retort, but not the words.

Fiona huffed, her face becoming a lighter shade of her red Becky's Bakeware blazer. "I thought we were friends! I'm not letting this happen, Nadine. You're messing with tradition, and it won't look good for you." She stomped off.

For all of Nadine's bravado, she looked rattled. She checked her watch, then drove away on her scooter. I watched her zoom toward the curtain of cypress trees, and wondered who she was about to tick off next.

CHAPTER 3

Baz went back to working on the ramp while I kept him company. He stopped to take off his zippered sweat-shirt, revealing a T-shirt that had the words "Hot Wax" in fat orange letters in a retro font.

"Is that T-shirt from Bea's Hive?" I asked.

He looked offended. "No! Hot Wax—it's a band. Alt rock. Keep current, Wil."

"Since when do you listen to alt rock? Oh my gosh. This is about turning thirty again, isn't it?" The thought of turning thirty soon had been freaking Baz out and he'd been driving me nuts about it. I had no sympathy—I was entering my mid-thirties. "You're gonna start listen-ing to Gen Z music now?"

"I'm barely millennial. And they're good! If you like that kind of thing."

"Which you don't. Baz, turning thirty's not so bad. Trust me."

"How do you remember? It was ages ago for you."

I tap-punched him on the arm.

Archie came over, still carrying his costume over his arm.

"Since when did you join *Dancing with the Stars*?" Baz ribbed, chuckling at the costume.

"Very funny," Archie replied.

"Watch out, Baz, Mrs. Schultz might recruit you too," I warned, secretly hoping she would. I was used to seeing Archie in all kinds of costumes—he used to be his high school's mascot and was up for wearing almost anything. I guess sheen was where he drew the line. "I thought you were getting changed," I said to Archie.

"I tried to, but the pageant moms kept giving me the stink eye, like I was a creep hiding in the bushes. I'll just wait for the other guys to get here and see what they do."

"Good idea," I said.

"Why don't you just get dressed in the museum? It's a five-minute walk," Baz suggested.

"You think it's open? I've been wanting to check it out," Archie said.

"Me too. And if it's not open, the other guys in the dance should be here by the time we get back," I said.

"See you in a few," Baz said with a wave.

Archie and I began the trek over to the museum. Once we walked beyond the row of trees that lent it some privacy, we could fully see the late-1800s Queen Anne–style house that served as the museum. Although the Victorian details gave the house a kind of majesty, it also looked sorely in need of a buff and a paint job, especially on its octagonal widow's peak.

"I wish Yarrow Glen had a haunted house," Archie uttered.

"It's haunted? What have you heard?" We'd already dealt with Nadine and the pageant chaos—I wasn't prepared to deal with ghosts too.

Archie laughed. "Nobody's said so, but look at it."

His impression of it wasn't exactly wrong. The setting sun and the faded white paint on the pecling clapboard gave the house a gray appearance, as if we were seeing it through the lens of a black-and-white photograph. The eaves threw shadows on the two-story mansion. Except for the carriage house and the barns, this home had stood alone on the property when it had been a ranch. I could imagine the weathervane squeaking in the wind atop the widow's peak.

"Mrs. Schultz told me it was built in the late 1800s by some rich guy who gave it to his daughter as a wedding present," Archie told me. "But after they started building it, the costs skyrocketed with all the decorative features, so he changed some stuff, like built one of the rooms without any windows and made a fake widow's peak just big enough for a staircase up to the widow's walk. I bet that's where the ghost walks around. Bwahahaha." He gave me his best spooky laugh and wiggled his fingers in my face.

I pushed him away playfully. "Maybe a pyromaniac ghost. It looks like there's some fire damage on that side. The house could use some TLC, but it's got great bones."

Now that we were up close, I could appreciate the Queen Anne features—the eyebrow detail over the tall second-floor windows, the ornate railings that led up the six steps to the front porch, the cornices snug in the eaves. Hanging beside the front door was a sign indicating it was now the Lockwood Historical Society Museum with posted hours.

We tried the door and smiled at each other when it opened.

Stepping inside, I felt like Dorothy opening the door to Munchkinland for the first time—the drab gray house had turned Technicolor. The wide enclosed entrance hall had rich paneling on the staircase and a bright red carpet with a matching runner leading up the stairs. The lower landing featured a stained-glass window. A small desk with a chair pushed against it sat abandoned by the inner wall. A welcome plaque and old metal fan, unplugged, took up most of the space atop the desk.

"Hello? Anyone here?" I called out.

"Hello?" Archie echoed.

Archie and I walked past the desk and took a left through the doorway leading to a wide hall, with large rooms on either side. We stepped into the first one on the left.

"Is this what they used to call a parlor?" Archie asked.

"Your guess is as good as mine."

The tall, bowed windows facing the front of the house would've let in the sunlight had they had a good washing. A chandelier hung in the center of a seating area, which was now surrounded with cabinets filled with Lockwood memorabilia. A two-gallon stoneware milk jug labeled "Nineteenth Century" rested on one of the shelves. Framed newspapers hung on the walls, folded so that only the headlines showed. I stepped closer to read some of them: "Town Buys Steadman Ranch." "Lockwood Historical Society Museum Opens." I took in the headlines farther down the wall: "Stacey Drooper Crowned Miss Dairy Princess." "Grace Kelp Crowned Miss Dairy Princess." "Shelby Cook Crowned . . ." My eyes followed the line of framed newspapers, each with the name of another Miss Dairy pageant winner. My attention was directed to a switch in headlines. "Police Sergeant Womack Saves Child, Hailed a Hero." "No Arrests Made After Fire Destroys Historical Society Museum Kitchen."

That last headline likely explained the damage I'd noticed to the widow's peak. The headlines were interesting, but the room was cloyingly warm. Archie and I continued across the hall into the next room, which gave us a start. We jumped back, then laughed at ourselves once we realized almost instantly that the mannequins dressed in clothing of different eras weren't real people. We quickly left that room to find the next. Archie was drawn to a narrow table pushed against the wall facing the back side of the house where another stoneware milk jug was displayed among smaller tin ones.

"Look! There's a pocket door behind this table. It must be a secret room! The ghost's room?" He widened his eyes dramatically before he chuckled.

The table was pushed up against a closed pocket door with an old-fashioned key in the lock.

"Yeah, let's get Team Cheese on that," I said sarcastically, going along with the joke, then concluded, "It probably just leads to the widow's walk."

Continuing through the wide hall, we passed another room with some period dining room furniture. Off that room was a smaller room, perhaps once a library.

"Boy, this house is huge," Archie said.

We followed an odd smaller hallway, which eventually led to a vestibule where the back door was.

"This has gotta be the bathroom," Archie said, standing next to a closed door I'd passed. He opened it and stepped inside before finding the light switch. "It's not a bathroom, but I think I found the room with no windows."

I followed him into a plain, windowless room that looked like it was being used as a storage library. Tall shelves filled with hardbound books and photo albums created shadowy aisles that the three strips of lighting on the ceiling couldn't penetrate.

We walked past a few rows of filled bookshelves. "This must be some kind of records room," I said.

"It might not have any windows, but it's got a door," he said, pointing down one of the aisles to a three-foot-tall wooden door on the opposite wall. "You think that's the cubby where the ghost lives?"

"I'm certain you're right," I said sarcastically, as I followed him to check it out. It didn't budge. "If this house was built in the late 1800s, this could be one of those doors they used to deliver milk. The delivery carriage could be pulled right up to it. This room may have even been used as a pantry storage room at some point."

Archie dropped his costume on a low stool and took out his phone. He turned on its flashlight to better peruse the books. "This room's cool. I can't believe people keep track of all this town stuff."

I walked farther into the large room to see how many aisles of books it held. My sneaker crunched something underfoot. I bent down to see I'd stepped on what looked like some broken pieces of stoneware. When I looked down the aisle, the clay jugs lining the bookshelves explained it. I walked down it to check them out. The first one I saw read "Lockwood Dairy Days. 1982." They each had the same writing on them with a different year. Archie found me in the aisle.

"What are these?" he asked, passing behind me as he checked them out.

"They must make a jug for each year of the Dairy Days festival."

I continued through the aisle, about to tell Archie

to change into his costume. We were letting the time get away from us. As I exited, I was confused to see a rust-orange scooter in the back corner of the room. I walked toward it, past more aisles of shelves, before seeing the floor was covered with haphazardly strewn books. The crunch of broken pottery was again underfoot. I came upon the final long shelving unit laying on the floor atop piles of books and journals and broken pottery. My heart picked up speed.

"What happened?" Archie was behind me, staring at the heap, frozen in place. "You think someone's under there?"

"That looks like Nadine's scooter," I said, pointing to it.

Suddenly we snapped out of our disbelief and raced closer to the shelving unit to get a better look at what might be underneath. I silently prayed that it was only books and broken stoneware.

"Nadine?" I called out in panic.

Archie and I lifted either corner of the shelving unit, but we couldn't get it past our knees. It was heavy and cumbersome. I tried to get a firmer grip, but slipped on a book and lost my footing, landing with a thud on my tailbone. The heavy shelf fell on my thighs.

"Willa! Are you okay?" Archie carefully put his corner down and came to my side. I shimmied out from under the shelf, my thighs tender where it had made impact. I stayed on the floor and took out my phone. "I'm okay but if Nadine is under there, she's in trouble." I hit the emergency button on my phone to call for help, but nothing happened.

"No signal."

Even in the poor lighting, I could see Archie's face had turned paler than usual, making his freckles and the irregular-shaped port-wine stain birthmark on his left cheek stand out. "I'll go get help," he said, taking off.

I stood and scanned the fallen shelves and the mounds underneath them, steeling myself for what I might find, but I couldn't distinguish a body among the debris. I didn't dare try to raise the shelves again.

I looked more closely at the scooter, hoping to convince myself that this was a spare and somehow the bookshelf fell on its own. Since Nadine ran the museum, maybe she wanted an indoor-only scooter, and it was simply parked there. However, splattered mud on the fenders rid me of that hope.

Mud? We'd been in a drought for weeks. My eyes suddenly alighted on the same stains on the floor around the scooter that I hadn't picked up on when I'd first noticed everything else out of place. A smudged trail led from the scooter to the fallen bookshelf. Was that . . . blood?

The door had been closed and the lights were off when we got to the room. If Nadine had come in here and had an accident, the lights would've still been on.

Still hoping somehow Nadine wasn't here, I trotted over to the light switch to see if it was one of those motion sensor ones that automatically turned off after several minutes of no movement. No, it was a basic, old fashioned light switch. As my hope dwindled, my heart picked up speed.

I went back and kneeled beside the fallen shelving unit, swiping the flashlight feature on my phone. I crawled around all four sides, shining the light underneath the foot of space, most of it filled with books and broken pottery. I'd never looked so hard for something I didn't want to find.

The light fell on a shape among the books and shards of stoneware jugs that made me pause. I couldn't distinguish it right away. I stared at it until my brain recognized it as Nadine's blood-soaked hair. A strangled cry escaped my throat.

CHAPTER 4

"Nadine! Nadine, can you hear me?" I called. I listened hard for any response. Instead, I heard hurried footsteps clomping through the museum. I was relieved to see two uniformed Lockwood police officers arrive ahead of Archie and another familiar face from Yarrow Glen, Officer Shepherd—Shep, as everyone called him—who was out of uniform, working security for the festival.

I scrambled to my feet. "Nadine's under there."

"Is she conscious?" the female officer asked.

"I don't think so."

"Move out of the way, Willa," Shep said, as he and the male officer grabbed hold of the shelves' thick frame. The female officer spoke into the radio at her shoulder, calling for an ambulance, and then helped her Lockwood colleague to slowly heave the unit. The male officer lost his footing amid the slippery bound journals as I had, but his colleague stepped in just in time. Archie and I held a collective breath until they worked their way inward to get the shelving upright. The same breath was knocked out of me once I saw the form in the center of the heap.

"We'll hold it, Williams," the male officer said,

prompting Officer Williams to take broad, careful steps to reach her. She tossed the books away that were covering much of the body, revealing Nadine lying face down. The bit of hair I'd first noticed was the only part of her head not matted with blood. A portion of her skull was crushed in. My hand flew to my mouth in horror, and I pulled Archie away. "Archie, you should wait outside for the ambulance. Let them know which room we're in," I said, wanting to get him out of the room.

He nodded and seemed relieved to go. As I watched him exit, another officer, this one in a white uniform that fit snugly over his muscular frame, came through the room.

"I heard the call. Harding, Williams, what's going on?" He stopped short upon seeing Nadine's body. "That's not . . ."

"It's Nadine Hockenbaum, Chief," Officer Williams said, rising from a crouched position where she'd been checking Nadine for signs of life.

The Lockwood chief of police hurried over to Nadine. He crouched over her and felt her neck for a pulse, even though Officer Williams had already done so. His head drooped and he squeezed his eyes shut before sighing heavily. A moment later, he stood, obviously having shoved aside whatever feelings the death had brought. "Tell them no sirens. Every vendor is on the festival grounds. We don't want to draw attention."

"Yes, Chief Womack." She used her radio to follow his orders.

"Let's be careful here until forensics has done their job," he said to Shep and his two police officers. "First I have to speak with Mayor Sonny." He stepped away from Nadine's body and seemed to notice me for the first time. "You are?"

"I'm Willa Bauer."

"She's from Yarrow Glenn, Chief Womack. She and Archie Driscoll alerted us to the situation," Shep explained.

"We tried to lift the bookshelves to see if anyone was trapped underneath, but we couldn't lift it very far. I'm sorry if we contaminated the crime scene," I said.

"Who said it was a crime scene?" His eyes, a disarming aqua blue, narrowed.

"Well, you said you have to get the forensics team out here."

"That's procedure for any death, especially if it's an accident that occurred on town property."

I was used to dealing with Yarrow Glen's lead investigator, Detective Heath, and he was used to me and my questions and opinions. With Chief Womack, I hesitated about speaking up, but I'd had a little time to think about this possible accident before discovering Nadine. The more I thought about it, the more I considered that it was no accident.

"I think it might not have been an accident, Chief Womack. If she'd come in here by herself looking for something, the light would've still been on when Archie and I came in. But the light was off and the door was closed." I forced myself to glance at Nadine's body again. "And wouldn't she be in the opposite position than she's in now if she'd been climbing the shelf when it fell? Or even if she was walking away, her feet would be closer to the bottom of the shelf, not her head."

Chief Womack looked at Nadine's body and seemed to consider what I said. Saying these things aloud made me more convinced I was right. I rushed on with one last possibility to my theory. "That's her scooter over there, isn't it? And I think there's blood on it."

I started toward it, but Chief Womack put an arm in front of me, halting my steps. He walked behind the shelf that Shep and Officer Harding were still holding steady in order to reach the scooter.

"On the fender and the floor," I told him.

Shep cut me a look that made me second-guess my prior confidence.

The room was quiet as Chief Womack surveyed the scooter and the worn wooden floor under it.

"If that's her blood, it could mean she was killed on her scooter, and the murderer moved her and pushed the shelf on top of her to make it look like an accident," I said.

Officer Williams craned her neck to get a look at the scooter.

Chief Womack continued to stare at it. "Who would want to murder Nadine?" he said quietly, obviously speaking to himself.

Heavy footfalls sounded from an adjacent room. Chief Womack stopped examining the scooter and made a beeline to the doorway, where he met the paramedics.

"I'm going to keep you out here for now," he said to them. "Shep, can you escort Willa Bauer outside and stay with her? Where is the friend you said you were with?"

"I'm here," Archie's voice came from outside the doorway.

"Stay with the two of them," Chief Womack said to Shep.

Shep and I left the room, then exited the museum with Archie.

Once we got outside, Archie said, "She's dead, isn't she?"

I nodded, my stomach souring at the picture it left in my mind's eye. I wrapped my arms around his shoulders and gave him a squeeze. I looked back at the porch steps we'd just descended. "How'd she even get into the museum?" I asked.

"There's a wheelchair accessible ramp at the back door," Shep answered.

I inhaled the fresh air and slowly let it out. The museum had been a little musty, but it was the disquieting feeling that had settled into my bones that I was trying to replace. "Someone needs to tell her cousin."

"That's never an easy thing to do." Shep's crooked nose crinkled at the thought. Not much stayed hidden behind his eyes—I saw his unease. He wasn't an intimidating presence, but he was the officer called on to break up bar fights or calm a heated couple in the throes of a domestic dispute. Shep's relaxed approach with people was well-known in Yarrow Glen. When I'd first met him, he'd reminded me of a golden retriever, loyal and friendly. However, this past year and a half of getting to know him as Detective Heath's sensitive and smart right-hand man had deepened my perspective of him.

"Will you be telling her, Shep?" I asked.

"It'll be Chief Womack or someone he assigns to do it. Dairy Days is a district-wide effort, so some of us from the Yarrow Glen force are hired as off-duty security for the festival, but this isn't our jurisdiction."

Archie stuck his hands in his shorts pockets and concentrated on the stone he was moving around with the toe of his shoe. We hardly knew Nadine, but any death was upsetting.

"Willa? Archie. Shep. What's going on?" Mrs. Schultz strode toward us from the side of the house, glancing back and forth from the ambulance to us, a look of concern replacing her usual toothy smile.

When she caught up to us, I gently explained what happened. Shep let her lean on him to withstand the emotional blow. Archie and I took turns answering her questions.

"Is everyone at the pageant wondering what's going on?" I asked her.

"I don't know. I was sent to the prop room on an errand. I just left there and saw the ambulance and then all of you."

"The prop room?"

"It's in the museum where the kitchen used to be before the fire. It's closed off now from the rest of the house and it's used as storage space."

"The secret door," I said to Archie, making the mental connection to the door we'd joked about.

"Not as exciting as a ghost," he replied, looking disappointed.

I decided it was time to let them in on my theory of murder. I told Archie and Mrs. Schultz what Shep had heard me tell Chief Womack.

"I've never seen anything like it by a civilian. You laid it out like you were Hercule Poirot," Shep said afterward.

I couldn't quite tell if he was outraged by it or impressed. I was so used to conferring with Detective Heath at the scene of a crime, it didn't occur to me not to ultimately be as forthright with Chief Womack.

"Except Poirot would know who did it. Unfortunately, I don't," I replied.

Amid the silence that ensued, Chief Womack appeared at the front doorway. His lips were pulled down in a grim line. He stepped onto the porch, his squinted gaze staring past us toward the trees. He took out a handkerchief to wipe the back of his neck. When he returned it to his pocket, his focus landed on us. He stuck his sunglasses over his eyes and walked down the steps to meet us.

"I need to know what you saw and heard before you went to find help," Chief Womack said.

"We didn't see or hear anything," I replied.

"Nothing. We were looking for somewhere I could change into my costume for the pageant rehearsal. It must've happened before we got here, or we would've heard all that stuff fall," Archie said.

"It couldn't have been much before we arrived. I saw her drive off in the scooter only about ten or fifteen minutes before we started walking over here," I added.

Chief Womack turned his focus on Mrs. Schultz. "It's Mrs. Schultz, isn't it? You've been working with the pageant for a few years now. With Beatrice?" His tone had softened.

"That's right." Mrs. Schultz smiled at the friendly recognition.

"Did you—"

The growl of an engine turned our attention to a sedan that bumped over the grass and came to a halt next to the ambulance and very near the house.

A man with a burly, round build pulled himself out of the car. I recognized him as Mayor Darling, or Mayor Sonny as everyone called him—he preferred the familiarity of his childhood nickname. The wide smile I recalled he had while presiding over last year's festival was gone, however. His bushy brows knit together, and his eyes immediately found Chief Womack. I wasn't familiar with the smaller guy dressed in khakis and a polo shirt who emerged from the driver's seat and kept pace behind the mayor.

Chief Womack leaned closer to Shep. "Keep an eye out for the forensics team, and make sure nobody else enters the museum. You three, stay here too," he said to me, Archie, and Mrs. Schultz.

"Will do," Shep answered.

"What's going on, Pete? What's this about Nadine?" Mayor Sonny called to Chief Womack as he strode toward him as quickly as his large body would take him. He looked like an overweight bouncer ready to throw out an unruly patron. Chief Womack put a steadying hand on his shoulder and led him into the museum, talking in quiet tones. The smaller man only glanced at us before following them up the stairs, but the worry on his face was apparent.

"Who's that with the mayor?" I quietly asked Shep.

"Tyrell James, the town's events director. He's in charge of Dairy Days."

"No wonder he looks worried," I murmured.

"No kidding. It's only his third year in the position. It's a lot for anyone to have on their shoulders under the best of circumstances, and this is about as far from the best as you can get." At the reminder of what had just transpired, Shep let out a slow breath, causing a light whistle to escape through his teeth.

His hands went to his hips as he turned toward the trees, beyond which were the festival grounds and the stage where I imagined people were starting to wonder about Nadine. The trees shielded the house from the stage, so no one from the pageant may have even had an inkling anything was amiss.

"What do we do now?" Archie asked Shep.

"Get comfortable, I guess," he answered. "It's going to be a while. You know how this goes, Willa. A lot of things need to happen before they can take the body away. Forensics haven't even gotten here yet."

The words were no sooner out of his mouth than a commotion by the door made us turn. Paramedics maneuvered a stretcher, now carrying Nadine's covered body, out of the house and to the waiting ambulance.

I recalled several months ago when a friend of mine had died of anaphylactic shock at our town park that Detective Heath had cordoned off the whole area and interviewed everyone involved. It was the procedure when finding a dead body, whether foul play was evident or not. The only reason my friend had been taken to the hospital was because they'd hoped to save her. But if there was no chance, as in Nadine's case . . .

I leaned into Shep. "Why are they moving her body already?"

"I don't know. That's . . . unusual," he said carefully, sounding confused too.

Chief Womack, Mayor Sonny, and Tyrell exited the house behind them. The mayor and Tyrell looked even worse than when they'd entered. They conversed while huddled on the porch, and then all heads swiveled to look at us. The mayor broke their circle and approached us with Tyrell at his heels. Chief Womack looked reluctant to follow, but eventually did, remaining a step behind the mayor.

"I understand you were the one to find her?" Mayor Sonny addressed me.

"Yes," I replied.

He clasped his hands in front of him and looked at me earnestly, his doughy face scrunched grimly. "An awful thing. You must still be in shock."

"Why was the body moved?" I asked. I couldn't help it—it was the first thing on my mind.

The mayor's bushy eyebrows shot up in surprise. He quickly rearranged his expression to one of solemnity again. "There was nothing that could be done for her."

"But isn't there procedure that needs to be followed?" I pushed on.

His voice didn't waver from the soothing cadence of a somber pastor in the receiving line of a wake. "Of course. Chief Womack will make sure that it is. In the meantime, I'm personally asking you not to discuss the details of the horrible aftermath of this accident." He looked each of us in the eye.

"Accident?" I repeated, stunned. My surprise went to Chief Womack, who'd all but called it a homicide just minutes ago. He lowered his gaze so it wouldn't meet mine.

Mayor Sonny continued, ignoring my interruption. "We have to inform the next of kin—her cousin, who's also a part of our festival. Gruesome details will only whet the public's appetite for more information. We don't want this to overshadow the festival."

"You're continuing with Dairy Days?" Archie asked, sounding incredulous.

"We have to," Tyrell, the festival director, spoke up.

The mayor raised his hand to stop Tyrell from saying anything else, all the while keeping his focus on us. "This is a tragedy, not only for Nadine's family, but for the entire Lockwood community and for Dairy Days. She was an integral part of this festival. Nadine would want it to continue. I'm certain of that."

Mayor Sonny paused and lowered his head. He passed a deep breath, then shut his eyes, remaining motionless. Was he conducting a moment of silence?

Praying? I almost closed my eyes too, when his head snapped up and he looked over at the festival director. In a sharp, clipped tone, he said, "Tyrell, we've got a lot to do." He turned to Chief Womack. "Pete, keep me updated."

The chief nodded and Tyrell followed the mayor to the car before they sped off in a cloud of dust. I noticed the ambulance had already quietly made its exit.

Chief Womack seemed reluctant to turn his attention back to us. He rubbed a hand across his closely trimmed beard. The muscles in his thick neck stood out. "Shep, do you mind getting Mary Ann and bringing her to my office?"

Shep gave a single nod, and with a sympathetic glance toward us for what had happened, he headed toward the festival grounds.

Chief Womack then turned his attention to us. "You three are free to go."

"Free to go?" Archie asked with surprise.

He wasn't the only one.

"I'll be in touch to get your official statements in a few days," Chief Womack said.

His attitude about Nadine's death had taken a one-eighty since speaking with the mayor.

"You don't think it was an accident too, just because the mayor wants it to be, do you?" I said, not ready to be dismissed.

"We'll be thoroughly looking into Nadine's cause of death," he said deliberately.

"So why not take our statements right now?"

He paused to study me or maybe to gather his patience. "You said you didn't hear or see anything. You showed me what you found in the room. Is there something else?"

I looked at Archie who shook his head quickly, seemingly happy not to have to talk further with the police.

"Well, no," I said.

"Mrs. Schultz? Did you see or hear anything before you entered the room?" he asked, half-turned to leave.

"I didn't go to the museum with them. I was looking for a milkmaid pail in the prop room."

"You were on your own in the museum?" Chief Womack's interest peaked. He no longer seemed in a hurry to leave.

"Yes. But I didn't see anybody or hear anything either, not until I heard a car drive up. I didn't think much of it until I came out and saw it was an ambulance."

"How long were you in the room?" he asked her.

She glanced toward the museum. "Hard to say. I didn't look at the time."

"Five minutes? Fifteen? Thirty?" Chief Womack offered.

"Oh no. Not that long." She tapped her forefinger to her chin in thought and sighed in frustration. "It was between five and fifteen, I suppose."

Chief Womack's head tipped to the side, and he looked at Mrs. Schultz's feet, clad as usual in ballet flats, because she liked to show off her "good ankles."

"Where's the bucket?" he asked her.

"The bucket?" Mrs. Schultz looked around her feet where his attention was, confused by his question.

"The bucket. You said you went to look for a bucket."

"Oh! The milkmaid pail. I never found one, but I didn't want to keep looking, because I knew Beatrice needed me back at the tent with the girls."

"Huh. Okay."

I didn't like the way he seemed to be contemplating Mrs. Schultz's story.

"Chief Womack, I have to put in my two cents. I don't think you should wait until Dairy Days is over to investigate. The murderer could be walking around the festival all weekend, right under our noses," I said.

"That's more of a ten-cent comment. But it's even more reason to keep as much of our team as possible on the festival grounds. I would like to interview *you* further, Mrs. Schultz."

"Why Mrs. Schultz?" Archie said, sounding protective.

The chief continued to question her. "Was anyone with you? Did you walk to the museum with Ms. Bauer and Mr. Driscoll?"

"No. I came by myself," she answered forthrightly.

"Did you see her go into the prop room?" he asked me and Archie.

This line of questioning was ridiculous. "Mrs. Schultz said she didn't hear anything, so it had to have happened before she got there. Even on the other side of the house, she would've heard it."

"If she went to the prop room like she says," he countered.

I felt as if Chief Womack had put me in a chokehold with one of his beefy arms. "Whoa. Hold up. What are you saying? Are you suspecting Mrs. Schultz?"

"Surely that's not what he's implying. Is it Chief Womack?" Somehow Mrs. Schultz remained remarkably calm.

"I'm just doing my job. Make up your mind, Ms. Bauer. Do you want me to investigate or don't you?"

Was he using this line of questioning as a threat? "I want you to investigate the right people!" I demanded.

"I don't know how they do it in Yarrow Glen, but you're not making the decisions here. I am. You three should come to the Lockwood police station on Tuesday morning. Got it?"

I said no more. I'd already made a mess of things. What if pushing Chief Womack to look into this murder meant Mrs. Schultz was now a suspect?

CHAPTER 5

Later that evening, I was relieved to be back at Curds & Whey, standing at the stove in my shop's kitchenette with Baz, Archie, and Mrs. Schultz nearby. I'd also brought down my betta fish, Loretta, from my apartment upstairs. Although she was perfectly happy spending all day in the company of her crush, Ted Allen, leaving Food Network's *Chopped* streaming on my TV for twelve hours wasn't very energy conscious. Besides, I missed her, and she enjoyed spending time in the shop.

It was late, and none of us had had a proper dinner, so I'd insisted on cooking to satisfy our appetites. Preparing something cheesy had a calming effect on me, eating something cheesy even more so. We often used the kitchenette to have meals together after shop hours, as it accommodated us more comfortably than my "cozy" apartment upstairs. This space at the rear of Curds & Whey was normally used for sample prepping, special events, and cheesemaking classes. We were currently in the planning stages to turn it into a café space to serve cheeseboards and drinks.

"Are you sure you don't want to sit down, Willa? You and Archie had quite a shock," Mrs. Schultz said from the other side of the marble-topped island.

I was more concerned about Chief Womack's accusation about Mrs. Schultz, but I didn't want to bring it up and worry her, since she didn't appear to take much stock in what he'd said.

"You don't have to be tough around us," Baz said, coming over to help. His second encounter with me had been over a dead body and it had bonded us quickly.

I rejected their offers. "You know I prefer to keep busy." Even though my hopes of seeing Nancy Fuller up close and personal were surely dashed, I'd been channeling her motto—*Fresh is best unless you're stressed*—while thinking of what to cook as we drove back to my shop. Luckily, I'd thought of an alfredo recipe that was easy *and* freshly cheesy. While a pot of water was coming to a boil on the stove, I picked out a hunk of Parmigiano-Reggiano, Asiago, sharp white cheddar, and some smoked mozzarella.

"Can I have something to do?" Archie asked. He also liked to keep busy, and he was a good cook.

I handed him the grater. "How are *you* feeling?"

Archie carefully began shredding the cheeses. "I'm okay. I didn't see much, thanks to you. It's still weird talking to her one minute and then knowing she's dead the next."

"It'll take some time to process."

I chopped up some fresh cloves of garlic from Lou's Market two doors down and took out some butter, heavy cream, and cream cheese from the refrigerator. Archie measured out the shredded cheeses as I poured fusilli pasta into the boiling water.

"What about you, Mrs. Schultz? Out of all of us, you knew her best," I said.

Mrs. Schultz was helping Baz set the farm table. "I only knew her from the pageants, and you saw how she was today—that was her normal mode. She was one to give orders more than have conversation, at least while she was directing the pageant." Mrs. Schultz shook her head. "I can't believe this happened to her."

"*I* can't believe they're still going ahead with the festival. It seems pretty cold," Baz added. He motioned for Mrs. Schultz to sit at one of the farm table's benches while he finished their task by bringing over four glasses of ice water.

Last September's Dairy Days was my first, as I'd been new to Yarrow Glen, so I'd been a little hesitant to rent a festival booth and close my shop for three days to participate. After an incident with a magazine critic who'd then been murdered right outside my newly opened shop, I'd wanted to do nothing else but focus on my business.

Just as I'd envisioned it, my shop's walls were wrapped in warm butterscotch wainscoting with a dark-paneled feature wall behind the counter. Turned-leg tables held towers of cheeses and jars of accompaniments like jellies and jams, along with attractive linens and handwoven picnic baskets. During the day, the large front windows kept the shop bright and the pleasant Northern California weather allowed us to keep the front door open most days. Stacked wheels and wedges could be seen from the brick sidewalk, along with long shelves of aged cheeses displayed in perfect rows, enticing passersby. Little did I know, my cheese shop dream would also provide me with the closest friends I've ever had.

Archie and I continued to cook in unison. He was just about done shredding the cheeses, so I began warming the ingredients in a pot, starting with the butter and cream.

I returned to thinking about Dairy Days. "Canceling any event isn't as easy as it sounds. Could Lockwood afford to cancel the festival?" I asked.

"I don't think so. All three towns in the district help with staffing it, but the money goes in and out through Lockwood. They'd have a lot of money to give back—everyone who paid to have a booth there, plus all the sponsors," Mrs. Schultz said.

"I guess you're right. Willa said they've got Nancy Fuller coming in to be the celebrity judge for the pageant. They must've paid her big bucks to do it," Baz said.

"Oh, the pageant!" Mrs. Schultz stuck her elbows on the table and cupped her chin in her hands, as if literally feeling the weight of her distress.

"What do you think they're going to do about the pageant without Nadine?" Archie asked.

Mrs. Schultz didn't have an answer.

Selfishly, I didn't care about the pageant. I was more concerned about Chief Womack's investigation and still worried whether he really thought Mrs. Schultz could have something to do with Nadine's murder. I didn't know how to bring it up so as not to needlessly worry her, however, so I stuck to talking about the pageant. "Surely, they'll cancel it. Dairy Days can still go on without the pageant."

"They can't cancel it," Mrs. Schultz replied, worry threading through her voice. "The prize for winning Miss Dairy Princess is a fifteen-thousand-dollar scholarship. For many of the girls, winning could mean the difference between being able to go to college or not."

"I forgot there was a prize attached." I had to remember to keep stirring so the cheese wouldn't stick to the pot.

Baz shook his head. "Ironic, isn't it? Having a huge

corporation like Spotted Cow Dairy sponsoring a festival celebrating the small, locally owned dairy farms and creameries?"

"Beatrice said it was Nadine who secured the sponsorship years ago. She wanted to help the girls. She may have been tough, but she really did do a lot for that pageant," Mrs. Schultz said. Her chin went back in her hands at the mention of Nadine.

The cheese had finished melting and melding into a shiny, creamy sauce. The stove's timer sounded to indicate the pasta was done at the same time we heard an old-fashioned ringing of a phone. My ringtone was "Sweet Dreams Are Made of Cheese," a take on the Eurythmics tune, so I knew it wasn't my phone. Mrs. Schultz, recognizing it as hers, went to retrieve her purse from the front counter. By that time, the ringing had stopped. She walked back to the kitchenette, checking her phone, as I drained the pasta.

"It's the Dairy Days director, Tyrell." A blip sound indicated a voicemail message. She put the phone to her ear and listened. She looked unpleasantly surprised as she anxiously played with her short curly hair. She ended the message. "He wants me to direct this year's pageant in place of Nadine." She reached for her glass of water, flustered.

"How do you feel about that?" I asked.

She took a sip and sat for a moment in thought. "It was an easier decision when he asked me to fill in for her temporarily after she broke her foot, even though Nadine ended up nixing it. She was determined to run it herself."

"It'll be like being back at your old job as a drama teacher at Yarrow Glen High. You'll do a great job," Archie said.

"That's not it, Archie. It feels premature to be discussing her replacement already."

"That's true, but Dairy Days starts tomorrow. They must have to make decisions fast if they want to keep the festival going," he reminded her.

Mrs. Schultz nodded, taking it in. "I suppose the practicality of it outweighs any sentimentality we'd like to have for Nadine's passing. The show must go on, as we say in the theater world." She took a breath and pulled her shoulders back to sit up straighter, as if fortifying herself in her decision.

Feeling uncertain about it, I stayed quiet while I poured the drained pasta into the pot and carefully folded it into the sauce. With each scoop of the wooden spoon, the alfredo worked its way into all the nooks and crannies of the spirals, coating the fusilli in the rich, cheesy sauce.

I portioned out the freshly made pasta alfredo. Baz popped off the bench to help me distribute the bowls and added another scoop to his own.

"It's got a few more cheeses than just cheddar," I warned him, knowing he liked to stick to the basics.

"Yeah, but it's not stinky cheese," he replied, heading back to the table with his nose close to his mound of pasta, inhaling its aroma.

I joined the others and we all tucked into our meals, the comfort of the hearty pasta especially needed this evening. I hadn't wanted to talk about it at dinner, but I couldn't keep my fears to myself. "I'm a little concerned about any of it going forward after what happened to Nadine," I said.

The others nodded in understanding.

"You're certain it was murder and not an accident?" Baz asked.

"Her body was positioned all wrong for it to have been an accident," I maintained.

"You said you thought there was blood on the floor and on her scooter?" Mrs. Schultz reiterated.

"Yes. And Chief Womack thought it was blood too. He didn't come out and say so, but I saw it in his face. He couldn't hide it—his face changed, like he was . . . kind of scared? I don't know."

"And don't forget the lights," Archie said.

"That's right. The lights were definitely off when you opened the door, right?" I asked him.

"It was pitch-black."

Baz left his seat momentarily to bring more freshly grated Parm to the table. "So what do you think she was killed with?" he asked.

We ate for a few moments in silence as we considered the question.

Archie spoke up. "I saw some big milk jugs in the museum. If you hit someone hard enough with one of them . . ." He shuddered.

"I did notice a couple of larger broken pieces of pottery compared to all the rest, but I didn't get a good look," I said.

"Who would be strong enough to push that shelf over? You both said it was heavy," Mrs. Schultz brought up. She seemed to be mostly pushing her pasta around with her fork rather than eating it.

"It would probably take two people," Archie speculated.

"Not necessarily. If it's narrow enough, high enough, and top-heavy, it wouldn't be too hard to knock over," Baz said. Being a carpenter and handyman, he knew more about such things than I did.

"Why was the mayor so quick to call it an accident?"

Archie asked. His appetite didn't seem hindered by the subject matter—his pasta bowl was almost empty.

"I have a feeling that was wishful thinking," Mrs. Schultz replied.

"Well, we just talked about how lucrative Dairy Days is for Lockwood. Announcing a murder on opening day tomorrow wouldn't do much for the festival. And next year is the fiftieth anniversary. From what I've been hearing, they've got big plans for it," Baz added.

"So Mayor Sonny has every reason to keep this murder under wraps," I said, shaking my head with disapproval. "It's always about money, isn't it? At least the forensics team was called in right away." I'd been relieved to see their van pull up to the museum just after we were told to leave.

"Chief Womack won't ignore the evidence," Mrs. Schultz said. Her conviction seemed to boost her spirits and she began to eat her alfredo again.

"Not for longer than three days anyway," I said. I couldn't help the retort—I didn't know why Mrs. Schultz had such trust in Chief Womack. It worried me that he was letting the case get cold—and that he had his eye on Mrs. Schultz as a possible person of interest. A botched investigation could mean trouble for one of our own. "I wish Heath was running this. If this happened in Yarrow Glen, he would never allow our mayor Trumbull to run *his* investigation."

"Yeah, she tried that once, remember?" Baz said with a raised eyebrow in my direction.

"Do I ever!" I replied. The case last winter involving a socialite and her fiancé, our mayor's nephew, was one I'd rather forget.

My mind and heart went to Heath. I missed him for

more reasons than this, but I didn't share that with the others.

Detective Heath and I had a complicated relationship. The reason I knew him at all was because I tended to get wrapped up in his investigations when I or one of my friends were entangled in a case. He would do his best to keep me away from the investigations, but I couldn't help it—when my friends are in trouble, I have to help. The proximity brought Heath and me closer, but ultimately, it tore at our budding relationship, regardless of our attraction. He'd finally asked me out on a date, but the case he was investigating got in the way, and then *I* got in the way trying to solve it myself when I'd promised him I wouldn't. I'd meant it when I made the promise, but someone else helped change my mind. Heath and I had disagreed about my involvement in his cases before, but we'd grown closer and we trusted each other more than ever, so this one was different. Although I had my reasons for doing what I did, I understood why he was upset. I hadn't realized just *how* upset until he kept his distance, not taking my calls and avoiding me in town since it happened four months ago. It hurt my heart when I thought about how long it had been since we'd spoken.

Archie put down his fork and looked around the table. "I know we kidded about this before we found Nadine, but do you think this is a case for Team Cheese?"

There were a lot of unanswered questions. However, there was a reason Heath never wanted me to get involved—it could be dangerous. "I don't think we should investigate. It really has nothing to do with us. As long as Chief Womack doesn't suspect *any of us*, that is." I allowed my gaze to slide to Mrs. Schultz, hoping she'd open up about her thoughts regarding Chief Womack.

"Oh, dear," she said, leading me to think she was about to do just that. Instead, she pulled something out of her dress pocket. "It's the envelope we found that I was going to give to Nadine. I just now felt it in my pocket. I completely forgot about it."

That quieted all of us. How quickly things had changed since this morning.

"Should I read it or give it to her cousin Mary Ann?" Mrs. Schultz asked.

"If it's nothing, it could just upset her," I said.

"Why don't you just see what it is?" Baz suggested.

Mrs. Schultz pulled the note out of its opened envelope. She read it aloud.

You can't ignore this. We have to talk. In private!
                                        Nadine

We looked at one another, wide-eyed.

If this was the reason she was at the museum, Nadine may have unwittingly set a meeting for her own murder.

CHAPTER 6

I was up at dawn for all the last-minute prep for our cheese booth at the Dairy Days festival. Normally, I would've been very excited for the day ahead, but on the tail of Nadine's murder and having to face Chief Womack as soon as we arrived, apprehension was my leading emotion. Mrs. Schultz insisted on giving Nadine's note to Chief Womack, but I wasn't about to let her go by herself—he already seemed suspicious of her, a detail she was choosing to ignore.

Baz, Archie, and I hauled the coolers with our grazing boxes onto the bed of Baz's pickup, along with signage and all our supplies, before I sent them off to the festival. Baz had offered to drive Archie and help set up our cheese booth, while Mrs. Schultz and I went straight to Chief Womack's temporary office at the carriage house to show him the note. Once we did this, I could fully concentrate on our Curds & Whey booth.

The fifteen-minute drive to Lockwood in Mrs. Schultz's Fiat took us through a quiet Main Street that consisted of a strip mall, a bank, and a gas station. Dairy farms populated much of the town, thus it was bigger in area than Yarrow Glen, but smaller in population, without a lively downtown like ours. Large events held on their sprawling festival grounds were the town's draw. Dairy Days was apparently its biggest moneymaker, although it relied on help from the other two towns in our district.

We pulled into the small lot we'd driven through yesterday on our way to the pageant stage. So much had changed since then. My body shuddered involuntarily as Mrs. Schultz parked her car in the lot in front of the single-story carriage house that served as Chief Womack's temporary office during events that took place on the festival grounds. Only one of the original bays still existed, likely for the chief's vehicle. The updated garage door was made to look like one of the old manual swinging ones. Where the other bays had been was now a front door flanked by windows. The eave above the door displayed the Lockwood Police seal.

As we stepped up to the door, it opened and a host of uniformed police officers and festival security, identifiable by their blue T-shirts with SECURITY written in capital letters on the back, began to stream out of the building.

One of the security officers paused and moved to the side. "Can we help you?"

"We're here to see Chief Womack," Mrs. Schultz said. Today, her dress and matching scarf were in somber shades of navy blue.

"Willa! Mrs. Schultz." Shep sounded surprised to see us as he stepped over the threshold.

Mrs. Schultz smiled at him.

"Hey, Shep," I replied. Even though he was heading to the festival with the others, it still calmed my nerves to see a familiar face.

The other helpful security guy fell in line with the others leaving the building.

"Do you need something?" Shep asked us.

"We need to see Chief Womack. Is he inside?"

"Yeah, we just finished a meeting. But the festival is starting in forty-five minutes. This probably isn't the best time."

"It's about yesterday," I said cryptically.

Shep sighed. He looked on as the last of his colleagues rounded the building toward the festival grounds. "Willa, I don't think you should get involved in this one," he said.

My reputation for involving myself in investigations preceded my presence.

"I'm sure the chief of police will be very interested to see what we have," Mrs. Schultz told him, pulling the envelope from her dress pocket, making it obvious Shep's reluctance wasn't going to sway her from speaking to Chief Womack.

Over Mrs. Schultz's shoulder, I noticed a thin woman in tight jeans and a black blouse cornering the building. I recognized Mary Ann at the same time Mrs. Schultz said to Shep, "It could be a direct link to the person who murdered Nadine."

Mary Ann froze, all but her eyes and her mouth— both had widened. Mine must've done the same, because Mrs. Schultz and Shep turned their heads to see what had made me go slack-jawed.

Mary Ann took cautious steps toward us. "What are you talking about? Nadine was murdered?"

Mrs. Schultz slipped the envelope back into her pocket. "Mary Ann. I'm so sorry. You weren't meant to hear that," she said.

Shep was beside Mary Ann instantly, keeping her propped up—she looked like she might drop to the ground at any moment. He walked her into the carriage house, and we followed. The simple interior consisted of a high-ceilinged room with utilitarian office furniture and a large whiteboard. A second room with a door was off the main room, from where Chief Womack emerged.

"What's going on?" he asked, immediately ascertaining Mary Ann was upset.

"Pete!" Mary Ann cried, reaching out to Chief Womack. "You told me she was dead. You didn't say she was murdered!"

He allowed Mary Ann to keep ahold of him, her unpolished nails digging into his forearms. "Let's sit down in my office. Shep, can you take Ms. Bauer and Mrs. Schultz out, please?"

"No, I want to hear what they have to say. What do you know about this?" Mary Ann's questioning stare alternated between me and Mrs. Schultz.

The grunt Chief Womack let out as he exhaled in frustration kept me and Mrs. Schultz silent for the moment. His hand brushed over his beard as it had yesterday just before he'd confronted us outside—he was obviously deciding how to handle Mary Ann.

"Let's sit down," he said to her again as he led her into his office and directed her into one of the two chairs across from his desk. He took out a box of tissues from the drawer and placed them in front of Mary Ann. He turned to Shep. "You're needed at your post. You should go."

Shep nodded then held his gaze on me and Mrs. Schultz for a moment before making the decision to leave.

Chief Womack pushed the box of tissues aside and half-sat, half-leaned on the desk next to where Mary Ann was seated. Mrs. Schultz and I remained standing just inside his office door, ignored by him.

"Please tell me what's going on," Mary Ann said to him.

"This is not something you should concern yourself with right now," he said gently.

"I'm afraid it's my fault. We didn't mean for you to overhear us talking about it. I'm so sorry," Mrs. Schultz said.

"Who would want to kill Nadine? Why?" Mary Ann pulled a tissue from the box.

"We don't know anything right now. Trust me, we will look into how this could've happened to Nadine. You know I want to know as much as anyone," Chief Womack said.

Mary Ann dabbed her eyes. "I know you do. Nadine considered Sophie her closest friend. Even though it's been years since your wife left. . . ."

Chief Womack's eye twitched at the mention of his wife, or likely ex-wife. "You're right, Nadine's death is still personal for me. Give us some time to gather what we need for an investigation," he assured her. A quick scowl in our direction let me know he wasn't happy with us.

Mary Ann turned her attention back to us. "Is there something you know? Did you see something? You said outside you had something to show Pete."

I saw Mrs. Schultz's hand fiddling with Nadine's note in her dress pocket.

I wasn't so sure it was a good idea to let Mary Ann know about the note. Anybody could be a suspect. "I was the one who found Nadine in the museum, so we're here to give Chief Womack a more detailed statement," I half-lied.

"It's all routine," he added, "You should be home resting. I'll have one of my men take you back to Nadine's."

She shook her head. "I have to be at the pageant. I can't let the girls down." She stood from the chair, her strength seemingly restored by the thought of the pageant.

"You don't have to worry about any of that," Mrs. Schultz said. "Tyrell's asked me to fill in and direct the pageant. I spoke with Beatrice last night. We'll take care of everything and make you and Nadine proud."

She cocked her head like a confused pet. "Why would he do that? Nadine would want *me* to take over. She made that clear to Tyrell when she broke her foot. What exactly are you trying to do, Mrs. Schultz? Are you trying to replace Nadine?"

Mrs. Schultz's cheeks flushed pink. "Of course not!"

"She's only trying to make things easier on everyone," I said as gently as I could muster.

"That's not what Nadine would want. I'm the only one who knows exactly how Nadine ran this pageant, how she'd want it to run in her absence. *I'll* be directing this pageant, Mrs. Schultz. I don't care what Tyrell's asked you to do."

Flustered at first, Mrs. Schultz retained her composure. "As long as you feel up to it. . . ."

"It's what Nadine would want. I'll do it in my cousin's honor."

Mrs. Schultz offered a sympathetic smile. "I'm here to help in any way you need."

Mary Ann's shoulders relaxed, and she took a few seconds with her eyes closed. When she opened them, her prickly demeanor had changed. "Thank you, Mrs. Schultz. I didn't mean to bark at you." She turned to Chief Womack. "Pete, be honest with me. Do you really think someone purposely killed Nadine?"

He paused momentarily before answering, "There is

some evidence to suggest that it might not have been an accident."

Her breath caught and her fingers anxiously worked the tissue she'd been holding as if she was making origami.

"I put two of our officers in the pageant area for the entirety of the festival," he told her.

"Do you think our girls are in danger?" Mary Ann's eyes widened.

"No, no," he answered quickly. "It's purely precautionary. In fact, for the sake of the pageant and the festival, I think it would be best if we kept this between us. We don't know anything for certain yet and Mayor Sonny prefers we not say anything publicly about the possibility of it being anything other than an accident."

He shot me a quick but meaningful glance that stopped me from voicing a contradiction. I kept quiet for Mary Ann's sake.

Mary Ann nodded. "I understand. I'm sure that's best."

"Once we get the report from forensics, we'll know what we're dealing with. If someone murdered Nadine, we'll find them," he continued.

Her lip trembled, which kept her from speaking at first. "We're very lucky to have you on the case."

"You just concentrate on the pageant and let me handle this."

She nodded in quick bursts and finally seemed reassured. "Rehearsal is set to start soon. We're having a short memorial for Nadine once everyone arrives. We should get over there, Mrs. Schultz." She started to leave the office.

"I need Mrs. Schultz to stay a little longer. I'll send

her your way soon," Chief Womack said, following Mary Ann to the doorway.

"Oh. Okay. I'm sure Beatrice will be needing you," she reminded Mrs. Schultz.

"I'll be there as soon as I can," Mrs. Schultz said.

"I'll check in with you later," Chief Womack assured her.

A brief smile crossed her lips before she finally turned and left.

Chief Womack closed his office door and said, "What is this all about? What kind of information do you have?"

"Possible evidence," I said.

Mrs. Schultz pulled out the envelope and showed it to him. "We found it under Beatrice's car yesterday. It might've fallen out of one of the costumes." She tried to hand it to him.

He refused it and walked around to open a drawer in his desk. He pulled out a pair of latex gloves, a clear bag, and some tweezers. He pulled on the gloves then held the envelope by its edges and used the tweezer to pull out the note. He unfolded it carefully and placed it in the clear bag before reading it.

You can't ignore this. We have to talk. In private!
                                                    Nadine

"I was going to give it to Nadine, but I forgot about it until last night. It looks like her handwriting. At least from the notes *I've* gotten from her," Mrs. Schultz said.

"Mary Ann would know," I added.

"Have you shown this to anyone else?"

"No," I answered quickly. No sense in getting Archie and Baz involved in this.

He stared at the note before lasering us with that stare again. "I'm going to ask that you keep the existence of this note to yourselves. Tell no one. Understood?"

We both nodded.

He fell heavily into his desk chair and motioned for us to take the two seats across from him. We did.

"Mrs. Schultz, when I spoke with Mary Ann last night, she said you had disappeared from the pageant rehearsal for quite a while yesterday morning."

Uh-oh. I was afraid of this. "She told you yesterday she sent her to get a prop," I intervened.

"Yes, that's what I recalled, but I asked Mary Ann about it last night and she said she didn't remember sending you to the museum. In fact, she was looking for you after you'd quietly gone to the museum on your own. Can you clear that up?"

"You don't have to answer him, Mrs. Schultz. Maybe we should get an attorney."

"Don't be silly, Willa. The request was from Nadine. She gave it to Beatrice who passed it on to me. Beatrice was too busy to go searching for a prop. I was too, but I'm low woman on the call sheet, so to speak, so I agreed to get it. You can ask Beatrice."

"Was it a note like this one?" he asked, pointing to the note in the evidence bag.

I did *not* like the direction this was going.

Mrs. Schultz answered without hesitation, "No, just a little memo note. Nadine was big on them."

"Do you have it with you?"

"No. It might still be in the pocket of the dress I wore yesterday. Or maybe I never took it from Beatrice. I don't recall."

"If you find it, I'd appreciate it if you'd give that to

me," he said with a smile, as if he was making pleasant conversation and not interrogating her.

"Mrs. Schultz, I don't want you to say another word," I said. The time for fake pleasantries was over. "I don't like what you're implying, Chief Womack. We came here to give you evidence to help the case. Why would we do that if one of us was guilty?"

He leaned forward, crossing his hands on the desk. "Why would you give me something to steer the case in another direction if one of you was the murderer? Is that really what you're asking?"

"Wha—?" It was probably to my benefit that my furious thoughts piled in my throat before they could form coherent words.

Mrs. Schultz was much more composed than I. "Now, Chief Womack, you seem like a much smarter man than that. That's not really what you believe, is it?" Her question echoed his in its cadence.

He leaned back in his chair, his fingers intertwined and resting on the six-pack abs I had no doubt were concealed by his uniform. "You're very intelligent yourself, Mrs. Schultz."

I could tell it wasn't meant as a compliment, but an observation. One that I didn't think boded well for Mrs. Schultz.

He glanced at his watch. "I'd like to get your statements now, but I have to get out there. The festival's about to start. Come to the police department in town on Tuesday to give your statements. And until then, remember, none of this information leaves this room. Got it?"

We agreed and left the building before him. Mrs. Schultz and I went back to her car. The door to the carriage house bay opened, revealing Chief Womack's Expedition.

"Do you want me to drive you to the vendor lot?" she asked as she started the car.

"No, let's not get mixed up in the festival traffic. You can park at the stage, and I'll walk over from there."

Mrs. Schultz wiggled her fingers in a wave as Chief Womack's SUV left the lot.

It would only take us a minute or two to get to the parking area, so I had to speak my mind now. "Mrs. Schultz, I agree with Chief Womack that you're very intelligent."

"Thank you, Willa. I like to think so."

I took a deep breath and plowed ahead. "So then why do you seem to be letting him get away with putting suspicion on you? I don't want to worry you, but isn't he making you nervous? The way he makes eye contact when he's asking you questions?" He was sure making *me* nervous.

"Why should he make me nervous? I haven't done anything wrong. I trust he'll get to the bottom of it."

She slowed the Fiat and pulled beside the last car in the makeshift row. "His eyes *are* piercing, aren't they? You don't often see an eye color like that."

"Mrs. Schultz! Are you being taken in by his good looks?"

Mrs. Schultz laughed. "Oh, Willa! I'm teasing you. Have you ever heard the phrase you catch more flies with honey than vinegar? Feelings play into suspicion, and I'd rather he have good feelings about me than antagonistic ones."

I got out of the car, properly schooled. "I should know better than to think you're not on top of your game. You'll keep your eyes and ears open today for anyone who *should* be under suspicion?"

"Of course."

"I'll come by later for any updates. Be careful."

"You too."

Mrs. Schultz walked toward the opening in the fence where she'd have to show her pageant badge to the security officer who stood guard. I started across the grounds to the opposite side where Archie and my cheese shop booth were located.

Mrs. Schultz was right—I wasn't doing myself any favors by being antagonistic to Chief Womack. But could I trust him not to pursue her as a suspect?

I pulled my phone from my sweatshirt pocket and stared at it, debating. The niggling that had started in my belly would soon be a knot of anxiety if I didn't do something. I opened the messages icon and tapped a text.

Heath, I need your help.

CHAPTER 7

I managed to make it to my booth just as the opening "Moo" horn sounded and people began to stream into the festival. Mayor Sonny, dressed in tails and a top hat that made him unintentionally look like the Wizard of Oz, did the honors.

Archie had a couple of costumes he liked to wear to our farmer's markets in Yarrow Glen's park, and today he'd insisted on bringing the cheese wedge one. He wasn't going to be outdone by the festival mascots, most of whom were in cow costumes. Once I arrived, he slipped the triangular costume over his shorts and Curds & Whey T-shirt. Only his arms, legs, and face poked out, but it was enough for him to do cartwheels and jump-kicks, and wave festivalgoers over to our booth.

A festival mascot wearing a milk carton costume joined Archie. The costume was more elaborate, covering the person in it from head to toe, much like a Disney theme park character, with only a shadow of a face visible behind mesh. The two of them easily got into a rhythm of dancing and high-fiving, as if they'd rehearsed, soon attracting a crowd. I was impressed by how they did anything in those bulky costumes.

It made my heart happy that Archie had something to do to take his mind off yesterday. But after about an hour, the temperature began inching its way up and I called him back to the booth.

"I know you love it, but I don't want you to get overheated," I said, handing him a water.

"It *is* pretty hot in this thing," he replied.

I held one out to the life-sized milk carton. "Water?" I'd assumed they were a festival mascot as I'd seen a costumed goat and sheep pass by, but the milk carton could've also been working for one of the booth vendors—the milk and cookie booth was a popular one. The person inside gave me a thumbs-up before taking the water bottle between oversized, white-gloved hands. Who knew milk cartons even had thumbs?

"If you don't want to take your lid off out here," Archie said, indicating the top of the costume that covered the milk carton's head, "you can come behind our booth."

The milk carton shook their head and started to walk off.

"Wait a second. What's your name?" Archie called after them.

The milk carton kept walking without answering.

"Darn, I wanted to find out who he was. He was awesome," Archie said to me.

"I doubt you'll have a hard time finding him again this weekend. How many acrobatic milk cartons are there?"

Disappointed, he went around to the back of our booth to peel off his costume before assisting me with a growing line of customers. Our Feeling Sheepish grazing box took an early lead for most popular. It contained the sheep's milk cheeses Rispens Gouda and the always popular Manchego, both of which I find hard to put down once I start eating them, and the stronger, bloomy rind Summer Snow. Accompaniments of pretzels, Marcona almonds, and a mini jar of cherry-elderflower jam completed the box. After another hour, the loudspeaker announced the start of Cow Chip Bingo, which cleared our booth of customers.

Now that I didn't have anything to take my mind off it, I started thinking again about Nadine's death and the Dairy Days pageant. I checked my phone for what seemed like the twentieth time—no text or call from Detective Heath. I guess our relationship was even more strained than I thought if he wouldn't even respond to my text for help.

"Archie, since it's slowed down, do you mind if I go check on Mrs. Schultz?" I asked.

Archie didn't answer right away. He was scanning the crowd. "Huh? Oh, sure. I got this."

"I'm sure the milk carton will return," I said, knowing just who he was looking for.

"How'd you know I was looking for him? I want him to show me that cool dance move he did."

I smiled to myself. Archie had been down for months since his girlfriend had gone off to Paris for the summer, then extended her stay through the fall. They'd decided to put their relationship on pause and see where they stood when she returned. So I was happy to see him in good spirits again.

I left our booth and walked across the festival grounds, passing booths selling various crafts and wares. I thought the one selling hats, mittens, and scarves handwoven from sheep's wool might have a tough go of it in this heat, even though autumn was right around the corner. Various food truck aromas wafted my way—French fries and smoked BBQ comingled with hints of cinnamon churros and chocolate chip cookies. I veered away from the long row of food trucks to stay on course.

I got caught up in a crowd streaming into a canopied area with tables and chairs. A woman stood at the front with a microphone and a big drum of numbered Ping-Pong balls. The sign in front of the tent read Cow Chip Bingo. I laughed at myself for having thought they were going to use real cows and their dried dung cow chips.

I continued on my way, leaving the activity of the festival to get to the stage at the edge of the grounds. The area was largely ignored by festivalgoers until Monday afternoon, when the popular pageant closed out the Dairy Days weekend.

I saw Mary Ann waving her arms like she was directing an incoming airplane to the tarmac instead of a couple of volunteers with a folding table for the judges. I peered closer at the groups of people milling about on the grass near the stage in hopes of spotting celebrity guest judge Nancy Fuller.

When the announcement came last month, I was super excited about the possibility of meeting Nancy Fuller. Although the Food Network show most often playing on my TV was *Chopped*—mostly because my betta fish, Loretta, was enamored with Ted Allen—I adored Nancy Fuller as a baking judge on the seasonal competition shows and as the star of her own show, *Farmhouse Rules*. She was a huge celebrity to snag. Her passion for farms and using farm fresh ingredients must've been why she agreed to be a guest judge this year. I hoped I could keep my fangirling in check.

Sadly, Nancy Fuller was nowhere to be seen. Instead, I saw Shep sauntering toward me, his thin frame in a

Dairy Days Security T-shirt and jeans, same as this morning.

"Hi, Shep. I just came to check on Mrs. Schultz. Any updates from Chief Womack?"

Shep crossed his arms and all but rolled his eyes. "About the *accident*, you mean? They still haven't labeled it a homicide. Precious time is being wasted. The first forty-eight hours are critical in solving a homicide. I'd be itching to get at it if it were our case. What went down this morning at Chief Womack's office with you and Mrs. Schultz and Mary Ann?"

Oddly, Shep's attention left me as soon as he asked the question. A smile of recognition broadened his face as he looked past me. "Detective Heath."

Heath? My stomach spun like that Cow Chip Bingo drum.

"Shep." I heard Heath's voice behind me.

He passed me, and he and Shep shook hands. Until he turned, I thought maybe it wasn't him after all—I'd rarely seen him wearing something other than a suit. Off-duty Heath wore jeans and a simple gray T-shirt that clung to his broad shoulders. I could practically feel my short, straight hair frizzing in the heat, but every strand of his thick, black hair was perfectly in place. His strong jaw was clean shaven. Why did he still have to be so darn good-looking? I tried not to stare but knew I was failing.

"Hi, Willa," he said.

He didn't exactly smile when he said it, but it was an improvement. At least he acknowledged me this time.

I wasn't sure how to act now that he was in front of me. I wanted to ask him about the text without sounding accusatory that he hadn't responded. I swallowed, trying to generate some saliva, my mouth now devoid of any.

I swallowed again. "Hi, Heath."

Should I have called him Jay, like he told me to when he asked me out on a date last May? No, definitely not. I always called him Heath. Given our current frosty relationship, he'd probably prefer I go back to "*Detective* Heath."

I willed my brain to think of something else to say—something innocuous but clever enough that maybe he'd decide to start a conversation with me. I kept staring at him, my mind drawing a blank. His dark eyes tended to do that to me, especially when they didn't leave mine, like now.

"Well," Shep said, breaking the spell that had me and Heath locking eyes. "I've got security duty." He and Heath did another quick bro handshake and Shep walked off.

Now that it was just the two of us, the tumbling in my stomach started up again. My saliva-maker wasn't working, but my stomach was working overtime. *Great.* Now if I could only think of something to say. "Are you here for the musical udders contest?" I blurted out. *Ugh. Really, Willa? That's what you came up with?*

His lips turned up in a slight smile, so it wasn't a complete waste.

"I got your text."

"You did? Why didn't you text me back?" So much for not sounding accusatory.

"I'm here, aren't I? I thought it would be better to talk in person. I talked to Shep about what happened yesterday. He said you and Archie found Nadine Hockenbaum's body. Are you okay?"

I wanted to take his show of concern as a sign his

coolness toward me was thawing, but did I dare hope for it? It certainly put a chink in my steely resolve to be impassive in the face of heartache and a dead body. I felt vulnerability creeping in.

"You'd think I'd be used to it by now, wouldn't you?" I said, throwing in a smile as if finding a body was nothing. Why be vulnerable when I could make light of it?

"I'd be more concerned if you *were* used to it." That sincere gaze caught mine again, this time only briefly.

For the first time, I wasn't interested in talking about a possible case with Heath. This time there was something more important to find out—where we stood with each other. "Heath—"

"Excuse me, Willa." He walked past me before I could get more out.

I stood like a fool, my mouth still open like I was trying to catch flies with it. I guess I was wrong.

Raised angry voices reached my ear and I turned to see the reason he'd left—he was making a beeline for the stage. I hurried over to see what was going on. Once I got closer, I could see a crowd of pageant moms and their contestant daughters had gathered around Mary Ann, who seemed to be screeching at the festival director, Tyrell. Fiona, the pageant judge I saw yelling at Nadine yesterday, once again wearing a bright red logoed blazer, was standing on the other side of Tyrell, who had adopted the stance of a boxing match referee between the two women. As soon as Heath saw Chief Womack striding over, he slowed his pace.

"She thinks this is her own Becky's Bakeware sellathon, and it's not! It's the Miss Dairy pageant!" Mary Ann yelled.

Mary Ann's shrill voice finally halted long enough for Tyrell to speak. "I understand that, but it's not enough to remove her as a pageant judge. I know Nadine didn't prefer Fiona to be a judge, but we have to think about what's best for the pageant this year," he said, working hard to keep his tone even. "Let's go somewhere more private to talk about this."

"Why make this private when you're publicly spitting on Nadine's memory? And you! What are *you* doing here?" Mary Ann pointed to a striking woman standing off to the side behind referee Tyrell and problematic pageant judge Fiona.

The woman, probably in her late twenties, wore a gauzy shirt along with cut-off denim shorts that showed off her long, dark legs. She transferred her phone to the opposite hand and pressed a coil of her cinnamon-brown hair behind an ear. "I'm just reporting on the festival, Mary Ann," she said in a non-apologetic tone.

"Just like last year, huh? I know what you're here for, Grace Kelp! You're here to smear the pageant again. I know what you tried to do to Nadine. She told me everything about you. Nobody is going to take down this pageant. It's not going to happen! Do you hear me?"

Heath started forward again, but Chief Womack intervened. He put a strong hand on Mary Ann's shoulder, as he'd done to Mayor Sonny yesterday. He hunched down to meet her at eye level. "Mary Ann, calm down. Get ahold of yourself."

This quieted her.

Beatrice stepped forward. "We're all here because we want the pageant to successfully continue."

The contestants nodded. One of the contestants I'd seen yesterday spoke up. "We loved Miss Hockenbaum. We'll do our best for her."

Mary Ann tried to choke back tears, but they fell anyway. Chief Womack handed her a handkerchief he'd quickly produced from his trousers pocket. She used it to dab at her cheeks and nose.

"She loved you girls, you know," she eventually said when she got her emotions in check. "She thought of each year's contestants as her own children since she didn't have any of her own. She was tough on you, but she did it *for* you, so you'd be at your best. She was the reason Miss Dairy has been so successful. Even though she's gone, we should still follow her wishes." She looked directly at Tyrell and Fiona. "That includes who judges the pageant."

Fiona moved in front of Tyrell. "Some of us are just as invested in these girls as Nadine was. I've been judging this pageant almost as long as she was directing it, so I wish you wouldn't dismiss my contributions. I don't want to speak ill of her now that she's gone, but her issues with me should've been kept strictly private. They had nothing to do with my position with this pageant. There is no one more qualified to be the head judge of Miss Dairy than me. I think Nadine let whatever personal jealousy about my Becky's Bakeware success get in the way of her professional decisions."

Mary Ann opened her mouth to hurl a response, but Tyrell went back to referee mode, this time holding his clipboard aloft like a partition between the two women.

"That's enough! I think we can all agree we don't need any more shake-ups right now. Let's agree to revisit this after this year's pageant, okay?" he said firmly.

"That sounds like a good plan," Chief Womack interjected, making his way into the brief pause in the argument. "I think it's time we all get back to what we were doing."

Fiona shrugged. "That's fine by me. Anyone who's not a part of our Lockwood community won't be involved in making the decisions for next year, anyway," Fiona said with satisfaction. "You'll finally be in charge now, Tyrell, as it should be."

"Fiona—" Tyrell was still trying to referee, but with Fiona's last comment, the bell had been rung. Mary Ann wasn't about to stay in her corner of the ring.

"If that's the case, Tyrell, then you'll have to decide if you really want a pageant judge who might have been responsible for Nadine's murder!" Mary Ann announced.

Uh-oh.

A buzz went around the group, as mothers and daughters became alarmed.

The overbearing pageant mom I'd come across yesterday put a protective arm around her copper-haired daughter. "Murder? Nadine was murdered?"

All eyes were on Chief Womack. Could he still put off the murder investigation now?

CHAPTER 8

"Everyone calm down," Chief Womack announced.

"How dare you accuse me of such a thing! I'm the number one Becky of Becky's Bakeware! I have a reputation to uphold!" Fiona yelled at Mary Ann. Her face was becoming perilously close to the red color of her Becky's Bakeware blazer.

Mary Ann was not to be deterred. "What would it have done to your reputation to get fired from the judging table of the biggest event in Lockwood? Is that why you murdered Nadine?"

"I'll sue you!"

"Murderer!"

Tyrell waved his arms to stop them, as if it would help Mary Ann's accusation dissipate into the air like smoke. "Stop using that word! Nobody was murdered!" Any semblance of him keeping his cool was gone. He stuck his face in Mary Ann's. "If you want this pageant to go on, you'd better stop making accusations like that! It was an accident, Mary Ann! An accident!" He raised his voice to make the pronouncement to everyone listening. "An accident! That's all it was."

Mary Ann looked shocked at her own words, and she stifled her mouth with the handkerchief.

"Tyrell's right. There's no indication that this was anything other than an accident," Chief Womack announced.

I understood his need to supply assurances, but that seemed to be taking it too far.

Mary Ann looked at the frightened faces of the contestants and suddenly seemed to awaken from her outburst. "Oh, my gosh. I'm so sorry, girls. I was being dramatic. There's nothing to worry about. I promise. I-I apologize, Fiona. Of course, I don't think you're a murderer."

Tyrell again winced at the word.

"I'm sorry, I'm not myself today," Mary Ann continued.

Mrs. Schultz stepped forward. "We understand. All of us are here to support you. Even Fiona." Mrs. Schultz looked sharply at Fiona—she could still pull out her teacher stare when she had to.

Fiona backed down slightly. "I'm here to support the pageant. These girls want a chance, and Nadine would want them to have it."

I felt a collective breath being held—it was up to Mary Ann to keep the peace.

Chief Womack gave it his best shot to make sure it would happen. "Mary Ann, maybe you *should* go home. It's too much to direct the pageant and grieve for your cousin at the same time. You're probably still in shock."

Mary Ann stared at the handkerchief in her hands. She seemed eased by his words of concern.

"Mrs. Schultz is very capable of taking over," he continued.

One sentence too many—she tensed back up. "No,

I can do this. I want to do this for Nadine. I'm so sorry about this. It won't happen again."

No one moved or spoke, unsure of what to do.

Beatrice snapped everyone out of it. "Come on, girls. Let's finish getting ready for dress rehearsal," she directed.

The contestants and their mothers looked to one another and then to Chief Womack to see if the direction should be followed. A confident nod and smile from him sent them back to the changing tent with Beatrice and Mrs. Schultz. It was apparent they trusted him.

Mary Ann faced Chief Womack and lowered her eyes. "I'm so embarrassed, Pete. I don't know what came over me."

"It's been a shock. You're still processing it. Are you sure you don't want to take some time to yourself?"

She shook her head. "No. This is the best thing for me, to finish Nadine's work. It's the least I can do for her. Besides, I don't really want to be alone."

He gave her a strong one-armed hug. She leaned in, as if she wanted to crumple in his arms.

"You're a strong woman, Mary Ann, just like Nadine was," Chief Womack said when he released her. "You'll be all right."

She backed away and straightened her posture. "Thank you. And again, I'm very sorry for the scene I caused." She headed toward the changing tent. She clapped and called, "Get a move on, girls. Let's go!", sounding very much like Nadine.

Chief Womack seemed satisfied that everything was under control and began to leave. I wanted to finish my conversation with Heath, but he'd caught up with Chief Womack and they walked off, conversing privately.

As the stragglers dispersed, I caught Tyrell, the festival director, muttering to himself, "No apology for me? Of course not. I'll just get blamed for it."

"What are you complaining about? She didn't accuse *you* of murder," Fiona said to him. "I made nice for the sake of the pageant, but if she says anything like that again, I'm warning you, I'm suing her, no matter how it affects the pageant."

"If she says that again, the pageant and this festival will be over anyway."

Fiona walked off, and even from where I stood, I could see Tyrell's chest heave in a deep sigh. He stuck his clipboard under one arm and used his other hand to reach for his phone. He tapped at it then held it above forehead level, doing a slow turn in place to get a signal. It must've failed, because he put it back in his pocket, obviously frustrated.

The reporter approached him, but he put a hand up to her. "You'd better leave the area before they come back, Miss Kelp," he said.

She hesitated as if she might not heed his request, but then walked off. Tyrell left in the opposite direction.

Baz came over to me and shook his head. "Crazy, huh? I'm glad that's over with."

"Is it, or has it just begun?" I wondered.

"You mean now that Mary Ann let the cat out of the bag? It looks like everyone took Chief Womack's word that there was no murder."

"Unless the murderer was here and knows they're onto him. Or her."

"I hadn't thought about that." He pushed his hair out of his eyes. "You think they could've been here?"

"Well, think about who had motive."

"That Fiona woman for sure."

"And what about that reporter that was just here? Grace Kelp."

"Yeah, what did Mary Ann mean when she said she knew what she had tried to do to Nadine?"

"I have no idea. Do you know Grace Kelp?" I asked him.

"No. I wouldn't mind an excuse to get to know her, though. She's gorgeous."

I looked in the direction she'd gone, but she'd faded into the festival crowd. "Darn, I should've talked to her before she left. Keep an eye out for her this weekend. If she's covering the festival like she said, she'll be around."

"You want me to go talk to her right now?" he said with a broad grin. He looked ready to take off.

I saw Heath and Chief Womack standing near the stage still talking. "No. Let's get closer to them and see if we can hear what they're talking about."

Baz and I meandered toward the stage, but we were still too far away to hear their conversation.

"Why do cops have the quietest voices?" I whispered to him.

"This is gonna get weird if we just stand here. Nobody else is around," Baz said.

"Come on, we're going to have to go onstage. Pretend you're showing me something."

We walked up the ramp Baz had fixed for Nadine and began to walk across the stage for a better listen. I moved my lips, pretending Baz and I were engaged in conversation.

He leaned closer to me. "I can't hear you."

"That's because I'm not really saying anything. I want to hear what *they're* saying," I whispered.

"Ah."

It was no use—I still couldn't hear them. I focused on Heath and attempted to read his lips. I sighed. Those lips . . . *That's not what you're doing right now, Willa!* I blinked away romantic thoughts of Heath at the same moment he suddenly looked up at me. *Oops!* I whipped around and knocked into Baz. It was too late—it would look even worse to run off the stage.

"Act like you're showing me something on the stage." I looked around for something to pretend to be interested in.

I pointed to the lights at the same time Baz knelt to the floor. I swatted at his shoulder for him to get up, but he pulled me down to his level and tapped the stage's surface.

"This is where the stage trapdoor is. It's how Nadine broke her foot. Oh, sorry." He started moving his lips without speaking.

"It happened here, onstage?"

Baz's lips kept moving and wouldn't quit.

"What are you doing?"

"Singing 'Supercalifragilisticexpialidocious' to myself. It looked like I was talking, didn't it? The stage is bringing out my acting chops." He smiled, impressed with himself.

Thankfully, the convo between Chief Womack and Heath had broken up. I left Baz and the charade and hurried down the stage steps after Heath.

"So? Any news?" I asked when I reached him.

He stopped walking.

"You couldn't hear for yourself?" he asked slyly.

My face flushed warm. I'd been caught. "You were too quiet, darn it," I admitted.

He smiled, despite himself.

"So, what are the police doing?"

"Womack's not letting me in on much. I have no jurisdiction here and I have to respect his leadership on this. I can't interfere," he said, serious again.

I sighed. Heath always played strictly by the rules, an admirable but sometimes frustrating quality.

"I'm going to stick around this weekend," he continued, surprising me.

"You are?"

Mary Ann's commands punctuated the growing voices of teenage girls and their mothers returning from the tent. Baz hightailed it off the stage before she could make any demands of him. Heath put a hand on my back and walked me away from the oncoming crowd of contestants.

"I want to keep an eye on things," he told me.

"Why? Do you think Mrs. Schultz is in danger? Or was I right in thinking Chief Womack considers her a suspect?" Both were horrible thoughts.

"No. Womack didn't say anything about Mrs. Schultz."

I followed his keen gaze toward Mary Ann as she consulted with Mrs. Schultz.

"Heath, what aren't you telling me?"

He brought his attention to me but didn't answer. His hesitation worried me.

"I should know if Mrs. Schultz is in danger. *She* should know. Is there anything you know that we don't?" I pressed.

He put his hands on his hips, one of his tells that he was angry or conflicted. Behind those dark eyes, I could sense him wrestling with whether to set aside his rules.

"If you don't have jurisdiction here, the rules don't apply to you," I prodded.

He seemed to consider this and finally said, "I spoke with Ivy."

I couldn't hide my surprise. Ivy was the district's coroner—I'd seen her at other crime scenes where she'd worked with Heath.

"Go on."

"Thus far the autopsy is inconclusive. There appears to be two head wounds. One that killed her and one that occurred postmortem."

"So I was right!"

Heath put his hands out to pump the brakes on my eagerness for a solid answer. "It could be, but it could also be that the shelf shifted after killing her and hit her a second time. Ivy's looking at the differences in the wounds."

"What about what I saw on the scooter and the floor? That's not inconclusive, is it?"

"No. That was Nadine's blood."

"So Nadine's blood wasn't only where she was found. What else do you need? If you know, Chief Womack knows, right?"

"Yes, but he's using the inconclusive autopsy as an excuse to keep a full investigation on pause."

"You've got to be kidding! Even now, you think? With Mary Ann having just blurted out the M-word?"

"Now more than ever. You saw the reaction it got. People will stay away from the festival for sure. He's getting too much pushback from Mayor Sonny and everyone else who's got a financial investment in the festival."

With no current access to cheese, which always calmed me down and helped me think, I gnawed my lower lip. It was a poor substitute. "Couldn't he have his officers investigate quietly, so the powers that be wouldn't know?"

Heath shook his head. "He made it clear his police resources are with the festival this weekend. It sounded like an investigation will have to wait."

I watched Chief Womack walking away in the distance, frustrated by all his excuses. "So why doesn't he accept your help, then?"

"That's not how it works."

"But Shep said valuable witness testimony and evidence could be lost if there's not an investigation right away." I felt my internal cylinders revving, but I couldn't back off. I had no doubt Nadine was murdered. "The autopsy might be inconclusive, but I know what I saw at the crime scene. The blood proves she was hit in the head and then moved to make it look like an accident. She was probably hit with one of those stoneware milk jugs. There were all sizes of them in the museum, some heavy enough to crush someone's skull. And I'm learning pretty quickly that Nadine had a few enemies. This has to be investigated. We should report Chief Womack to the authorities."

Heath looked around us. Even though we were alone, he moved me farther away from anyone who could possibly be within earshot. "Chief Womack and Mayor Sonny *are* the authorities. I know you don't like the way this is being handled and frankly, neither do I. But that's not the way to deal with this. Listen, Shep's filled me in. Womack agrees that her death looks suspicious. He's going to try to do what he can on his own, but he's between a rock and a hard place right now."

"*You* wouldn't be. If this happened in Yarrow Glen,

you wouldn't let our mayor Trumbull tell you how to run a murder investigation."

Heath didn't respond, but his expression told me he agreed. I was sure of it anyway. Maybe his desire for justice would override his need for playing by the rules this time.

"Are you going to investigate on the sly?" I asked quietly.

"No. How Chief Womack proceeds is up to him. I'm not here to interfere with his case."

Drats.

I tried to read his face but couldn't. "So if you believe the case is being handled and you don't think any of us are in danger, can I ask, why *are* you sticking around?" I held my breath, waiting for his answer. I allowed myself to feel a flutter of hope that it had something to do with my text for help.

"Some of my men are working security, and the person who murdered Nadine could still be at the festival," he replied.

"I see." It was silly of me to think it had something to do with me.

"I'm here to make sure the people I care about are safe." His gaze didn't leave mine when he said it and my squashed hope fluttered to life once again.

"I'm glad you're going to be here," I said. I wanted to say more, so much more, but how could I apologize, as I had months ago, without dredging up why he was mad at me in the first place? How could I tell him that I cared about him more than I had ever let on?

"I need to talk to Shep. Where are you going to be?" he said before I could corral any of my emotions enough to speak.

I put my head back in the game. "I came here to

check on Mrs. Schultz, and then I have to get back to my booth. I left Archie there by himself."

"I'll see you later, then. I'll find your booth. Be careful."

"I will be."

"I mean an average person's idea of careful, not your idea of careful."

I chuckled. I didn't have a comeback—he had a point. "I promise, I will be average-person careful."

He smiled at me before turning to leave. As I watched him go, I felt a warmth that wasn't just from the sun. I hadn't fully realized before how much I needed having Heath in my corner.

CHAPTER 9

Everything was back in motion, as the Miss Dairy contestants were in and out of the changing tent while their mothers clucked around them. Mary Ann was shuffling them out of the tent to start rehearsal, as Nadine had her do when she was alive, but with less timidity than she used to employ. I would've liked to ask her about the people who held a grudge against Nadine, but now was not the time. I wanted to fill Mrs. Schultz in on the forensics results. I didn't see her around, so I entered the tent.

I spotted Beatrice, pins between her lips, helping with last-minute adjustments. Mrs. Schultz was in a corner of the tent with the beautiful copper-haired girl—Tabitha, I thought her name was. The one with the overprotective mother. I stopped short when it appeared she and Mrs. Schultz were having a serious conversation.

Tabitha pulled on a strand of ringlets as she spoke earnestly. She looked distraught. "I've wanted this all my life, Mrs. Schultz. This is the only chance I have. We can't be in the pageant past our senior year. She's using Nadine's accident to get me to quit."

"Your mother might be a little frightened by what happened to Nadine," Mrs. Schultz said gently.

Tabitha waved off the defense of her mother. "She's been frightened since I was a baby! She doesn't want me to win and get the chance at a college scholarship. 'Cause then I'd move away, and she wouldn't be able to hover the way she does. Do you know what it's like not to be able to do anything on your own? The few times I've gone out, she makes me call her every half hour, even with a location tracker on my phone. She's ruining my life! This scholarship is my only way out. Please, tell her it's safe. Tell her I'm safe doing the pageant."

Poor girl. I felt for her, but I also understood her mother's worry. Since my brother's death years ago while driving with his friends on his college graduation weekend, my mother has regretted not having kept a closer watch on him. Heck, I regretted it—you're supposed to take care of your younger brother. It's something every parent has to balance, but one with potentially high consequences.

"Tabby? Tabby?" Tabitha's mother, in stretch pants and a long blouse, entered the tent, searching, a bit wild-eyed, in every direction.

Tabitha's gaze went heavenward. "See what I mean?" She left Mrs. Schultz and went to her mother. "Where would I go, Mom? You saw me come in here."

"I know, but you were taking an awfully long time." She linked her arm with her daughter's and escorted her out of the tent.

Mrs. Schultz noticed me, and I gave her a look of sympathy. I could tell she was troubled by Tabitha's plea.

"I overheard. That's tough," I said.

"Mothers and daughters. I talk to my own daughter three times a week, but it wasn't always such an easy relationship."

"That surprises me. I've heard about your great rapport with your students when you were a teacher and I see with these girls. Tabitha already trusts you enough to ask for your help."

"That's because I'm not their mother. The relationships with our mothers are complex, and the teenage years are the hardest."

I knew that firsthand. All I'd wanted to do as a teenager was get as far away from our farm in Oregon as possible. But the first chance I got during a semester abroad in France, I ended up hanging out in a town that reminded me of home, with a cheese shop owner who reminded me of my mother. I guess we all have to learn for ourselves.

"I bet you've always been a wonderful mother," I said.

"I tried my best. I'll speak with her mother, but I don't think it'll do much good." She sighed, her disappointment showing at not being able to help more. "What are you doing back here? I was surprised to see Detective Heath."

Making sure we weren't overheard, I told her about Heath keeping watch. "If you're nervous about sticking around, I could get you out of it. Being your employer, I could tell Mary Ann you're needed at the cheese booth. It's an easy excuse to bow out."

"You heard Tabitha. If I leave the pageant, it'll send ripples that there might be something to be afraid of. It's not just her, it's *all* the girls—this is the last year for the seniors to have a chance at that scholarship. I have to stay and make sure it goes off all right. Mary Ann really wants to do this in her cousin's memory. I think it'll be okay."

"You're sure?"

"Yes. And you said Detective Heath is here too, so that's extra assurance. What's there to be afraid of?"

I accepted her answer and left the tent. There was no reason to believe any of us were in danger. Except for the fact that Nadine's murderer could be in our midst.

CHAPTER 10

I headed straight toward the main festival area and our booth. Heeding Heath's advice to be average-person careful, I stayed with the crowds. I paused when I got to the butter sculpture, where several people were watching an older man in the refrigerated glass booth sculpt a large block of butter. It was in the early stages, but I could already see the form of a cow taking shape. I couldn't help but be enthralled.

"Moo!" A voice sounded in my ear.

I whipped around to see who the *moo*-er was. He turned his face away from me as if he hadn't done it, but his mop of curly black hair gave him away. A. J. Stringer. I should've known! The intrepid editor of our *Glen Gazette* always made a habit of sneaking up on me.

He turned toward me and laughed. "What's up, Willa?" He wore his usual white T-shirt and worn jeans, but this time, given the warm temperature, he wasn't wearing his ever-present green Salvation Army jacket. It was tied around the well-used leather messenger bag slung across his torso.

"What are you doing here? You're not covering a *lightweight* event like the festival, are you?" I said. A. J. still clung to his short-lived roots as a "serious"

L.A. journalist, even though our free local newspaper usually covered nothing more exciting than the latest seasonal fruits at the farmer's market. Along with his editor duties, he'd begun writing features about the murder cases I'd helped to solve. Piggybacking on the popularity of those *Case Closed* articles, he was now hosting his own unsolved crime podcast.

"I'm not here for the goat races. I'm here because of the murder."

I scanned the faces of the few families near us to make sure they hadn't overheard and moved us away from the butter sculpture so they wouldn't. I didn't want to scare anyone or get into trouble with Chief Womack for spreading the word *murder* around when I knew they were trying to keep it quiet.

"I was told the official word is that it was an accident," I said.

"You still don't believe I've got sources, do you?" he replied, happy to prove me wrong.

"With the Lockwood police too?"

"No, but it's all trickling over to the guys in Yarrow Glen's department. There are plenty working security here. Knowing you, Willa, you know even more than I do. Whaddya got?"

A. J. and I had a quid pro quo relationship when it came to investigative information. As a journalist and one with some connections, he was often able to get information I couldn't. Whatever I shared with him, he'd use to try to help me solve the case and wouldn't breathe a word of any of it in the paper or on his podcast until the culprit had been caught. But during the last case, he'd blabbed a confidential piece of information on his podcast, which unleveled our playing field. He owed me.

"You first."

He winced at my response, not liking it but accepting that he had some more making up to do before he could make demands of me. "All right. I got word that there might've been blood on the scene that doesn't align with where the victim was supposed to have met her accidental death."

"That was my take on it."

His eyebrows shot up. "You saw the crime scene? How did you get in?"

"Your sources didn't tell you?" I gloated. He wasn't the only one who had a surprise up his sleeve.

His eyes widened in realization. "No way! You found the body?"

"Yeah. Archie was the one who alerted the police."

"Wow." He shook his head in disbelief—or maybe envy, knowing him—but it was only momentary. "So what else is there to know?"

"Whoever tried to make it look like an accident wasn't thinking very clearly. The door was closed and the light was off when Archie and I went in. Regardless of the inconclusive autopsy, I know what happened to her wasn't an accident and so do Chief Womack and Detective Heath."

"Heath is in on this?"

"Not officially. He's sticking around though, which tells me he believes it's a homicide."

"Whoa. And you've got autopsy results? Man, I should put you on the *Gazette*'s payroll!" It was the first time A. J. admitted being impressed.

"Very early results. And keep that to yourself for now." A. J. still had to rebuild his trust with me, but I believed he truly regretted his former slip-up. I knew he was loyal to his other anonymous sources.

"You can trust me, Willa."

"I'm counting on that."

"Do you have any suspects?" he pressed on.

"A few. Her cousin, Mary Ann, has been a pretty good resource for who had issues with Nadine, but it made me wonder whether she's diverting suspicion from herself. She's determined to take Nadine's place directing the pageant."

"You think jealousy could be her motive?"

"That, or she got fed up with being bossed around. Although if that's the case, why did she agree to come down here every year to do it? She doesn't even live here, she just comes for the summer to help Nadine."

"Nadine could be paying her to do it. Maybe she needs the money. What does she do for a living?"

"We'll have to find out. It must be something she can take two months off from every year. Is she inheriting anything from Nadine? She mentioned that Nadine didn't have any other family."

"I'll look into that." A. J. reached into his messenger bag and pulled out a pad and pen. After scribbling a note to himself, he said, "I heard the reason for the scooter was because Nadine had a broken foot?"

"Yup. Baz said she fell through a trapdoor on the stage."

"Was her cousin around for that?"

"She was in town, but I don't know if she was there when it happened."

He made another note to himself. "Maybe the broken foot wasn't meant to be a broken foot," he said, eyebrows raised.

The group gathered by the butter sculpture was getting bigger, so I moved us farther away. "What do you mean?"

"Maybe that was the first attempt on Nadine's life."

Whoa. I stopped to consider this. "That could narrow down the suspect list if we knew who was there when it happened."

My eye caught the reporter Grace Kelp approaching us—the journalist with the long legs who didn't seem fazed by Mary Ann's accusations toward her of wanting to take down the pageant. A. J. saw her too and smiled.

"Hey, Grace," he said.

"Hi, A. J. Too bad for you—the early bird gets the worm. You missed the fireworks down at the main stage," she said.

He glared at me for neglecting to tell him something.

"It was just Mary Ann having a little breakdown," I informed him.

Grace took a second look at me. "You were there too, weren't you? I didn't get a chance to introduce myself between accusations from Mary Ann. I'm Grace Kelp. I write for the *Lockwood Weekly*."

She smiled and moved her cell phone to her left hand and offered her right. I shook it.

"I'm Willa Bauer. You know, the more I hear your name, the more it sounds familiar." I tried to place it, but couldn't come up with where I knew it from. I would've remembered meeting her before—she was stunning.

"Well, I'm kind of infamous in this town," she supplied with no irony.

"Infamous?"

"I'm a pariah around Lockwood, but they can't blame me this year if the pageant goes under. Nadine's death may have put a nail in Miss Dairy's coffin."

A. J. and I cringed.

"Ooh, sorry. Bad metaphor," she said, wincing. She grabbed the strap of a small leather backpack that had been slung over one shoulder, unzipped it, and pulled some fingerless leather gloves out of it. "I'm going inside the fridge box to interview the butter man about this year's sculpture and redeem my reputation. Wish me luck!"

"Luck," I said.

A. J. merely gave her a nod.

She pulled the gloves on as she walked away.

"What does she mean, she's a pariah?" I asked him after she'd gone.

"Last year she wrote a scathing piece on how outdated pageants are and said that Lockwood should retire the Miss Dairy pageant. The irony is, not only was she one of the Miss Dairy contestants when she was in high school, she was Miss Dairy Princess."

I snapped my fingers. "That's why I knew her name! I saw it in one of the headlines at the historical society museum. So she *won* the Miss Dairy pageant?"

"It paid her way through community college to get that journalism degree. Anyway, the *Lockwood Weekly* refused to publish her article, but she was able to get it in *All Things Sonoma* magazine right before last year's festival."

"Now that you say that, I remember reading it last summer." It was a good article, and I couldn't say I disagreed with her views on pageants. "I'm assuming Nadine was livid?"

"She wasn't the only one. Remember that scene in *Frankenstein* when all the people in the village arrive at Dr. Frankenstein's door with torches and pitchforks?"

I nodded.

"That was pretty much what happened," he said.

I could see why Mary Ann reacted the way she had about seeing Grace.

"If it was that bad, I'm surprised she's still allowed to work for the Lockwood paper," I said.

"Somebody must've pulled some strings for her. The fury has died down, but I'm surprised she showed her face at the pageant. She's got guts."

I wondered if she blamed Nadine for becoming an outcast in her own town and sought her revenge. Or maybe there was some history between them, seeing as how she had been a contestant in the pageant under Nadine's reign.

A. J. changed the subject. "Sounds like Grace has a leg up on me, so we'd better get cracking. First up, Mary Ann. Is she holding rehearsal?"

"Yeah, she and all the Miss Dairy girls are at the stage, but I've got to get to my booth. I've left Archie long enough."

"Suit yourself." He returned his notebook to his messenger bag and traded it for a voice recorder.

I caught him by the arm before he left. "Be careful asking questions. If whoever killed Nadine is lurking around, I don't want them to suspect people are snooping and get nervous. I'm concerned about Mrs. Schultz."

"Why Mrs. Schultz?"

"She's Mary Ann's right-hand woman now that Nadine is gone. And Archie's participating in the opening dance number for the pageant, so I'm a little worried for him too."

"You think they could be in danger?"

"I don't know, but I think Nadine's murder is connected to the pageant. I don't like my friends' close proximity to it."

"Ah, gotcha." He produced a Nikon camera from his bag and slung it around his neck. "I'll hang out as an innocent festival journalist and see what I can learn."

"Playing innocent could be a stretch for you," I kidded.

"Ha ha," he responded drolly. He was used to my sarcasm.

I was serious again. "You'll let me know if you find out anything important?"

I knew his lips wanted to say "quid pro quo," but he thought better of it. "You bet."

"Thanks, A. J."

He nodded and trotted off to get some scoop.

I kept telling myself this case didn't involve me, but without knowing more, I couldn't feel certain the people associated with the pageant weren't in danger, including Mrs. Schultz and Archie. I had to keep my eyes and ears open.

CHAPTER 11

I returned to our booth, where Archie gave me the rundown on what we'd sold. Our Goat Wild grazing box was selling well. It included a trio of goat's milk cheeses: the creamy, mushroomy Linedeline; Brabander Goat Gouda, one of my absolute favorites; and Tomme de la Châtaigneraie from France. The Tomme's distinctively nutty flavor is owing to the goats regularly foraging in a chestnut grove. The cheese is also aged on chestnut leaves, which gives it a beautiful, yellow-tinted rind. In fact, all of the grazing boxes were selling pretty well, with the exception of our Do I Smell? boxes, which wasn't much of a surprise. We'd only packed a few with Taleggio, mini Epoisses, and Limburger cheeses for more adventurous customers.

"Is Mrs. Schultz doing okay?" Archie asked.

"Yeah, she seems fine. She's determined to still help out with the pageant."

"You're not worried about her, are you?" Archie asked. I could see *he* was.

I was too, a little bit, but I didn't want to add to Archie's concerns. "I'm sure she'll be fine. Detective Heath is here. He said he's going to hang around this weekend."

"That makes me feel better. Did you find out anything new from him?"

"A few things." I let him in on what I knew. "I wish I knew the people involved a little more. I might have to ask Beatrice—I don't know anyone else from Lockwood."

We saw Baz walking over carrying two large cones wrapped in checkered waxed paper. When he handed one to Archie, I realized they weren't filled with ice cream. Was the heat making me see things?

"Is that a cone of mac and cheese?" I asked, getting a closer look. A sprinkling of bacon sat atop the elbow macaroni coated with gooey melted cheese.

"It was a tough decision between this and fried butter on a stick," Baz answered.

"Was it? I think you made the right choice," I said, laughing.

"I didn't know you'd be back, or I would've gotten you one too." He used the little wooden spork stuck in the top to take his first bite. The spork was tiny, but the cheese helped to adhere the macaroni together for a decent-sized bite, even for Baz and Archie, who were used to putting as much food in their mouth as it would hold.

Archie tore off a piece of the cone, which was soft. "The cone is garlic naan bread. Come on! It's genius."

That *was* pretty genius.

"We could do a take on this once we get our Cheeseboard Café up and running," Archie suggested.

"I think we'll stick with doing cheeseboards at first. I still have to create our initial cheeseboard menus, rearrange the kitchenette to put in more tables, and get a liquor license . . . There's so much to be done, and so far I haven't been able to find anyone to hire. I was lucky to find you and Mrs. Schultz. Things seem to be different in the employment world nowadays."

"We can do it ourselves." Archie's enthusiasm sometimes overtook logic. "I'm turning twenty-one soon, so I'll be able to serve the mead and wine."

"I don't want to open it until we have enough staff. You and Mrs. Schultz work too much, as is. With Mrs. Schultz helping with the pageant, we could've even used an extra person for our booth this weekend."

"When do you think you'll have the café open?" Baz asked. He was using a different method than Archie—eating all the mac and cheese first, so the pile had dwindled within his cone of garlic bread.

"I'm not sure. If we're lucky, before the holidays." My stomach knotted thinking of all I had to do. I suddenly craved a hunk of cheese, and here I was without any Challerhocker, my *Swiss-tacular* go-to stress reliever. I should've brought some extra cheese to have at my disposal.

"Not for three months? Aw." Archie's shoulders drooped in disappointment.

"Better to take our time and do it right." It involved some more financial investment on my part, which was a risk in the infancy of my business. But it was something I'd been thinking about for a while, and it felt like the right time. I yearned for customers to stay longer in my shop. So often they'd tell me how cozy it was, whether the sun was streaming in through the large front windows, or a dreary rain was highlighting the mellow lights from the wall sconces. They already enjoyed lingering, so why not add bistro tables in the kitchenette so they could snack with friends over mead or wine and new daily cheeseboard combinations?

"Archie, since you've got your lunch, go ahead and

take a break before you have to go to the pageant rehearsal. You've been holding down the fort long enough."

"Thanks. I wanted to stop at the milk and cookie booth first."

To my surprise, even with teeny sporks, they were already on their final bites of the macaroni and cheese cones. I shook my head. Although Archie had to be at least forty pounds lighter than Baz, they were both bulldozers when it came to eating.

Baz crumpled the now-empty wrapper in his fist. "Mrs. Schultz asked me to be on call for any problems that come up on stage or with the props, so I'm gonna head back there myself. We'll hit the milk and cookies and ice cream booths on the way," he told Archie.

Archie nodded and threw his spork and wadded-up paper into our small trash can before leaving the booth. "You want us to get you anything, Willa?" he asked.

"No, I brought a sandwich. Thanks. You guys have fun."

They walked off with a wave. It made me feel better to know that the three of them—Archie, Baz, and Mrs. Schultz—were sticking close to each other today, even if it meant they were all at the pageant.

I went through the coolers and reorganized what was left of the cheese. I updated our signs and crossed off the items we'd sold out of. With a lull in customers, I took the sandwich I'd made this morning out of my personal cooler. Cheese never failed to clear my head and this time was no different, even when it was something as simple as a homemade pimento cheese sandwich on white bread. I could've made this sandwich perfectly satisfying with four simple ingredients the way Southerners do it: pimentos, mayonnaise, black pepper, and freshly shredded aged cheddar cheese. However, I decided to give this one a creamier kick by adding cream cheese, Colby Jack, and a dash of cayenne. The first bite hit all my senses—creamy, spicy, and best of all, cheesy. I enjoyed the first half without interruption.

As I reached for my second half, wishing I'd made two sandwiches, I saw Tyrell, the festival director, striding toward my booth, clipboard in hand. He looked like he was on a mission. What could he want with me?

He stopped in front of my booth. "This is Curds & Whey, right?" He looked around the booth and finally saw the large sign attached. "Yes, good," he answered his own question. "Are you Willa Bauer? The owner of the cheese shop?"

His nervous energy made me nervous. "Yes. That's me."

"Great." He stuck out his hand.

I wiped my hands on a napkin to make sure he wouldn't get a pimento cheese handshake before putting it in his firm grip. Finally being face-to-face with him, I could see that he was younger than I'd assumed for his position—closer to thirty. His black hair was a thicker buzz cut, faded down the sides with a defined part shaven above the temple—neat and precise, like his well-fitting business attire. His outfit seemed uncomfortable for an outdoor festival, but there was no doubt he looked sharp. I could also see that he was taller now that he wasn't near Chief Womack or the burly mayor.

"I'm Tyrell James, town director of events. I'm in charge of the festival."

"We sort of already met. Yesterday? In front of the historical museum after Nadine's . . ." I let what happened to Nadine hang in the air.

This reminder certainly didn't help his nervous energy. "Oh, right, right. I thought you looked vaguely familiar. Well, now that we know each other, I need a favor."

My evident surprise finally slowed his fast pace.

"Sorry. I'm not being very polite, am I?" he said with an embarrassed grin.

I empathized as I could only imagine the pressure he was getting from Mayor Sonny to make sure this festival was still a great success, even after someone was murdered on the grounds. "You must have a lot on your plate. What kind of favor do you need?"

His tension that made him appear like a wind-up toy released in relief. "Oh, bless you. It's just a small favor . . . and a great opportunity! Nancy Fuller was slated to be our guest judge for this year's pageant," he began.

"Yes, I know." With all the negativity the pageant had been shrouded in, I was looking forward to the one bright spot—seeing Nancy Fuller in person. Was he bringing up her name because he was going to ask me to escort *the* Nancy Fuller around the festival now that Nadine was gone? Maybe we'd swap recipes and become besties. Maybe my fish, Loretta, would get to meet Ted Allen!

"We just heard from her people," he continued, interrupting my exhilarating thoughts. He leaned in closer to me across the table at the front of my booth and lowered his voice. "With Nadine's, ahem, death, Ms. Fuller won't be coming after all."

"Oh no." I felt truly crushed. No chance at becoming her bestie or meeting Ted Allen. "That's too bad, not that anyone could blame her. I mean, if Nadine was mur—" I stopped mid-*murdered*. The poor man looked like he was going to jump out of his skin at the word. I cleared my throat. "Sorry. I just meant, someone of her caliber needs to keep her reputation squeaky clean."

"So you were there for the impromptu show this morning?" He rolled his eyes. "Well, don't believe what you heard. Nancy Fuller was still willing to come, apparently, but her people insisted it wouldn't be a good look. Anyway, we need a new guest judge pronto. We usually prefer someone who's not in the district to avoid the appearance of conflict of interest, but we have to take what we can get."

"Aren't the other pageant judges from Lockwood?"

"They are. This was a new rule we implemented when we started adding a guest judge. It helps to even out the voting. I heard you've only lived in Yarrow Glen for about a year?"

"A year and a half."

"You don't know any of the girls or the mothers in the pageant, do you?"

"No." *What was he getting at?*

"Good, because we're low on choices right now and we've chosen you."

After pausing a beat to decide if I was offended, I said, "Me?"

"Yes. You're a cheesemonger, right? The guest judge needs to have some expertise in one of the dairy categories for the trivia round, and you do, so you're it!" Tyrell nodded like a bobblehead on a bumpy road. He raised his clipboard as if ready to make a checkmark next to my name on his to-do list.

"Well, with such a glowing compliment, how could I refuse?" I said dryly.

His pinched face cleared. "Great! Thanks!"

"I'm being sarcastic."

I practically felt his body re-clench. He must've thought his enthusiastic nodding would automatically earn my consent.

A couple in their twenties sauntered over to the booth holding hands. Tyrell stepped to the side while the woman lifted her sunglasses and squinted at the posted pictures of our cheese selection.

"Cheese is keto, right?" she asked me. She was already very slender.

"Yes, but some things in our grazing boxes aren't, like the crackers or jams," I explained.

"Can I get the box without those?"

"I'm afraid not. They're sold as is."

"Oh." She pursed her very pink lips, shiny with gloss.

Her boyfriend untwined his fingers from hers and ran his hand through his hair. "Just get it. I'll eat the stuff you don't. We've gone to every food booth here." He sounded out of patience.

She perused the pictures again. "Okay, can I get the Cheers to Cheese box?"

I pointed to the big black X over the picture of our boozy cheeses grazing box that she'd been staring at. "The X means we're sold out of it. I'm sorry. You might like the one with Monterey Jack and Colby cheeses? We've still got two more of those."

"Are you kidding?" She looked like I'd just offered her one of the cow chips that I'd mistakenly thought would be used in Cow Chip Bingo.

"Just get it, Brittany," the boyfriend said, leaning on one leg and then the other in impatience.

"Really? You want me eating a cheese named after my ex? Do you care at *all* about me?" She stomped away and her boyfriend followed, his head lolled back like an impatient boy following his mother through the grocery store.

Tyrell picked up where we'd left off. "So, is that a yes to being the guest judge?" he pushed.

"I don't know how I feel about pageants and I'm not sure I want to be involved in promoting them. I mean, they *are* antiquated." I'd never had a strong opinion about pageants, but my bruised ego decided I would today.

"Not you too! Listen, I respect your opinion and I'll work on it, but nobody's mind is going to be changed about having a pageant at Dairy Days in the next forty-eight hours, so can you help a guy out here?" He splayed his arms in a plea.

I caught a glimpse of the top page of his clipboard, covered in lines and arrows and checkmarks from top to bottom of a long list.

He saw that I'd noticed it. "Yeah, the Wi-Fi and cell reception are too spotty on the festival grounds to use my iPad everywhere, not that the battery in that eleven-year-old relic they gave me would last a whole day anyway." His gaze went back to his clipboard. "Maybe they can spare some change for a new one now that Nadine won't be funneling it all to the pageant."

That brought me back from daydreaming about the rest of my pimento cheese sandwich. "What do you mean, 'funneling it to the pageant'?"

He looked up from the clipboard, seeming to realize he'd said that last part aloud. "Sorry, that was crass of me. I know Nadine deserved to get the things she asked for to run the pageant. She was the one who secured the big milk sponsor for the annual college scholar-ship and the one who got the celebrity pageant judges to appear. She was one of the reasons Dairy Days has been growing the way it has. I'm not saying the praise is unwarranted, but she only had the pageant to run. I have the whole festival! I'm supposed to be the top dog here. Just because the last events director did it this way for his reign of thirty years, they think I should be able to." He looked at his ancient clipboard again and his frustration streamed into self-pity. "I don't know. Maybe I *should* be able to."

If this was all an act to get me to feel sorry for him, it worked. I sighed and, against my better judgment, said, "What does being a pageant judge entail?"

The question seemed to snatch off his glum blanket, flipping the switch of his anxious energy back on. "Can you come by the stage at the end of the day today? I'll debrief you on the pageant rules. It's simple. You just help judge and crown Miss Dairy Princess." He returned to bobbing his head.

Mrs. Schultz and Archie were doing their part so this pageant could still go on. I supposed I had to think about the girls and their scholarship. I'd planned to be at the pageant on Monday, anyway, as a spectator, so it wasn't really adding anything to my plate. I felt my head nod in rhythm with his. "I suppose I could handle that."

"Great!" Tyrell checked off an item on his list. "Thank you. You just saved my job. Whatever you do, *don't* change your mind."

He hurried off before I could do just that.

CHAPTER 12

I was able to finish my pimento cheese sandwich and sold all but a few of our grazing boxes to non-dieters before the majority of people began to depart the festival. Dairy Days was just about over for the day. I saw the life-sized milk carton standing on their own nearby, still waving to the crowd. They took their position seriously—it had to have been a very long day for them, even if they had breaks.

I took one of our remaining grazing boxes out of the cooler, the one we named Disguises. I hadn't made very many of this combination of cheeses—not everybody liked cheese that didn't look like it tasted, but they'd be well-rewarded if they tried them. I left the booth with the grazing box in hand and brought it to the milk carton.

"The day's almost over. Are you interested in some cheese? No charge." I positioned the box so they could see the contents through the lid's transparent window.

They tilted their head and peered at the box through the costume's mesh. "Is that one Irish Porter? I like that kind," a female voice said.

I was happily surprised at her knowledge. "You're familiar with Irish Porter?" It wasn't a common type.

The yellow cheese with brown marbling, caused by the dark beer infused in the cheese, took on the flavor of the malty brew. "Don't you think it looks like stained glass? Can you guess what the other cheeses are disguised as?"

She carefully took the container and held it between her oversized gloves to get a better look. "That one's pretending to be a blue cheese, but I think it's Morbier—it tastes more like Havarti, not blue. And this one looks like a piece of caramel, but it's that Norwegian cheese with a weird name."

"Gjetost," I provided, pronouncing it "yay-toast." It not only looked like a sweet treat, it tasted like one too—a combination of caramel and fudge. "Let me guess. Your parents own a creamery?"

"Nope. My parents are teachers. I just like cheese. When you grow up in Lockwood, you tend to eat a lot of it."

I laughed. "I knew I liked you! Will you be here tomorrow?"

The top of the milk carton crinkled in a nod.

"I'll bring a special selection for you. Come by the booth on your lunch break and you can have it."

"Thanks a lot! I better get back. See ya."

She walked away with the grazing box, and I returned to my booth giggling to myself that Archie had assumed the person in the milk carton suit was a guy.

We'd sold out of cheese, and no one had gotten killed today—I'd chalk that up as a successful day. I realized I hadn't seen Heath again, which was a disappointment. I began to pack up as Archie and Baz returned.

"You just missed our milk carton friend. I gave her one of our last grazing boxes," I told Archie.

"Her?"

"Yup. Lesson learned—don't judge a milk by its carton," I teased.

"Shame on me. You think she'll be around tomorrow?" he asked, scanning the area for her.

"Yes. I told her I'd make a special box for her. She loves cheese and she seems pretty knowledgeable about it."

"Cool." He and Baz gave me a hand stacking the displays into the now-empty coolers to make fewer trips to the truck.

"Thanks for all your help, Baz. This would be a lot more challenging without you and your truck. How did rehearsal go?" I asked.

"Total chaos," Archie replied. He lifted an empty cooler and headed to the truck with it.

Baz gave me more details. "Mary Ann's in way over her head, but she won't admit it. Mrs. Schultz and Beatrice are running around like crazy. It's like Mary Ann's turned into Nadine, barking orders. I don't know who's worse, her or those moms. They never stop making demands."

"That doesn't make me excited to go over there, but I'm meeting Tyrell. Is rehearsal finished?"

"Yeah, I think they were done for the day."

"If Mrs. Schultz is still around, I'll ask her for a ride home, so you and Archie don't have to wait for me."

"She was still there when we left," he said.

"I'll text her." I pulled out my phone and sent a text. Normally, I'd never text Mrs. Schultz, knowing that she didn't make a habit of keeping her phone on her, but after Nadine's murder, she'd agreed to have it handy. A red exclamation point appeared after the text. I hit send again but the same thing happened.

"It's not sending."

"The cell signal is bad over there. Head over now so you don't miss her. Archie and I can handle this."

"You sure?"

"It'll take three trips to the truck, tops. We got this."

"Thanks, Baz. I'll catch up with you later."

I hoped agreeing to be a pageant judge wasn't a mistake. That pageant seemed like a lightning rod for bad things happening. I'd feel better if I could be there even once without something dreadful occurring.

CHAPTER 13

For the second time that day, I traversed the grassy grounds to get to the stage. Festival stragglers streamed to the parking lot as vendors shuttered their trucks and packed up their booths.

My first glimpse of the vacant stage made me think I'd come all this way for nothing, but as I got closer, I picked up on the rise and fall of continual chatter. I continued behind the stage where mothers and their daughters were leaving the tent to go home. I was relieved to see Mrs. Schultz hanging the returned costumes on the clothes racks outside the tent. At least I hadn't missed her. Now where was Tyrell?

"Hi, Willa. What brings you by?" Mrs. Schultz asked, surprisingly cheerful. Her short, curly hair was the only thing looking a little wayward.

"I'm supposed to be meeting Tyrell here. I've been chosen to replace Nancy Fuller as the guest judge."

"Congratulations! I heard she wasn't going to make it. That's disappointing, but this is exciting for you."

"I don't know if *exciting* is the right word." I allowed my lack of enthusiasm to show.

"Well, it's nice of you to help us out of a bind," she replied.

"I'm going to need a ride home too, if it's not too inconvenient. Archie and Baz are packing up and driving back."

"Of course."

I was dragging a little from the nonstop day and the heat, but Mrs. Schultz didn't look like she'd been through a whole day of the chaos that Baz and Archie described, especially considering the way it had started out.

"Tell me your secret. How are you still so energetic after a busy day like this?"

"The stage invigorates me, Willa. The theatrics . . . the drama . . ." She leaned in and said, "Even if it's not all on the stage," then winked.

I chuckled in understanding. I'd missed Mrs. Schultz's presence while working today. Her positive disposition tended to rub off on me.

Mary Ann appeared from inside the tent, holding a notebook. Her black blouse had come partially untucked, as had her hair from its ponytail band.

She gave me a fleeting glance before speaking to Mrs. Schultz. "Only a couple of girls are still changing in the tent. We didn't get through nearly what we should've today." She studied the list in her notebook.

"I think we did fine. They'll have the routines down before the pageant," Mrs. Schultz reassured her.

"We're still short a few guys for the opening number, but I suppose if we pair them up two girls to each guy, it won't look so bad." She sighed and snapped her notebook closed. "Thank goodness the girls already had so many rehearsals with Nadine." Upon glancing at me a second time, she stopped to acknowledge my presence.

"Hello." I waved at her uncertainly. "I'm Willa Bauer, your new guest judge."

She scrunched up her face as if I'd just delivered some bad news. "*You're* the cheese shop owner in Yarrow Glen?"

"That's right."

The lukewarm invitation had been bad enough. If Mary Ann was going to give me pushback, I would gladly relinquish my new position.

"This is embarrassing. I didn't make the best first impression this morning, did I?" she said, surprising me.

Her distraught expression had been in regard to herself, not me. I'd have to change my attitude too, then.

"Considering the circumstances, it's understandable. I haven't given it a second thought," I answered.

"That's very kind of you. It's been an extremely stressful two days."

"I imagine so. I'm very sorry for your loss," I said.

"It's lucky my job is giving me some leeway on finishing my work this week. Small favors, I suppose," she said.

"You do the pageant *and* work a job?" Mrs. Schultz asked, impressed.

"Yes. I'm an analyst. It's a lot to juggle, but I can work remotely, so I'm able to be here most of the summer."

"That sounds like a good career, especially if you have the freedom of working from anywhere," I said. What I really wanted to ask was, *How much do you make, and did you need your cousin's inheritance?*

"I get freedom from the office but not the work. I shouldn't complain. I've been able to always support myself. Are you here to take Mrs. Schultz home? I know Beatrice had to leave early for a dentist appointment."

"She's actually giving me a lift home. Tyrell said I should come by, and he'd show me the ropes," I answered.

Mary Ann rolled her eyes. "What would Tyrell know about being a pageant judge? All he does is get in the way, like he has with Fiona. I can't believe he went against Nadine's wishes to get rid of her as a judge." She stopped herself. "Sorry, I told myself I wouldn't bring it up again."

Please, bring it up so I don't have to! "Who could blame you?" I prodded. "I heard Fiona say they were friends. If that was true, Nadine must've had an especially good reason to want to dismiss her."

"They *were* friends! I wish I knew why, but Nadine didn't want to discuss it. And if Nadine didn't want to talk about something, there was no sense in asking about it again. Fiona must've done something against the pageant rules. It wasn't just that she was peddling Becky's Bakeware to the contestants' mothers. They'd been having that argument for years, but it was Fiona's livelihood and they *were* friends, so Nadine overlooked it. This had to be something bigger. Nadine was very strict about certain rules. It didn't matter who you were, she'd cut you out if it meant preserving the pageant's good name."

"That sounds a bit harsh," Mrs. Schultz said.

"She felt it was up to her to protect the integrity of the pageant, but it was never easy for her," Mary Ann said.

"She'd gotten rid of judges before?"

"Not judges. She's had to disqualify a few contestants over the years. This is the first time she's had to take action with a pageant judge. Especially because it was Fiona, I could tell it was eating at her." Mary Ann's severe expression faded, no doubt clouded by her memories of the final weeks with her cousin.

I went over yesterday morning in my mind since Mary Ann seemed willing to talk. "Do you know what her announcement yesterday was going to be?"

For a moment she looked confused and then seemed to recall it. "The announcement. That took me by surprise like everyone else. It was probably going to be about replacing Fiona as a judge. Whatever she had going on, it was weighing on her. People might be surprised to hear this, but she was a sensitive person. She hadn't been herself in the last few weeks."

"What do you mean she wasn't herself?"

Mary Ann seemed sorry she'd brought it up and backpedaled. "Nothing you could put your finger on if you didn't know her like I did." She shrugged, making an attempt to explain. "She was quiet. Preoccupied. That wasn't like her. I think that's why she didn't see that the trapdoor on the stage floor was open and had that accident—her mind was on something else. It must've been about Fiona. I think she'd been struggling with her decision for quite a while. It's the only reason I can think of that she'd let her go."

"What is Becky's Bakeware, anyway?" I asked.

"It's one of those direct sales products that you sell from home," Mrs. Schultz supplied.

"Oh, and they have parties to sell them to their friends?" I nodded, recalling a few invitations I'd gotten through Facebook from people I was barely acquainted with.

"That's right. Fiona's been selling it for a long time.

She's very serious about it and she'll tell anyone who will listen that she's the number one Becky in the Valley," Mary Ann said.

"If she was working for Mary Kay, she'd have one of those pink Cadillacs by now." Mrs. Schultz chuckled.

Mary Ann and I looked at each other and then at Mrs. Schultz, not understanding the reference.

"Have I aged myself? Mary Kay Cosmetics was one of the earliest direct sales companies. That and Avon. The very top salespeople would be rewarded with a pearly pink Cadillac. It was a status symbol. When you saw one on the road, you knew a top Mary Kay agent was driving it," Mrs. Schultz answered.

"A pink Cadillac was an *incentive*?" Mary Ann said, wrinkling her long nose.

"Back in the day, yes," Mrs. Schultz replied.

"I'm sure Fiona has earned whatever top incentive Becky's Bakeware offers. The town won't let her have a booth at the festival, so she brings her bakeware around the pageant every year," Mary Ann said.

"I can see how that could be considered a conflict of interest if buying Fiona's products garnered favor with her as a judge," I agreed.

"Even the appearance of a scandal could harm the pageant," Mrs. Schultz added.

"Nadine was too fair to do anything extreme unless she knew for a fact Fiona was breaking the rules. She must've found out something definite. I asked her what was bothering her, but she said she didn't want to talk about it." Mary Ann shrugged again.

I wondered what Fiona could've done for Nadine to take the "extreme" measure of wanting her out as a pageant judge. Then I wondered if Fiona decided to get rid of Nadine before anyone else found out what it was Fiona had done.

Two women, mother and daughter, stepped out of the tent. I recognized them from yesterday—Barbie Mom and her mini-me, Annabelle. It was hard to forget a name like that or the fuss Barbie Mom made about the dress Beatrice had worked on for her daughter. She looked no happier today as she approached us.

"I know you've had a heck of a day, Mary Ann, but were you able to find that milk pail for Annabelle?" she asked in a polite but firm tone.

"I promised you I'd look, but if I can't find an extra, she'll have to make do with the one she was assigned. Maybe she can ask one of the other girls to trade with her," Mary Ann said.

The politeness she'd mustered when she asked the question didn't stick around. Barbie Mom huffed loudly, causing her daughter to stiffen and back away. It looked like Annabelle knew more was coming. She was right.

"We tried that. Nobody's willing. First she gets the oldest dress and now she gets a subpar milk pail. There's no excuse to sabotage her like this just because she's the prettiest one of the bunch!" she said.

Annabelle shrank behind her mother in embarrassment and began gnawing on her nails.

Mary Ann kept her cool, especially compared to this morning. "She's not being sabotaged. She gets to wear her own clothes during the judging portion. These costumes and props won't affect who wins, but even so, I don't think hers is any worse than the others."

"I volunteered to help with inventorying the props after last year's pageant and I know for a fact there were at least thirty pails in the prop room. There's got to be a better one than what she was assigned," Annabelle's mother insisted.

"Like I told you before, I'll look before I leave today," Mary Ann said with finality.

She forced herself to be placated and switched her bristly tone. "I know you've been through a lot in the last twenty-four hours, and I don't mean to add any stress on you. I'm just trying to make things fair for Annabelle."

"I'm doing my best," Mary Ann answered. I noticed dark shadows under her eyes for the first time.

I suddenly felt a deep sense of empathy for Mary Ann. Since Nadine's death, I'd briefly considered her as a suspect and been annoyed with her, but I hadn't thought too much about what she was going through.

It must've hit Annabelle's mother at the same time too. She reached around Mary Ann and gave her a hug that consisted of a series of pats on the back, followed by a sympathetic smile. Then she turned and began to walk away. "Come on, Annabelle. And stop biting your cuticles! You're going to ruin your manicure."

Mary Ann pinched the bridge of her nose, eyes closed, then took a breath. The restorative gesture only lasted a few seconds—until she saw Tyrell heading our way. I, on the other hand, was glad to see him.

He approached and dispensed with greetings. I was learning Tyrell was too busy for niceties.

"Mary Ann! Good, you're still here. I thought we'd take our new guest judge through the paces of the judging portion of the pageant." He gestured to me as the new guest judge.

Mary Ann's fatigue turned to impatience. She glared at him. "I've had a very long day. I have to go to the funeral home this evening to make arrangements for my cousin, and I still have to rifle through the prop room to satisfy one of the pageant mothers before I can leave. So you're welcome to run through it with her, but I need to go."

"Well, I-I . . ." he began to stammer.

"You don't know what to do, do you?" It seemed to satisfy her to say it, but she paused, allowing the bite of her words to soften. "Tyrell, I don't blame you. This is only your third year. But just because you're the festival director doesn't mean you know anything about the pageant, not like Nadine did." The thought of her cousin seemed to ramp up the fight in her again. "If she were still here, she would never have accepted you overriding her decision to dismiss Fiona." She obviously wasn't ready to let that go.

"I did it for the pageant, Mary Ann. I might not know the ins and outs of the Miss Dairy pageant, but I know how to pull off a successful event. People will question why Fiona's not a judge anymore, especially if she makes it clear to everyone she didn't leave of her own accord. Accusing Fiona of murder in front of everybody doesn't exactly keep scandal rumors out of the mouths of Lockwood citizens and promote a successful event, does it?"

Mary Ann's hackles receded at this truth.

Tyrell continued, "As the festival director, I have to look at the bigger picture. I rarely get the credit when things go well, but when things go wrong, you can bet I get all the blame."

Mary Ann didn't have a comeback, but Tyrell looked like he had bottomed out.

"If you're not going to help, then here," he said. He unclipped a packet of papers from his clipboard and shoved them at me. "These are the rules. Read them over. We'll debrief you Monday before the pageant gets started," he said to me.

I took the papers he gave me, and he marched away.

CHAPTER 14

Mary Ann watched Tyrell go and let out a hearty breath. She pulled on either side of her ponytail to tighten it. "Have we dealt with everybody? I'm afraid to go into the tent to see if anyone else is still here. I don't have the energy to do battle anymore today."

"Let me have a look," Mrs. Schultz said, patting her on the shoulder before stepping inside. She emerged within moments and announced that everyone had gone.

I helped them wheel the racks of costumes inside the tent, and we fastened the ties that closed the canvas flaps that served as the door.

"Since I didn't find it yesterday, we can help you look for the milk pail before we go," Mrs. Schultz said to Mary Ann. She looked at me for confirmation that I was okay with her suggestion. I nodded.

"Are you sure you want to share in Barbie's wrath if we don't find one?" Mary Ann said.

I laughed.

Mary Ann and Mrs. Schultz looked confused.

"Barbie. Wait, is that actually her name?" I asked.

"Barbara, but she goes by Barbie," Mary Ann said.

"Huh."

A car's engine got our attention as an Expedition rolled up to the orange fencing.

"That's Chief Womack." Mary Ann brightened. The grim lines on her face seemed to vanish. She pulled on her ponytail and ran her hands over the wisps of hair that had escaped from it just as he got out of his car. She smiled as he approached, perhaps the first time I'd seen it. "Pete! What brings you by?"

"I noticed a couple of cars still over here, so I came by to check that everyone was on their way out since our officers have left."

"That was thoughtful of you," Mrs. Schultz said, giving him a toothy smile. "We were just about to pop into the prop room to look for that pesky milk pail I couldn't find yesterday for one of our contestants."

It satisfied me to witness him realize the truth about why she was at the museum yesterday morning. Mary Ann was right here to back it up. I think it satisfied Mrs. Schultz too.

Mary Ann stepped between the two. "One of the mothers asked for my assistance, and of course, I'd never say no to a request."

Mrs. Schultz and I passed a look between us. That was certainly a nicer take on what had happened.

"The prop room in the museum? We've kept the house under lock and key since last night," Chief Womack said.

I was glad to hear him announce that it was still off-limits. Maybe he *was* quietly investigating.

"Oh no. Can't we just sneak into the prop room, Pete? It's got its own entrance and it's blocked off from the rest of the house. We couldn't disturb anything even if we wanted to." Mary Ann's plea was wrapped in a flirty tone.

Chief Womack crossed his beefy arms and contemplated her request. "You've made a good point. For you, I'll allow it."

Mary Ann beamed.

"In and out, though, okay? I'm not comfortable with anyone being here on their own after festival hours," he said.

"Yes sir!"

"We understand, Chief. We'll be out in a jiffy," Mrs. Schultz said.

He smiled, seeming to be amused by her. I couldn't tell if they were getting along or *playing* along.

"I'd accompany you, but I've got somewhere to be right now before our appointment," he said to Mary Ann.

"It's so nice of you to help me with Nadine's funeral arrangements. It's hard with neither of us having any other family. I don't have anyone to lean on."

He briefly put a hand on Mary Ann's shoulder in condolence, as I'd seen him do before. "I'm glad I can be here for you. She spent a lot of time at our home when she and Sophie were friends."

I recalled Sophie being mentioned before at his office—Chief Womack's ex-wife?

Does she know?" Mary Ann asked him.

"We don't stay in touch."

Ah, definitely ex-wife.

"The sun is starting to set. You'd better get going. You ladies be careful."

"Thanks, Pete. See you later," Mary Ann said.

"Thank you, Chief Womack," Mrs. Schultz said sweetly. She was laying on the honey as I was keeping my vinegary thoughts to myself.

"You're welcome." He gave us a parting smile and left in his hefty SUV.

We watched him go, particularly Mary Ann. She picked up a heavy tote bag that was lying against the tent, stuck her notebook in it, and started walking to the car. We followed.

"That man is such a saint," she said. "His wife, Sophie, ran off without a word—gosh, it has to be more than fifteen years ago—and he's never said a mean word about her. I can't imagine why. It's not like they have any children they have to be cordial for." She rooted around in her bag for her key fob and unlocked the car remotely. "I'm surprised Nadine was ever friends with her. She sounds horrid. Pete's too nice for his own good."

"You can never be too nice," Mrs. Schultz commented.

"He does seem very nice, and you were right, Mrs. Schultz; those eyes are arresting, pardon the pun," I said.

Mrs. Schultz chuckled. "You ride with Mary Ann. I'll meet you there." She took my pageant judge directions to her car for me as she continued on to her Fiat. Mary Ann started her car and waited for Mrs. Schultz to start hers before we headed across the field to the historical society museum.

"Sounds like Mrs. Schultz might be interested in Pete," she said casually. "He's not even fifty, you know. Is she one of those cougars?"

I giggled before realizing she was serious. "Mrs. Schultz?" Anyone who knew her knew she was as traditional as they come.

"Well, she wouldn't be the only one in Lockwood. He is a gem. Who knows why he chose Sophie." Mary Ann pursed her lips and didn't say more as she pulled up to the side of the museum with the damaged widow's peak and parked the car.

The side entrance door must've led directly into the kitchen-turned-storage room. One of its two windows was boarded up. We exited the car at the same time as Mrs. Schultz.

"Have you ever thought of dating Chief Womack?" I asked Mary Ann as we walked to the side door.

"Me? I don't even live here." She began rummaging in the bag for a key to the museum door.

"But you've spent every summer here for years now, right? You must have to work closely together for the pageant."

"Sure, I've known him for years. That doesn't mean I'm after him." She sounded a little defensive.

Mrs. Schultz raised her eyebrows at me, likely wondering about our car conversation that led to this.

"I don't think you're after him. You just seem to have a strong opinion about his ex-wife," I continued.

She dropped the tote bag that was hanging from her arm on the ground, so she could get a better look inside it. "It's because of Nadine. They were best friends and Sophie not only up and left Pete, she left Nadine too, without a word. She was here one day and gone the next. Nobody even saw her move out and nobody in Lockwood ever heard from her again. What kind of person does that?" She rooted around the tote bag. "Ugh. I should've done this in the car where there was more light."

"*Nobody* has seen or spoken to her?" I glanced at Mrs. Schultz. Call me a skeptic, but that sounded suspicious.

Mary Ann jiggled her tote bag. "Nope. Nadine said

she had some mental health issues—depression, I guess—so maybe she just wanted a new life. But to just fall off the face of the earth? Nadine was upset about it for a really long time. She didn't like to talk about her. Ah! Found them!" She held up a key ring. "Now to find the one that fits." She stuck one in the lock.

"Was there a fire on this side of the house?" I asked.

Mary Ann tried another key. "Yeah. It used to be the kitchen. An electrical fire started there. They had to rewire the entire house. They used up the budget just doing the rewiring, so they couldn't refurbish the kitchen. Since it's not needed for the museum, Nadine convinced them to let us use it to store props."

"I read the headline about the fire when I was looking around the museum," I said. "What a shame."

Mary Ann craned her neck to look up at the widow's peak and pointed to the top. "They plan to refurbish the widow's peak. Well, it's a faux widow's peak—nothing but a spiral staircase in the center leading up to a widow's walk. I hope they do, because it's a great view from up there, but they're going to have to make sure fixing it up doesn't entice kids again."

"Is that what happened?"

Mary Ann nodded. "This used to be an old door—easy to pick the lock—and teenagers would sneak in on a regular basis to get into the kitchen and go up to the top. It was sort of a make-out spot. Two kids were up there when the fire started, and it spread fast. They got out, but not without injuries. They weren't even teenagers hooking up, they were young kids—a boy and his little sister. They were very lucky they made it out with only a few burns."

"I remember hearing about that when it happened. How awful," Mrs. Schultz commented.

I recalled another headline on the museum wall declaring Chief Womack a hero for saving a child. I wondered if it was he who rescued the kids.

Mary Ann wiggled the knob after a third key. The door pushed open.

The waning daylight didn't permeate much beyond the open door. Archie's comment about the house being haunted filtered through my thoughts. Mary Ann entered without the hesitation I had. On the counter to her left, she grabbed a battery-operated lantern and illuminated it, causing the shadows to recede to the edges of the large room. She went to the corner of the kitchen counter and turned on an old lamp that didn't do much good.

At first glance, it was as cluttered as Beatrice's vintage thrift shop, without the panache. Filled bins and boxes dotted the floor. Large hand-painted theater sets leaned against the lower kitchen cabinets. A tall rack of tattered curtains made of heavy fabric in different colors partially divided the room. Against the back wall stood a tall free-standing cabinet. I shuddered—I'd make sure to stay away from it. It would take me a while to be okay around tall shelving units again.

"There's a lot here," I said.

"It's a shared space with the community theater. They also use the stage," Mrs. Schultz explained.

"It's organized when we start rehearsals, but by this time, it's . . . well, you can see. Let's get looking," she said.

Mary Ann searched the far side of the kitchen, carrying the lantern with her. The room filled with shadows again.

"Are there any more lanterns?" I called over to her.

"Yeah, there's a couple on the floor in the corner over there by the door to the widow's peak." She pointed near where I was still standing.

I went over to them. "You mean the gas lanterns? That's risky for a place that's already seen a fire."

"Don't ask me. I just do what I'm told." She disappeared behind the rack of curtains.

I had no idea how long the lanterns had been there, so I decided it was safer for us to do without. We used our phone's harsh flashlights instead and began to search the tables, shelves, and bins for a milk pail in good condition.

Mary Ann came into view again. "The funeral home just texted me. I must've gotten the time of the appointment wrong. I've got to go. I'm not looking forward to telling Barbie that we didn't find it."

"We can keep looking. You go ahead and go," Mrs. Schultz said.

"Are you sure? I'd really appreciate it. You can lock this door from the inside without needing a key. Be sure it's closed all the way before you leave, okay?"

"We will."

"Thanks." She handed Mrs. Schultz the lantern. "Good luck finding it." She hurried out and shut the door behind her.

The slight breeze from the movement of the door wafted a hint of must and smoke that had lingered in the stained walls. A shiver brushed my spine. Mrs. Schultz turned off her flashlight and tucked her phone in the pocket of her flared skirt. The shadows spread, becoming black holes.

"We should get on with this," I said, rubbing the

goose bumps off my neck. The place was creeping me out.

"Honestly, nobody's going to see or care about the chip in Annabelle's pail," Mrs. Schultz said. "After what Mary Ann has been through, the petty demands from these mothers astound me."

We split up and kept looking.

"What do you think about what she said about Chief Womack's ex-wife?" I asked from across the room.

"It's sad."

"It makes you wonder about him a little bit, doesn't it?"

"What do you mean? Because she left him?" Mrs. Schultz asked.

I began searching through a bin of road signs. "Because nobody's seen or heard from her since then."

"What are you saying? You think he did something to her?"

"Isn't it weird she didn't say a word to Nadine before or after and has never contacted her? They were best friends." I left the bin and started searching another.

"Well, yes, that *is* odd."

"I wonder if 'we don't keep in touch' really means he doesn't know where she is. Or she doesn't want him to know where she is." I stopped searching. My thoughts had trailed off to Chief Womack and his vanishing wife.

Mrs. Schultz, who was searching the kitchen cabinets, stopped to look at me. "What are you saying, Willa?"

"I'm not sure. I just have a weird feeling about him. We know he doesn't mind bending the rules or the truth, like when he told everyone at the pageant that Nadine's death was an accident. We know he's the only one in charge of this non-investigation. And now we learn his wife disappeared fifteen years ago under mysterious circumstances."

"Mary Ann didn't use the word *disappear*."

"What else do you call it when someone is there one day and gone the next? All I'm saying is, the more I find out about Chief Womack, the less I trust him. There's something suspicious about this thing with his wife."

Mrs. Schultz moved on from the cabinets. "Don't we have enough to try to figure out Nadine's murder without adding to the list what happened to Chief Womack's wife fifteen years ago?"

I sighed. "All right. I guess you're right."

I wiped my dusty hands on my shorts. I'd completely lost interest and hope in finding the milk pail anymore. My mind was still on Chief Womack, regardless of what I'd said to Mrs. Schultz. The room seemed to be darkening by the minute and the harsh light from my phone kept producing a glare whenever it met with anything metal, making it actually more difficult to see. I decided to try to go with the weak light of the single lamp and whatever peripheral light Mrs. Schultz's lantern would provide instead. I tapped off my flashlight just as a click sounded from one of the dark corners. I immediately tapped my phone repeatedly to return the flashlight and swung the light around the room.

"Was that you?" I asked Mrs. Schultz, still aiming the light all around the room.

"No. It sounded like it came from over there." She held up the lantern, directing it toward the tattered rack of curtains concealing whatever or *who*ever was behind it.

I hurried over to Mrs. Schultz. I had the urge to take her hand and run out of the museum to her car, like anyone who was average-person careful would do. But if someone was hiding back there and heard what I'd said about Chief Womack, I needed to know who it was. I swept my light across the bins and found a wooden oar. A good enough weapon since I could blind them first with my flashlight.

"Stay behind me," I whispered.

Who could be hiding here and why? Was it the same person who was lying in wait for Nadine yesterday?

With a wide berth, we began to creep around the curtain. My heart picked up speed with each step. As soon as we crossed its barrier, I swept the beam of light around the space. My other hand held the oar aloft, ready to swing.

Nothing was there. Just a bunch of signs leaning against the wall. Mrs. Schultz came closer and lifted the lantern, which illuminated the entire corner behind the curtain. My rapidly beating heart took longer to get the message that we were alone. I finally put my arm down.

"One of the signs is on the floor. Maybe we heard it fall over," she said.

"Whatever it was, can we call this milk pail search a fail and go, please? They really need to put a light in the ceiling if they want us to go looking for things." I walked to the door, more than ready to go. Any ghosts didn't have to tell me twice.

"Let me just take one last quick check over here. I hate for Mary Ann to have to put up with Barbie tomorrow," Mrs. Schultz said. She started pulling out the smaller bins that were on the shelves of the tall cabinet.

"Be careful over there," I warned. I knew I was be-ing overly cautious about the tall cabinet, but were the shadows playing tricks or was the cabinet shaking? "Mrs.—"

Before I could warn her, the cabinet toppled forward.

CHAPTER 15

The crash resounded in the small space, followed by a scream of surprise that I think came from me. My momentary shock was immediately blanketed by relief when I saw Mrs. Schultz standing on the other side of the cabinet, mouth agape, staring down at it.

"Are you okay?" I asked. Somehow, I was short of breath, although I'd been frozen in place with panic.

She did a quick once-over of herself, as if to make sure. "I think so. It was pure luck that I stepped out of the way before it came down."

I looked at the space where the cabinet had been standing, noting the molding on the wall. What I thought I'd seen as soon as the shelf had fallen suddenly made sense. "That's the pocket door."

I stepped over broken porcelain and glass that had tumbled from the cabinet and some plywood, as the cabinet itself had also broken in several places—it wasn't as sturdy as the shelf that had fallen on Nadine. I wanted a closer look at the door. Mrs. Schultz raised the lantern to aid my trek. A reflection of light bounced off the dull brass hardware. I hooked my finger through the recessed handle and pulled on the door, but it didn't budge. Mrs. Schultz steadied me as I climbed back over the shards of furniture to return to my original spot.

"I thought I saw something move over here right after the cabinet fell," I explained. "The sound we heard could've been the door opening." I looked back at the door. "I'll be right back."

I left the kitchen and ran around to the front of the house and up the porch steps. I tried the handle. It was locked. I moved to the window and cupped my hands to the sides of my face to peer in. The entry room and stairs were empty, but nothing else was visible from my vantage point. I tried looking through the sitting room window, but it was too cloudy. I trotted back to the side of the house, where Mrs. Schultz was waiting outside the door, her arms wrapped around her.

"Nothing," I said, feeling dejected.

"What were you hoping to find?" she asked.

"I thought maybe I'd see who opened the door and pushed the cabinet. They could still be inside. You saw the door slide closed too, after the cabinet fell, right?"

"I'm afraid I didn't. I wasn't looking at the door. Are you certain?"

"Yes! At least I think I am." The more I thought about it, the more I questioned myself. "How else would that cabinet have just fallen over like that? It was the same thing that happened to Nadine, and that was no accident."

"We should find Chief Womack," Mrs. Schultz suggested.

"He told us he was leaving right away," I reminded her so I could nix her suggestion. "I'm calling the police. I don't mean to frighten you, Mrs. Schultz, but I think Nadine's murderer has attempted to strike again."

And I wasn't so sure the culprit wasn't the chief of police.

I called 9-1-1 and the two Lockwood officers I recognized from yesterday's crime scene arrived shortly and introduced themselves. By the way they were inspecting the room and looking at us and each other, I could tell they were skeptical. Officer Harding tried the front door of the museum, but it was locked, just as I'd told him it would be. He tested the linoleum floor with the toe of his boot.

"This floor's very uneven and this cabinet isn't deep. Are you sure you didn't accidentally lean on it or knock something into it? It could've been top-heavy."

"I was all the way over here by the door when it happened," I said.

"And you, Mrs. Schultz? Were you next to the cabinet?" Officer Williams took over the questioning.

"She was right in front of it. That's the point. She was almost crushed by it," I said, feeling myself losing patience.

"Did you move out of the way when you saw it shaking?" Officer Williams continued.

"I have to admit, I didn't notice it shaking," Mrs. Schultz said, glancing at me apologetically. "Luckily, I happened to step out of the way seconds before it happened. Maybe I sensed it?"

"So maybe you pushed on it as you were stepping around it without realizing it. It's not a very sturdy cabinet," Officer Harding interjected, picking up one of the plywood pieces that had broken off.

"I don't think I did, but I suppose it's possible."

"That doesn't explain the person who was behind that door," I spoke up.

"What did they look like, Ms. Bauer?" Officer Harding asked.

"I told you, I didn't see them. We heard a noise and then the shelf fell and I saw the pocket door closing."

A look passed between the officers again.

"But when you went to the front of the house, nobody was there," he confirmed my earlier statement.

"The door was locked. I couldn't get in. That doesn't prove somebody wasn't inside." I crossed my arms and felt my body stiffen in defense.

"The door was locked," he repeated.

"If they were still in there, they wouldn't want to be caught. They'd lock the door behind themselves."

"The door has been locked since yesterday. Nobody can get in or out without Chief Womack's permission."

Chief Womack had access. Interesting, but I wasn't about to tell the Lockwood police my suspicions of Chief Womack. Besides, there were plenty of people who could've gotten into the house. "He's not the only one with a key, right? Nadine and Mary Ann had one, so there must be others. Museum volunteers? Pageant volunteers? The person who cleans the place?"

"You think the cleaning service tried to harm you?" Officer Harding said with a smirk.

Now I was getting annoyed. They were being purposefully obtuse. "No. I'm just saying, there are other keys out there."

Officer Harding put his notepad away and said, "Ms. Bauer, as I recall, you found Nadine Hockenbaum yesterday?"

"Yes."

"It's understandable, then, why you might still be a little wary of tall shelves and jump to this conclusion."

"I'm not jumping to anything!" I heard the shrillness in my voice and took it down a notch. "I know what I saw."

"Officer Williams and I will go inside the museum and check the pocket door for any signs of recent entry."

"Thank you. I remember seeing a table in front of a closed pocket door when Archie and I were in the museum yesterday. It must be this door. It had a key in it, I think. Check the back door too. I didn't think to see if they ran out that door. It's a straight shot to run to the parking lot." *And Womack's office at the carriage house.*

"We'll check on it," Officer Harding promised.

"Okay. I'm coming with you," I said, ready to walk out.

Officers Williams and Harding didn't move.

"We have to get the chief's permission before we can go inside the museum. Once he gets in touch with us, we'll check it out for you. Right now, it might be best for you two to go home and get some rest. You've had a scare. We'll be in touch with any developments," Officer Williams said.

I was about to protest their condescending advice, but Mrs. Schultz broke in.

"Thank you, Officers, for coming so quickly," she said, smoothing over my impertinence.

I kept my mouth shut after that as Officer Williams insisted on walking us to Mrs. Schultz's car right outside the museum. We thanked the officer, although there was a bitter taste in my mouth afterward.

"I could've sworn I saw the door closing. I'm sorry if I scared you," I said after we got into Mrs. Schultz's Fiat.

She turned on the ignition and slowly drove over the dirt trail toward the museum parking lot and the road. "It was the cabinet falling over that scared me, not you. We still don't know what really happened."

"I wish they could've gone inside the museum right now. I guess we'll have to wait to see if they find any evidence that someone was there."

"What could they possibly find that would unequivocally say someone was there tonight? Unless they took pictures of more than just Nadine's crime scene, anything they find could be attributed to everyone who went through there yesterday."

"You're right. There's no reason for them to believe me."

"What do *you* believe? I trust you, Willa."

I went over it in my mind again. "I guess I don't know one hundred percent. I *felt* someone there, but maybe I was just spooked because of the noise. I guess I can't say for sure that I saw someone. Maybe Officer Harding was right."

"For the heck of it, let's suppose you're right and someone pushed that cabinet deliberately so one of us would end up like Nadine. Who knew we would be there?"

"Your car was parked outside, so anybody could've seen it."

"But who would still be around? It had to be someone who knew we would be there."

"Chief Womack, for one."

"Oh, Willa." Mrs. Schultz was still not on board with suspecting Chief Womack of any wrongdoing.

"Okay, then, Mary Ann. Maybe leaving early was just an excuse."

"Why would Mary Ann want to hurt me or you?"

"She did get mad at you this morning when she thought you wanted to take over for Nadine."

"We worked well together all day. I'm sure we put that misunderstanding behind us. Besides, it was Barbie who asked Mary Ann to go to the prop room in the first place. I volunteered to go with her. It wasn't planned," Mrs. Schultz said.

"You're right. Barbie believed *Mary Ann* would be in that room."

"Yes, but why would Barbie try to hurt Mary Ann?"

"Okay then, maybe Tyrell?"

"That makes a little more sense. There's no love lost between him and Mary Ann," Mrs. Schultz said. "Does that mean Tyrell could've killed Nadine?"

I thought about it. "He did seem to resent Nadine's powerful role in Dairy Days. She seemed to have more sway than he did in decisions regarding the festival or at least the pageant. He even said how festival money that he could've used was funneled toward the pageant."

"That sounds like a real possibility. On the other hand, wouldn't another incident make his job even harder?"

"Good point." Every theory that got traction had a speed bump.

"We have to find out a little more about the suspects. I don't know anything about Tyrell. Do you?" I asked.

"No. I haven't had much interaction with him," Mrs. Schultz said.

She slowed to a stop at a red light at the edge of downtown Lockwood.

"The problem is, I don't know whether to *suspect* Mary Ann or protect her. We need to find out more about her and Nadine," I said.

"Let's call Beatrice and see if we can stop by for

a chat. She should be able to tell us something about the cousins." As soon as the light turned green, Mrs. Schultz accelerated the punchy little Fiat, and we headed to Yarrow Glen.

CHAPTER 16

Once we arrived in downtown Yarrow Glen, Mrs. Schultz parked her car in one of the diagonal spots in front of Beatrice's thrift shop. Bea's Hive of Thrifted Finds was across the street and a few shops up from Curds & Whey. I'd called Beatrice on the way over and she seemed happy for us to visit.

The stairs to Beatrice's apartment were inside her shop, so we pushed a buzzer on the inner doorway frame. Her shop only had standard-sized windows in the front, so the contents of the store were unknown until you stepped inside and found yourself in a maze of vintage curiosities. Beatrice didn't accept just anything for her shop—she curated the best of the mid-to-late-twentieth century.

She answered the door momentarily in a colorful caftan and her hair out of its braid. She let us in the front door, setting off the cuckoo clock that had been revamped to "cuckoo" three times when the door opened. Now *that* would drive me cuckoo.

"We're sorry to bother you so late, Beatrice," I said, noting her attire.

"It's not late. I just like to get comfortable when I'm

done for the day, whatever time that may be. Over a half century wearing a bra will do that to you."

I chuckled as she led us up the staircase to her apartment on the second floor and straight into a small kitchen that looked right out of the nineteen sixties. Much like me with my cheese, vintage wasn't just Bea's shop, it was her passion. She guided us to sit at the round linoleum table and brought out a plastic pitcher.

"Sweet tea?" she offered. "Or would you rather have hot? It's really starting to cool down after dark."

"Sweet tea is fine. Thank you," Mrs. Schultz said.

I nodded in agreement.

Beatrice cracked an ice tray, filled three flowered cups with ice, and poured the tea. "What's up? Have you heard any more about what happened to Nadine? She was a pill to work with, but I still hate the way she died." She returned the pitcher to the fridge, then opened one of her knotty pine cabinets and came back to the table with a bottle of rum, a splash of which she added to her tea.

"It's my treat for going to the dentist. They don't give out lollipops anymore." Beatrice always managed to surprise me. She extended the bottle to us, but we declined. As she returned it to the cabinet, she said, "I hope I don't go in an accident like that, but with this place, it's not so far-fetched. I can see it now—someone finds me a week later buried under a black-and-white television set and a pile of *National Geographic*s." She shook her head at the thought and sat with us at the table. "Or was it murder, like Mary Ann said? If some lowlife took her out, I sure hope she'd done something to them that still sticks in their craw."

"I'm with you, Beatrice, but we haven't heard anything. The police are still trying to figure out if it was intentional or not," Mrs. Schultz said.

"They need one of those TV detectives to look at the crime scene and declare it a homicide on the spot— Columbo or Jessica Fletcher." Then she looked at me. "Or Willa."

"What?" I felt caught in the spotlight. What did Beatrice know?

"I've read A. J.'s *Case Closed* articles. You've come across a few murders since you've been in town and helped solve them too. You and Archie found Nadine, didn't you?"

"We did, but then the police came, and we had to leave."

All true.

"Too bad. This case could use your sleuthing skills. Unless that's why you're here, to get some insider information?" Beatrice's eyes glowed at the idea.

Apparently, we had underestimated Beatrice. I sipped my drink and my mouth puckered at the amount of *sweet* in the sweet tea.

On the way to Beatrice's, Mrs. Schultz and I had agreed we'd keep what happened tonight to ourselves until we heard more from the police. But pretending we'd come to hear her pleasant reminiscence about Nadine and Mary Ann wasn't going to cut it. She was too sharp for that. Beatrice might be a target too, so it wasn't a bad idea to let her in on some of our concerns.

"I don't know anything for certain, Beatrice, but we have to admit, we're worried about the possibility of murder, especially for the safety of everyone at the pageant," I said.

"We've had Jeff Harding patrolling the pageant

area," Beatrice replied. "I've known him since he was a kid. He's not that bright, but he's beefy enough to scare someone away."

Still bitter about how condescending he was to me earlier, I inwardly cheered her assessment.

"And I've been keeping an eye out for anyone suspicious. Poor Mary Ann. She's been surprisingly difficult, hasn't she? I didn't know she had it in her—I swear, she's channeling Nadine," Beatrice added.

"Were she and Nadine as close as she claims?" I asked.

"I think so, despite how Nadine treated her when they worked together. I never heard Mary Ann complain when she came here to help with the pageant. If she hated it, she's returned for the torture year after year."

"I wonder why," I said.

"They were family—they only had each other. Neither one has a husband or children. She would talk to me sometimes about growing up with Nadine in Crescent City. I think Mary Ann was used to being bossed around by her. She never joined in with complaints about her during the pageant. If anything, she'd defend Nadine. Family sticks together." She took a healthy sip of her drink.

"Mary Ann said that's why the pageant meant so much to Nadine. The girls were like her children, and that's why she was so tough on them," I said, recalling the little speech she gave after her outburst this morning.

"It might be the same reason Nadine was tough on Mary Ann too. She was older than Mary Ann by a good ten years. Maybe she was a tough love kind of person, and we only recognized the *tough* part."

She made some good points. Maybe I needed to

focus on our other suspects. "Do you know anybody who'd want to sabotage the pageant?"

"Other than Grace Kelp, you mean? You heard she wants to abolish beauty pageants, even the pageant she won?"

"Yes. I saw that confrontation today," I replied. I couldn't see the *Lockwood Weekly* journalist killing just because she believes pageants are misogynistic. "What about the pageant judge, Fiona, the Becky's Bakeware saleswoman? Mary Ann doesn't know why Nadine wanted her kicked off the judging table. Was she doing something that could hurt the pageant?"

"I don't know what happened there. There were always some complaints from the mothers at the end of every pageant thinking *their* daughter should've won, but that's to be expected. I'm not sure why Fiona would be singled out, except that she was the head judge."

If Beatrice hadn't heard any gossip about wrongdoing by Fiona, then there was likely none to be had. Could I trust Mary Ann's perspective on her cousin? Was Becky's Bakeware the reason she wanted her gone or was it a secret about Fiona only Nadine knew? Did Fiona kill her to keep it from being revealed?

Deep in contemplation, I took a swig of my drink, forgetting the overpowering sugary flavor. I did my best to hide my unpleasant surprise.

A thump from the other room made me start. Another person in hiding?

"You okay? It's just Sweet Potato," Beatrice said, reaching to the floor. I turned to see her orange cat saunter into the room and go right to Beatrice's hand.

I knew Beatrice had a cat—I'd seen her downstairs in the shop. Maybe I *did* need some of Beatrice's rum tonight.

Sweet Potato accepted smushy rubs from Beatrice, then made her way to me and Mrs. Schultz for a quick full body swipe against our ankles before she munched on some dry cat food.

"Now it's my turn," Beatrice said. "Why all the questions?" She peered at us from over her plastic cup as she sipped her spiked tea. When we didn't answer right away, she continued with more questions. "You think it *is* murder, don't you? You *do* have a nose for these things, Willa."

I'd promised Chief Womack I'd keep quiet about the crime scene and the note we'd found, so I couldn't share any inside information with her. I needed him on my side, especially if I wanted him to take me seriously about what happened tonight—assuming he wasn't involved, that is.

"The police haven't told me anything." That wasn't a lie—they hadn't. "But the possibility worries me. Since we don't know yet exactly what happened, everyone should stay alert."

"Yes. Play it safe and be careful, Beatrice," Mrs. Schultz said.

Beatrice took in our warning. "We'll use the buddy system, you and I," she said to Mrs. Schultz.

I took another sip of my drink, this time to be polite. "Thanks for the tea and the information, Beatrice."

CHAPTER 17

Mrs. Schultz drove home, and I started to walk the block to my apartment above Curds & Whey when I read a missed text from Baz that he was at our local pub, The Cellar, if I felt like having some food with him. I turned around and walked the two and a half blocks up Pleasant Avenue and across Main Street to the historic Inn at Yarrow Glen where The Cellar was located.

The turn-of-the-twentieth-century inn was tucked between rows of evergreens. An inviting porch and an identical second floor balcony wrapped around the entire white, symmetrical structure. The simplicity of the exterior was broken up by two large urns flanking the front door—the summery yellow and white flowers had already been traded for hearty mums and wide-leafed blooms in fall colors of wine reds and rust oranges, providing bursts of color.

I stepped into the modest lobby. A spindle staircase was to the right, and the sitting area anchored by an arched fireplace was to my left. It was comprised of a Chesterfield sofa and two wing chairs on either side of what looked like an antique walnut coffee table. The highly polished wood floor was covered with a dark print rug. A matching runner led to the ornate reception desk at the rear of the lobby, where Baz was chatting with Constance Yi, the twentysomething reception clerk. She saw me enter and waved, causing Baz to notice too. I walked over to them.

"Hi, Constance."

"Hi, Willa."

"Don't tell me you're already done with dinner," I said to Baz.

"I haven't been down yet. Archie bailed on me, so Constance has been keeping me company."

"Can you join us for dinner?" I asked Constance. They seemed like they were vibing, and I didn't want to break it up.

"I wish! I took my break early tonight," she replied.

"You want me to bring you up one of the spiked milkshakes they're serving for Dairy Days weekend?" Baz asked her.

She knew he was kidding and giggled in response. "I wish!" she said again. "You two have one for me."

"*That* I can do. Next time I'll come as a genie so I can grant your wish. See ya later."

"I'll get my three wishes ready," she said to him, giggling again, as we left the reception desk.

We cut across the sitting area and down the short hall to the red door with a tattered piece of paper taped on it, listing the acoustic bands that would be playing in The Cellar each weekend after eight. There was no sign indicating the door led to a pub, which wasn't a problem for its clientele. Although the inn had changed hands many times, The Cellar, which originally held the inn's wine, continued to be the top hangout among locals. Guests of the inn were directed to it by Constance.

Descending the steps to The Cellar often gave me the feeling of going to some secret society. The stone walls and stone floor gave it a somewhat gothic feel, highlighted by the wrought-iron ring chandeliers that hung from the ceiling. It was like an English pub plopped into a medieval dungeon. It packed as many tables and chairs as would fit, leaving only narrow pathways to get to and from the bar. An acoustic folk band was playing background music in the rear of the room beyond the long bar, ignored by most of the chatting patrons except for scattered clapping at the conclusion of each song. Several oak-lined arched nooks broke up the long wall, with a booth tucked into each cozy space.

It wasn't as busy as usual for a Saturday night. People may have already stuffed themselves at Dairy Days, although that wasn't stopping Baz. He handed me the narrow specials menu that was housed on the table between the ketchup and the salt and pepper shakers. Their regular menus were there also, but we'd been here often enough to know them by heart. The title at the top of the menu announced they were offering new items for Dairy Days weekend: the Brie fondue caught my eye.

"I'm starting with one of these Dairy Doozy milkshakes," Baz said.

"It was nice of you to offer to get one for Constance." I said it with my eyebrows raised and a lot more implied than the words themselves indicated.

He looked up from the menu and pushed his hair out of his eyes. "Whaddya mean?"

"Just that you two looked . . . cozy."

He took my meaning right away. "Constance? Nah. She's a buddy. Like you." He went back to focusing on the menu. Was it because he was hungry or because he didn't want me to see the truth in his eyes? Since Baz was always hungry, I let it go.

"Okay." My woman's intuition was telling me they were feeling more than buddy chemistry, but I didn't push it—I hated when people implied that Baz and I had to be more than close friends just because we weren't the same gender. Despite what Harry told Sally in that movie, single men and women *can* be friends.

"Besides, she's only twenty-four," he said.

"Oh, so you *do* like her!" And to think I was going to let it go.

"No, I'm just saying if I *was* interested, she's only twenty-four."

I rolled my eyes. "Is this about you freaking out over the big three-oh? So what if she's younger? Haven't you been trying to 'recapture your youth' for the past two months? Isn't that what that mullet's all about?"

"Mullet?" He pretended to look highly offended. "Okay, so maybe trying to do the surfer dude hair wasn't the best idea. But my twenties are practically in the rearview mirror. It's either grow my hair or work out, and I'm not working out. My burger belly and I have become too close of friends for that," he said, patting his stomach, which slightly bulged under his T-shirt.

Liz, one of the regular servers, arrived at the table to take our order.

"Speaking of . . . you go first," I told Baz.

"I'll have the strawberry Doozy milkshake and my usual cheeseburger," Baz said without missing a beat.

Liz nodded.

"I'll do the strawberry Doozy milkshake too. And the Brie fondue." It had been a long day.

"The fondue's for two," Liz informed me.

"You underestimate her," Baz joked.

"He'll help me eat it," I said.

When Liz left the table, Baz said, "A lake of cheese *and* hard liquor? What's going on?" He was familiar with my emotional eating habits and the fact that I rarely drank. "Is what happened with Nadine getting to you?"

"Literally. Mrs. Schultz narrowly escaped a similar fate."

This straightened his slouched position in the booth. "What happened?"

I proceeded to tell him what I thought happened earlier at the museum. "But I'm second guessing myself whether it was intentional or an accident," I finished.

"Your mind could be playing tricks on you. But what if you're right? There seem to be an awful lot of accidents around the pageant."

"Tell me more about the first accident—the one where Nadine broke her foot. You said she fell through a trapdoor on the stage floor?"

"Yeah, that was really dangerous. Luckily, I was just arriving for my first day on the job, so she couldn't blame me for it."

"Did you see it happen?"

"No. I got there the same time as Chief Womack."

"Chief Womack was there?" This sparked my interest. "Who called him?"

"Nobody. He said he was checking the festival grounds when he heard her cry out. It was lucky for Nadine. It was way before rehearsal was supposed to start that day, and she and Mary Ann were the only ones there."

"So Mary Ann saw it happen?"

"No, she came running up when I got there. She had

no idea—she said she was still getting their stuff from the car. She said the first thing Nadine always does is walk the stage as soon as she arrives. She was lucky that she only broke her foot. It could've been worse."

"Like murder?"

Confusion crossed Baz's face. "You think Nadine's accident wasn't an accident?"

"A. J. got me thinking it might've been the first attempt to murder her. When it didn't succeed, they tried again, and well, we know how *that* went."

"Too bad that doesn't narrow down our suspect list. If everyone knew it was Nadine's routine to walk the stage, that trapdoor could've been opened at any time from the night before to that morning."

Liz returned with our spiked strawberry milkshakes in all their pink glory. We immediately took sips. The kick from the strawberry vodka and Irish crème liqueur went down easy with the creamy ice cream, made richer by the addition of a white chocolate liqueur. I sucked up more than I should have.

"How does Mrs. Schultz feel after what happened tonight? Is she gonna continue with the pageant?" Baz asked.

"She wants to. I'd like to talk her out of it, but I can't say for sure that it wasn't some random accident tonight."

"A cabinet just happened to randomly fall over while you were in there? That would be quite a coincidence."

I shrugged. "I know, but the police want proof. I'm going to have to wait for them to tell me what, if anything, they find to show that someone went into the museum, unlocked that door, and pushed the cabinet over. And I have to wonder if they'd even tell me or just keep it to themselves."

"You could ask Heath to find out for you. You two are talking again, I noticed."

"We are, thank goodness. But he already made it clear he doesn't want to interfere in Chief Womack's investigation."

"Okay, then. Let's tick off our full list of suspects for Nadine's murder based on what happened tonight too." Baz counted them off on his fingers to make sure he was getting it right. "We have pageant judge Fiona; event director Tyrell; and you said something about pageant mom Barbie."

"Yeah, but there's no motive."

"Not one we know of yet. We gotta count every possibility."

I shrugged. "All right then, Barbie and her daughter, Annabelle."

"And Mary Ann, who might be a suspect or a possible target," he added.

"Right. And don't forget Grace Kelp, the *Lockwood Weekly* journalist Nadine turned the town against. I don't know if she knew Mary Ann was going to the museum, but if she did, she could've certainly been fed up with her, especially after Mary Ann accused her of still trying to take down the pageant."

"Did you ever find out what that was all about?"

"Yeah. A. J. filled me in on that."

"Did I hear my name?" As usual, A. J. Stringer seemed to appear out of nowhere at the same time Liz came to the table with Baz's burger platter and the platter of dippers for my Brie fondue—toasted cubes of seasoned French bread, roasted vegetables, and shrimp. Another server helped her with the warming stone on which she set the fondue pot of luscious cheese sauce, then left us to our feast.

"Just in time to join you for dinner. What luck!" He patted me on the arm with the back of his hand to scoot me over in the booth.

"What are we having?" A. J. peeked into the fondue pot. I gave him my plate. My stress level had been bigger than my stomach and the milkshake was filling me up. He accepted happily, picked up a fondue skewer, and got right to the dunking. "What's the word?" he said after his first mouthful.

"You tell us. You're the journalist."

"I didn't get anything today. I tried to interview Mary Ann but there was too much going on for her to give me much. I interviewed a few of the moms. Some of them are wild." His eyes bugged out and he chuckled, then went in for some more fondue as he spoke. "Talk about stage moms! And then there's that Fiona Carson, walking around in her red blazer, pushing her Becky's Bakeware on everyone. It was like *Dance Moms* meets the Home Shopping Network. A bad combination." A. J. laughed and shook his head.

"Was there anyone in particular interested in what Fiona was selling?" I wondered if there was any connection between who bought the most of Fiona's bakeware and who won the pageant that year.

A. J. popped a cube of cheese-covered bread into his mouth before digging into his messenger bag and pulling out his small notebook. "Barbie Patterson. Her daughter's Annabelle. Are you thinking Fiona's got some kind of racket going with her Becky Bakeware stuff and Nadine discovered it?"

"I'm not sure, but she, Tyrell, and Mary Ann are my top three suspects right now."

He went through his notes. "I checked into the inheritance motive. Nadine lived on a town employee salary and still owed a mortgage on her house. Mary Ann was the likely one to inherit, but I doubt it would be much."

"That takes *that* motive out of the equation," Baz said between bites of his burger.

I went back to thinking about Fiona. "Do you think Grace Kelp would know anything about what went on between Nadine and Fiona to make Nadine kick her out as a pageant judge?" I asked A. J.

"Possibly. She had insider access to the pageant last year when she was doing that story on it."

"I thought it was a cutthroat piece. Why would they give her access?"

"She didn't tell them that was the angle she was going for, which was why Nadine and the whole town were even more ticked off at her," he explained.

"I thought Grace Kelp was one of our suspects," Baz said between bites of his cheeseburger.

"She is, but she could still be a good resource," I said.

"A reliable one, though?" Baz questioned.

"You could be right. She's obviously sneaky, but I'd love to know some of what she knows."

As I knew he would, Baz paused eating the second half of his burger to dig into the fondue. He tried some on his tongue before deciding he liked it and loaded up his fondue fork with shrimp. "It could make things even murkier if she lies to us," he said.

A. J. put a forefinger up. "The best way to get people to tell the truth inadvertently or lie badly is to catch them off guard. I do it all the time."

This I knew to be true. He was great at catching people—namely me—off guard. "How would we do that with Grace Kelp?" I asked.

"The first way is to loosen her up. Find something

to be on her side about. The second is to employ the element of surprise."

"I guess we can ask her some questions if we run into her at the festival tomorrow," I said.

"Why wait until tomorrow? Let's go to her apartment tonight. Show up at her door." A. J. looked ready to leave the booth and do it right at that moment.

"Showing up at her door uninvited? What would make her talk to us?" I asked.

"She knows A. J.," Baz countered.

"Like I said, what would make her talk to us?" I re-iterated.

"Ha ha. Fine. You got a better idea?" A. J. put me on the spot.

I went for my straw again, but there was nothing left in the glass. "Is there a pub in Lockwood?"

"Yup. Just one, and more townies hang out there than we've got here. She's still persona non grata with a lot of folks—she's not going to be spending her Saturday night there."

"It sounds like we'll have to be satisfied with seeing her tomorrow at the festival," Baz said, dripping some of the melted Brie onto his fries.

"If she's there." As I considered our options, I un-spooled the napkin that was wrapped around my regular fork. Who was I kidding? My appetite had no bearing on whether I'd eat cheese or not. I used the fork to drench bread cubes in the creamy Brie peppered with chives, and let the buttery sauce coat my tastebuds. The menu said it was made with pink grapefruit juice, so there was no wine or beer to compound the effects of my milkshake.

After I was satiated with my first bite, I said, "Maybe it's the alcohol talking, but we could do what

A. J. suggested. I do have something in common with her—I'm not a fan of pageants either, and Tyrell asked me to take Nancy Fuller's place and be the guest judge for the pageant."

"*You're* going to be the *celebrity* judge?" A. J. made sure to appear plenty shocked. I did my best to ignore the ribbing.

"I'm the *guest* judge. Anyway, my point is, I could ask her what I should do about the invitation. We could bond over our dislike of beauty pageants."

"Is bonding with one of our suspects a good idea?" Baz said. "I mean, I know I've saved your butt before, but I'd rather not have to pull out my hero cape again so soon if I can help it."

"That's why you two will be with me. If she really does want to take down this pageant, maybe I could pretend I'm willing to help her do it, seeing as how I'll be one of the judges. Let's see how far Grace Kelp is willing to go to make sure the pageant tanks."

Our server, Liz, appeared with an extra fondue skewer, and Baz, A. J., and I finished off the fondue. I left The Cellar with enough cheesy padding to keep down any stress I had about Nadine's murder, not trusting Chief Womack, and investigating it all without messing up my relationship with Heath again. Cheese always does the trick.

CHAPTER 18

A. J. had refrained from the Dairy Doozy milkshakes, and he knew where Grace Kelp lived, so he offered to drive. I was relieved not to have to ride in the beat-up Jeep Wrangler we'd wiped out in last year—he'd traded it for a newer Renegade.

We headed toward Lockwood, passing the quiet Main Street to eventually arrive at a quaint complex of townhomes. Sidewalks emerging from each unit's stoop cut through pockets of grass and led to numbered parking spaces. A. J. slowed the car as we tried to read the door numbers from the sporadically illuminated porch lights.

"I was only here once before, but that was in the daytime. You can't tell at night which units are the dark gray and which are the light ones. I think this is Building 3."

"Why don't we ask that guy?" Baz suggested.

There was a man walking away from us toward one of the townhomes. Baz rolled down his window.

"Wait a second, Baz. I recognize him," I said. There was something about the urgency in his gait . . .

"That looks like the festival director, Tyrell," A. J. said just before I was certain.

He pulled the car into an unused space, cut the engine, and turned off the headlights.

Tyrell pushed a Big Wheels trike out of his path and approached the stoop just as the porch light came on. The figure of a woman I recognized as Grace appeared in the doorway. She pulled him into the house and shut the door behind them.

"Why is Tyrell visiting Grace on a Saturday night?" I asked.

"You think they're a couple? She didn't look surprised he was at her door," Baz said.

"They could be, but they didn't act like it after Mary Ann had her outburst this morning. I heard him call her Miss Kelp," I said, confused.

"Now we know who pulled the strings for Grace to keep her job at the *Lockwood Weekly*," A. J. muttered.

After thinking more about their connection, I said, "Tyrell has to be publicly in favor of the pageant, but what if he's secretly trying to sabotage it?"

A. J. rejected my theory. "Who's going to risk their job *and* a murder charge for some moral high ground about a pageant?"

I wasn't giving up on it that easily. Where one secret was discovered, more were usually buried. "What if he did it in the name of love? Nadine turned everyone in town against Grace and maybe she'd still be stoking the flames against her. Grace obviously refused to be run out of her hometown, so maybe the next best thing was chopping off the head of the dragon and killing Nadine."

"Let's go in and confront them," A. J. said, unbuckling his seat belt.

"I don't think that's a good idea. They're not going

to cop to anything. They'll only know we're onto them," I said.

"Willa's right. It could be dangerous," Baz agreed from the back seat.

A. J. thought for a moment and nodded in agreement. "This element of surprise could be too big. Better to talk to them tomorrow and see how much truth they're willing to tell."

CHAPTER 19

The next morning, Archie, Mrs. Schultz, and I arrived at the shop early to make the day's grazing boxes. I was glad to see we'd done so well, even with the local creameries selling their own cheeses at the festival. Along with duplicating yesterday's favorites, we also packed some themed by country.

"Great job with the French grazing box, Archie," I said as we finished packing his cheese choices—Brie de Nangis, a milder Brie; the rich, nutty Ossau-Iraty; and one of our favorites for its sweet and salty undertones, Comté.

"Oui oui," he replied in his best French accent.

Mrs. Schultz and I laughed.

"Let's use that for the name—the Oui Oui grazing box," I suggested.

He went to the laptop and typed the name under the photo collage he'd made for it.

"Is that the last of them? Can I print them out?" Mrs. Schultz asked.

"Yes. Thank you both for starting so early. I know we all have a long day ahead of us still."

"I love being at the festival. We get to be outside all

day; it's hardly work," Archie said as he secured the boxes.

"This is the most time I get to spend with you two all day. I didn't mind coming in early," Mrs. Schultz put in as she took the laptop from Archie.

"Thanks, you two. I hope whoever I can find to add to our crew is as great as you both are," I said. Truth be told, I was a little nervous to be adding to our Curds & Whey family. I knew from working at many different cheese shops over the years that one person could change the whole dynamic. We had such a good thing going with just the three of us, but there was no doubt we'd need extra help.

"You'll find someone great," Mrs. Schultz said. She patted me on the shoulder and headed to the back of the shop through the stockroom door, laptop in hand, to my closet of an office.

"That didn't take long," Archie said, closing the last box.

"We have just one more box to make. I promised our milk carton friend I'd bring her one. I was impressed with her knowledge of the cheeses I offered her yesterday, so I want to make her a special box." I surveyed our selections, waiting for the right ones to speak to me.

"She's definitely going to be there, then?" he asked.

"She said she would be."

I saw a smile cross Archie's lips. "We could find something to go with the rest of this fig bread," he suggested.

"How about Moody Blue for her grazing box?" I suggested. "It's smoked over fruit wood. I think it would pair well with the fig bread."

"We could do a box of smoky cheeses for her," Archie suggested.

"Good idea. We can call it Around the Campfire." I picked up some smoked Gouda and Idiazabal, a sheep's milk cheese from Spain with notes of burnt caramel and bacon.

Mrs. Schultz came back with the printouts for the grazing boxes and as Archie was finishing assembling our special grazing box, there was a knock on the front door.

"That's probably Baz," I said as I walked to the door to unlock it. The man I saw through the four-paned window was tall and fit, his black T-shirt clung to his broad shoulders—definitely not Baz. I was still getting used to the casual Heath, the one without a suit or a stern warning telling me to stay away from an investigation. My stomach was already doing the jitterbug even before I turned the key in the lock. I opened the door. "Heath. Hi."

"Hi, Willa. I'm glad I caught you before the festival," he said.

"Just. I thought you were Baz—we're using his truck again today. Come on in."

He entered the shop, and Archie and Mrs. Schultz said hello.

"What brings you by, Detective?" Mrs. Schultz asked.

"I heard what happened to you two yesterday. I came by to make sure you're all right."

I lowered my head so he wouldn't see how happy it made me that he was checking up on us.

"Not a scratch on us, but that's very nice of you," Mrs. Schultz replied.

I made an effort to look at him without the smile

that was pulling at the corners of my mouth surfacing. "How did you find out about it? Is there any news?"

"The officers wouldn't go in the museum to check if there was any evidence of someone having opened the pocket door and pushed the cabinet," Mrs. Schultz explained.

Heath nodded, indicating he already knew. "Shep is buddies with one of the Lockwood officers who was on the scene. After Shep told me about what he learned, I made some inquiries. Let's just say, the chief didn't appreciate my input."

"How rude!" Mrs. Schultz sniped. She crossed her arms. "That gets my dander up."

"Why, Mrs. Schultz, I don't think I've ever seen your dander up," Heath said with a hint of a smile. He was being cheeky, but it was true—Mrs. Schultz was from the "make peace, not war" era. She always looked on the bright side, which undoubtedly helped her through a thirty-five-year career teaching hormonal teenagers.

"What's a dander?" Archie intervened.

"It means Chief Womack's ticked her off, Archie," I said.

He nodded.

Mrs. Schultz leaned into her annoyance, raising her chin and keeping her arms crossed. "It's not often something makes me mad, but this has. You're only trying to help."

Heath slipped his hands into the pockets of his jeans. "Don't be too hard on him. I can't say how I'd feel if he questioned how I was proceeding in an investigation. He was polite when I had questions about Nadine's death yesterday, but I wore out my welcome with this second visit."

This soothed Mrs. Schultz's anger. "I suppose he's allowed to run things as he sees fit."

"The feature articles that came out about Nadine's death in the *Lockwood Weekly* and the *Glen Gazette* didn't help his attitude. As of this morning, he's decided to tighten the reins and keep everything in-house from now on. Their officers are forbidden to discuss it, not even with our guys working security at the festival. I won't be getting any more information going forward. Sorry."

"I'm sure he'll let us know what he's found out about our close call," Mrs. Schultz said. Even when she tried, she couldn't help her positivity.

"I've been checking my phone since last night to see if he tried to get in touch," I said. "Nothing."

Heath had delivered plenty of bad news to me in the past, so I knew what that look on his face meant.

"What is it?" I asked.

"It didn't sound like they were taking the complaint very seriously. Shep's friend, one of the responding officers, seemed to think you were spooked because of witnessing Nadine's death."

I scoffed. "Don't tell me. According to them, nothing happened last night, just like Nadine's death was an accident, right? They're really going to sweep everything under the rug all in the name of keeping Dairy Days afloat, aren't they?"

Mrs. Schultz's arms went back to her angry, crossed position. Both our danders were up.

Another knock brought our attention to the door. This time it was Baz. Archie let him in then went back to stacking the cheese kits into the coolers.

"Hey, guys. We all set? Hi, Detective Heath." Baz's

quick glance to us said, *What's he doing here?* It was rarely good news when Heath paid a visit to my shop.

"Heath just came to check on me and Mrs. Schultz after what happened yesterday," I answered his unspoken question.

"The cheese is packed up," Archie announced.

Baz took a cooler, as did Heath. Archie and I shared the task with the third large cooler. We got them loaded onto the bed of Baz's truck.

"I'm going to Beatrice's. We're driving together," Mrs. Schultz announced.

"Good idea. See you later," I called after her.

"Do you mind if I talk to you privately for a minute, Willa?" Heath asked.

I told Archie and Baz to go on ahead—I knew Archie had rehearsal before the festival opened—and I'd text when I got to the festival so Baz and I could meet up to get the coolers to the booth. Heath and I returned to the shop, and I closed the door behind us, anxious to hear why he wanted to speak with me alone.

CHAPTER 20

I led Heath to the kitchenette at the rear of the shop. I suddenly wondered if he wanted to talk to me about last night, if he thought I was responsible for being in that dangerous situation.

"I hope you're not mad about me and Mrs. Schultz being at the museum. It was all aboveboard—we were not sleuthing! We really were just looking for a prop," I said. I wanted to move forward with Heath, not back.

"Willa." He squeezed my shoulder, stopping me. "I'm not mad. I know what happened wasn't your fault."

My expanding worry shrank away. I leaned against the counter at my back. "We might never know what really happened, will we? Not with Chief Womack dragging his feet."

"Despite cutting me off from any information, I do think he's trying to investigate under the radar."

"Under the radar? Why? He's the chief of police!"

"The mayor hires the chief of police, so Mayor Sonny is his boss, and he's given him strict instructions to wait until after the festival concludes."

"Isn't Chief Womack supposed to be some hero or something?" I recalled the old headline I'd seen at the historical museum. "What kind of police officer doesn't investigate?"

"He checks out." Heath sat on the farm table bench across from where I stood.

"What do you mean, he checks out?"

"I did a quick search."

"You looked into Chief Womack?" This was a side of Heath I hadn't seen before.

"Normally, I wouldn't interfere in another police department's investigation, but if he had reason not to investigate this death properly, I wanted to know about it."

"What did you find out?"

"He's been on the force in Lockwood for twenty-two years without a smudge on his record. In fact, he was the youngest sergeant to be hired as the chief of police. From what Shep's heard, his men respect him."

"What about his wife who disappeared never to be heard from again, like, fifteen years ago?"

"I didn't know anything about that. All I have is that he's married."

"He's still married?" My initial surprise was overtaken by my certainty that I'd been right about him. "According to Mary Ann, she suddenly wasn't living there anymore, and nobody's heard from her since. Don't you think that's suspicious? What if he's still legally married because she's not alive to sign a divorce petition?"

"Whoa. Slow down. You think Chief Womack killed his wife fifteen years ago?"

"I don't know. I'm just saying, she seems to have disappeared and everyone just took his word for it that she left. They seem to like to smooth things over in Lockwood, don't they?"

Heath was quiet in contemplation. "It's a leap, but I'll look into it," he said. I could tell he meant it. "You should still keep an open mind."

I thought about other suspects we hadn't looked into enough. "What about Mayor Sonny? Maybe the festival's not the only reason he doesn't want Nadine's death investigated."

"From what Shep's heard over the years, Mayor Sonny can play hardball, but he's clean."

Even though everyone knew Shep was a police officer, he was one of those unassuming guys people felt comfortable talking to where they might not have with another cop around. If there were gossipy rumblings, Shep would've heard about them.

"Mayor Sonny also has an airtight alibi. He was at a meeting attended by eight other people within the hour the incident with Nadine occurred," Heath added.

I nodded, mentally crossing off Mayor Sonny from the suspect list. "He came to the crime scene with Tyrell, the festival director. Do you know if Tyrell was at that meeting too?"

Heath stood to pull his phone out of his pocket and tapped it.

"No mini notebook today?" I asked. He always had it tucked in his suit jacket pocket during investigations.

"No suit, no paper notebook. The notebook's on this." He lifted his phone and looked over the names. "No, Tyrell's not on the list."

"Interesting." So Tyrell didn't have an alibi. I thought about the other suspects I had. "This is how little I know about the case. I don't even know who has alibis. This is why we need the Lockwood police to get on this investigation. If Chief Womack has a spotless record and Mayor Sonny's not a bad guy, why won't Womack stand up to him? Would he really lose his job?"

"There's another reason, and you can't tell a soul—not even Baz or Mrs. Schultz or Archie."

I had to think about that, because I wasn't about to break another promise to Heath as I'd done months ago. I rarely kept things from my closest friends, but if Heath was willing to confide in me, I had to trust him. I gave him my word. "Okay."

"Shep heard this before the moratorium on information going beyond the Lockwood force. In Mayor Sonny's panic, he mentioned Mayor Trumbull's name."

"Why would he talk about *our* mayor? And what do you mean? Mentioned her name how?"

"That she might've been responsible."

I guffawed. "How is the mayor of Yarrow Glen responsible? He can't be serious."

"He claims that ruining Lockwood's reputation just before the big fiftieth anniversary year was her ploy to get the festival moved to Yarrow Glen."

Mayor Trumbull made no secret that she thought a percentage of the profits for Dairy Days should be shared among the three towns in the district, since the volunteer load was spread among us and some of our town's resources were used. She'd even tried to get the location changed to Yarrow Glen a few years ago, but our small park wasn't suited for such a large event. She was only doing her job as our mayor. I was certain she'd never sabotage the festival, and certainly not in such a hideous way.

I shook my head. "That's ludicrous."

"Luckily, Chief Womack thinks so too. It's the reason he's making it appear that he's holding off on the investigation. If talk starts to pick up that Nadine's death might be murder, Mayor Sonny might publicly pin it on Mayor Trumbull to get the heat off Lockwood."

I sunk onto the bench. "That would be disastrous for her. Does she have an alibi, just in case?"

Heath sat next to me. "She doesn't know anything about this, so I quietly looked into it. She was at Apricot Grille. Plenty of people saw her." Apricot Grille was our local upscale eatery. "But you know how quickly sensational headlines get picked up before the details of their truth are even mentioned," Heath continued.

I nodded. Especially after her proximity to her nephew's murder last winter, I wasn't sure her reputation could weather this.

"Womack is hoping once the spotlight's not on the festival anymore, Mayor Sonny will calm down and let his team do a proper investigation," Heath continued.

"So Chief Womack's actually doing us a favor?"

"That's the conclusion I've come to."

"That makes me second guess my suspicions of Chief Womack. If he was guilty, he'd run with the suspect Mayor Sonny's put in his lap, wouldn't he?"

"Maybe, but that would sensationalize the case. It's possible he doesn't want it to be scrutinized by the public."

It made me feel good to know that Heath was keeping an open mind about Chief Womack. "You're right. He could have his own reasons for not wanting to point the finger at Mayor Trumbull. It still doesn't help the fact that the more time that passes, the colder this case gets."

"Listen to you, Detective Bauer." Heath tapped me on the arm with his elbow, a slight smile on his face.

"I know, I know. You don't like when I stick my nose in."

"In this case, *someone's* nose needs to be in it. After what happened to you and Mrs. Schultz last night, whoever killed Nadine might not be done."

"You believe me that I saw someone?" I searched his eyes for the truth. They didn't leave mine.

"I believe you know what you saw. You make some bad decisions, and you jump to a lot of conclusions, but you're not a hysterical person."

Forget conclusions, I wanted to jump into his lap. But that wouldn't do. "Thank you for that." I pulled my gaze away from his so I wouldn't change my mind about his lap. *The case, Willa. The case.* "How are we supposed to find out anything if the Lockwood police won't share information with you?"

He splayed his hands and gave a little shrug. "I'll have to do it the old-fashioned way. Snoop."

I did a double take, not sure I heard him right. "Are you saying you're going to take off your badge and put on your sleuthing cap?"

"Do you have an extra?"

I didn't know what to make of this. "Are you being serious?"

The smile that had played on his lips disappeared. "I'm not comfortable letting this murder take a back seat for the weekend, especially when there are so many people from our community involved in the festival and Mayor Trumbull's reputation could be on the line."

"I can help you, Heath. Now before you say no, hear me out. Even though I've been minding my own business, I've got some suspects in mind. And—"

"I'd like your help."

"You would?" I guess I needed to stop being surprised that he kept surprising me today.

"I'll need you to be my eyes and ears. The minute people see me, they clam up," he said.

"People recognize you without your suit? *I* almost didn't," I kidded.

"I think I have cop energy, no matter what. I don't have glasses or a cape to fool people." That hint of a smile was back.

"I'll spring for the tights." *Did I just say that?*

He burst out laughing and we giggled together. That full-on smile of his slayed me.

My phone dinged a text from its place on the marble island. I got up from the bench and retrieved it. "It's from Archie."

"Do you need a ride to the festival? I'm going anyway," Heath offered.

"Sure. That'd be great." I opened the text and read it. "Archie forgot his . . ."

"His what?"

I looked up at Heath and smiled. "Well, it's not a cape, but I know how you can be at the pageant undercover."

He looked at me with suspicion. "Am I going to regret this?"

I walked to the other side of the farm table where Archie's cheese wedge costume lay forgotten on the other bench.

"You're not putting me in that thing, are you?" Heath asked. I might've even seen a little fear in his eyes.

I let him off the hook. "I don't think you'd fit into this, but I've got another idea. Let's get going."

I took the costume and left the shop with Heath.

CHAPTER 21

We began the short drive to Lockwood in Heath's car. "You said you have some suspects in mind?" Heath asked.

It felt good that he trusted my opinion.

"Sure. I've got plenty, but none of the motives seem serious enough to kill for. And if I'm right and Mary Ann or Mrs. Schultz was a target, that complicates things even more."

"How was Mary Ann a target?"

"One of the pageant moms, Barbie, asked Mary Ann to go to the museum's prop room to exchange one of the props for her daughter. She didn't know Mrs. Schultz and I had gone with her or that Mary Ann had left the prop room early. She may have laid in wait on the other side of the door and then when she heard who she thought was Mary Ann, she made her move. But I don't know what the motive is."

"Isn't there a large scholarship on the line? Money's always a motive. Any other pageant moms having issues?"

I thought about it. "There's Lynette, who doesn't want her daughter, Tabitha, in the pageant—she's very overprotective of her—but to kill to shut down the pageant? That seems like a stretch."

"Who else knew you would be at the museum yesterday?"

"Barbie's daughter, Annabelle, was there when Mrs. Schultz spoke to Mary Ann. And Tyrell, the festival director, knew. He's moved to the top of my list after last night." I told Heath about our venture out to Grace Kelp's townhome. "Why do you think they'd be meeting in secret?"

"Maybe they're friends? Lovers?"

"That's what A. J. thought. I heard Tyrell call her Miss Kelp at the festival yesterday morning, so if they're lovers, they must want to keep it a secret."

Heath was staring at the road ahead, but I could tell he was considering this new information about Tyrell and Grace.

"There's also Fiona, one of the pageant judges who Nadine tried to get removed," I continued. "I overheard the two of them getting into it, and it seemed like whatever the reason that Nadine wanted her dismissed as a judge, Fiona didn't want it to get out. Nadine could've been holding some secret over her head."

"So you have the pageant judge Fiona, the festival director Tyrell, the journalist Grace who might be working with Tyrell, and possibly two pageant mothers. And Nadine's cousin, Mary Ann, might be a suspect or a possible target," he confirmed.

"That's what I've got so far. Not very helpful, is it?"

"On the contrary, it's extremely helpful to narrow it down."

"Narrow it down? I have six possible suspects."

"Out of an entire town? That's a good start."

Heath glanced over at me and gave me an encouraging smile.

I looked out the passenger-side window, feeling satisfied, and thinking how surprisingly comfortable it felt to be working this case with him side by side.

I stood waiting next to the small tent that had finally been erected for any guys participating in the dance number to change into their costumes, which was located farther than it needed to be from the much larger one for the pageant contestants. Everyone else in the show was already in costume and milling about near the stage.

"I can't believe I'm doing this," Heath said, as he stepped out wearing the cowboy costume Mrs. Schultz had wrangled from Beatrice, chaps and all.

I pressed my lips together, trying not to show my delight. Heath could never look bad, but this costume was certainly a change from one of his tailored suits.

"You mean in all your years as a police detective, you've never gone undercover?"

"Not as Woody from *Toy Story*," he said dryly.

I held in my laughter. "This is the only way Mary Ann will let you near the girls. Nadine was very strict about men not hanging around and Mary Ann's taken that to heart."

"This isn't enough to disguise me if Mary Ann recognizes me. She saw me with Womack yesterday, and some of the others may have too."

"True, but it's the same costume as some of the others. If you wear the hat far enough in front of your face"—I reached up and tipped his hat down—"you'll be able to hang out with everyone else while they're on the sidelines without drawing attention to yourself. At least you'll be able to eavesdrop. As a judge, I'm not supposed to be mingling with the contestants, so I can't hang around for too long."

He looked longingly back at the tent before finally acquiescing.

"We'll meet up later?" I asked.

"You bet." He stuck his thumbs in his belt loop, elbows out, and started walking with bent knees and toes outward like a life-sized Woody doll. I burst out laughing. The last thing I expected was Heath to be a goofball. After a few paces, he looked my way and tipped the brim of his hat like a cowboy-gentleman, then resumed his regular gait, which was anything but goofy. My laughter dissipated but my heart sped up as I watched him go.

I spotted Mrs. Schultz and Beatrice by the girls' tent, so I walked over to thank them.

"Detective Heath is on his way to blend in with the others. Thank you for finding a costume for him," I said.

"Can someone that tall, dark, and handsome blend in even if he's wearing the same outfit as the others?" Beatrice asked.

"He's going to try," I said with a happy sigh.

Beatrice went inside the tent to corral the last of the contestants. Tabitha strode out of it quickly, looking pinched. Her mother was, not surprisingly, only a few steps behind.

"Nothing's changed with Tabitha and her mother?" I asked Mrs. Schultz when they passed us. I recalled how the girl had pleaded with Mrs. Schultz to intervene with her mother, so she'd stop shadowing her.

"No, poor girl. I spoke with Lynette, but one talk from me isn't going to change seventeen years of behavior. At least she's agreed to let her stay in the pageant." Mrs. Schultz watched them with concern on her face.

"Gosh, my mother sent me off on my own to the farmer's market to sell our cheese when I was that age, a few years younger even. Of course, I begged her to so I could get out of doing the farm chores on weekends. Mom always said, 'To reap its benefits, independence should be nurtured.'" I couldn't imagine my mother trailing me like that.

"It's not good for her or Tabitha, but I sympathize with Lynette. Did you know Tabitha went missing when she was a child? I remember reading about it when it happened—a toddler wandering off—but Beatrice reminded me that Tabitha had been that child," Mrs. Schultz said.

Beatrice emerged from the tent, alone. "My ears were buzzing."

"I was just telling Willa about what happened to Tabitha when she was a toddler," Mrs. Schultz explained.

"Oh yes. That was awful. They couldn't find her for about nine hours," Beatrice supplied. "They had police dogs and half the community searching the woods for her, myself included."

"Oh no! That must've been horrible for her parents," I said.

"I can hardly imagine the panic they must've felt until she was found," Mrs. Schultz said, surely thinking of her own daughter at that age.

I rubbed away the goose bumps that had sprouted on my arms at the thought of it.

"When I spoke with Lynette yesterday on Tabitha's behalf and assured her that it was safe to have her daughter in the pageant, she confided in me about why she has a hard time letting go. She told me she blames herself, which is why she's barely let her daughter out of her sight since. She knows she should, she just can't bring herself to do it," Mrs. Schultz explained.

"I thought she was just being one of those helicopter moms, but it makes more sense now," I said.

"You never know what people are privately wrestling with," Beatrice added.

Attempting to figure out who to suspect in Nadine's murder, I spent a lot of time judging people on their behavior alone. This was a lesson for me, although it only complicated matters in trying to solve a case—I could only go by what I saw or heard.

"Beatrice, do you mind if I steal Mrs. Schultz from you for just a few minutes?" I asked. I wanted to ask Mrs. Schultz her impressions of our suspects in last night's incident at the museum.

"Not at all. I've got to tidy up the tent now that all the girls are onstage. It's a mess in there."

"Thanks."

"I'll be back in a jiffy," Mrs. Schultz told her as we walked toward the cluster of parked cars by the plastic fencing.

"Did you find out something new from Detective Heath?" Mrs. Schultz asked me as soon as we were out of earshot.

"No. I wanted to ask how things have been so far around here. Has anyone acted suspiciously since you arrived this morning, like Mary Ann or Barbie? Was Mary Ann surprised you weren't injured?"

"If she was surprised, she didn't show it. Barbie seemed no different—she was still focused on getting Annabelle a new milk pail. I think if it was her, she would've made sure we found the milk pail before pushing the shelf," Mrs. Schultz kidded.

We saw one of the moms walking from the tent toward the cars. To my surprise, it was Tabitha's mother, Lynette, alone.

"I didn't see Tabitha come this way. Maybe she's finally convinced her mom she can be on her own," Mrs. Schultz said.

As she got closer, we could see her scanning the row of cars parked behind the orange fencing. She glanced at us but quickly looked away, as if she didn't want us noticing her either. It was obvious Mrs. Schultz wasn't who she was looking for. Her gaze landed on a shiny pale blue Subaru we heard rolling up to the fence. She went over to meet it as Fiona—easily recognizable in her Becky's Bakeware blazer—stepped out of the car.

Mrs. Schultz scowled in disapproval. "Fiona knows she's not allowed to fraternize with the contestants or their mothers."

"You'd think she'd be extra careful after almost getting canned. I bet I can guess what they're doing." I stood on my tiptoes to get a better look over the other cars.

"A Becky's Bakeware transaction," Mrs. Schultz stated what I was thinking.

"I wonder how much Lynette has to buy to earn her some judging favors from Fiona. Come on, let's get closer and see what's happening."

We strolled to the opening in the fence and closer to the cars. Fiona and Lynette were standing behind her car. Although I pretended to head toward Heath's car, they spotted us right away. They went silent, offering uncomfortable smiles as they waited for us to be on our way.

I opened the back door to Heath's car and took out Archie's cheese wedge costume. "I forgot the costume," I said loudly to Mrs. Schultz. We had no other excuse to be there.

Mrs. Schultz wasn't as cowardly. "Fiona. Why are *you* here?" She walked up to Fiona's car, and I followed. Lynette looked like a deer caught in the headlights.

Fiona's impatience turned to annoyance. "Not you too, Mrs. Schultz. Mary Ann's got everyone on patrol now?"

Mrs. Schultz wasn't daunted. "Judges aren't supposed to be mingling with contestants. You know the rules."

"She's a little old to be in the pageant. No offense, Lynette," Fiona said.

"You know what I mean, Fiona—the contestants *and* their mothers. The rules are clear."

"Pageant rules aren't going to get in the way of my business. Perhaps you're not aware that I'm the number one Becky in the Valley. If someone who just happens to be associated with the pageant needs my bakeware, I'm going to provide it. I took the Becky's Bakeware oath and I'll do no less."

The oath? I pictured a line of Becky's Bakeware women swearing an oath—one oven-mitted hand raised, the other on a cookbook.

"What are you selling? I could use some bakeware," I said to Fiona. I was lying. Cheese was my comfort food, so I rarely baked, but I hadn't taken a baking oath, so I didn't feel bad about fibbing. "I'm Willa Bauer, by the way." I offered my hand. Fiona shook it and gave me a fake smile in return. I put my hand out to Lynette.

"Lynette Finley," she introduced herself, shaking it.

"Any recommendations? What are *you* buying?"

"Oh, uh . . . pie—"

"Storage containers," Fiona spoke over her. She opened the hatchback of her shiny Subaru and brought out a stack of five plastic containers in different sizes, shapes, and opaque rainbow colors. They were held in place by a satin ribbon with a bow at the top. "These are our bestsellers. See how pretty they're packaged?" She handed off the stack to Lynette who almost dropped them as they shifted within the flimsy ribbon.

The sound of a car engine turned our heads to an SUV approaching. I recognized it as Chief Womack's car.

Fiona scurried to the driver's seat, opened the door, and sat halfway in the car with one of her legs sticking out. Her hurried pace made me think for a moment that she was about to hightail it out of there, but she must've been rooting around for something— after a minute, she emerged with a brochure. She pushed it into my hands.

"Here's my brochure with the highlights of what I sell. My card is attached," she said.

Chief Womack parked his SUV a few cars down.

"Here." Fiona handed Lynette a square piece of paper about the size of a sticky note that had been hidden in her hand. "Here are the care instructions. I have to go."

"But—" Lynette began.

"Read them carefully. See you later!" Fiona closed the hatchback and got back into the driver's seat, and this time she did intend to drive off. We saw the white taillights and cleared out of her way as she backed up and drove off.

Chief Womack had gotten out of the car. He had to have seen us, but he ignored us and walked toward the tent. Lynette looked oddly relieved.

"I should get back to Tabitha if rehearsal's starting," she said. "I'll put these in my car first so Mary Ann doesn't throw a fit."

Care instructions, my Asiago! What did Fiona give to Lynette?

"Do you mind if I take a look at them?" I asked her in a rush of words before she had the chance to leave.

I reached for her stack of containers before she could answer. With the clumsy cheese costume over my arm, it was easy to purposely hit the middle of the stack, so they'd tumble out of the ribbon. It was a perfect swipe—the ribbon was useless in keeping them together. Lynette tried to prevent them from falling, and in doing so, the note in her hand wafted to the ground too. Her purse slipped off her shoulder and she saved it first. I dove for the note: B25@1. I pretended I didn't look at it as I gathered the containers and the unattached ribbon.

"I'm so sorry. How clumsy of me," I said, handing everything back to her.

She threw me another uncomfortable smile before rushing over to her car, her arms wrapped around the containers and her fingers gripping the note from Fiona.

"What was that about?" Mrs. Schultz said to me, knowing clumsiness wasn't the reason I'd knocked over the containers.

I took my phone out and typed "B25@1" in the notes section so as not to forget. "I wanted to see what was on that paper." I showed her my phone. "Does that mean anything to you?"

She thought for a second. "No, nothing that I can think of."

"It's got to mean something. It certainly wasn't instructions on whether those containers are dishwasher safe. Fiona gave her some kind of code. I just have to find out what it means."

"I'll keep thinking on it. Right now, I have to go. I bet Chief Womack's here for the dress rehearsal. I'd better get his trench coat in case Beatrice is busy with the girls."

"A trench coat? Is he playing Columbo?"

Mrs. Schultz laughed. "No, a trench coat like the ones they wore in that movie *Tombstone*. He's going to briefly make an appearance as a Wild West sheriff. Maybe this wasn't the year to try something new with everything that's gone on."

"Chief Womack's going to be at rehearsal? I'd better warn Heath." If the chief thought Heath was interfering in his investigation, he could make things uncomfortable for Heath professionally. We walked at a quick pace, Mrs. Schultz toward the wardrobe tent and I toward the stage.

CHAPTER 22

As I passed the tent, I noticed Chief Womack was with Beatrice at the wardrobe rack. I wanted to question him regarding what he intended to do about what happened to me and Mrs. Schultz last night, but right now I was more concerned about letting Heath know Womack would soon be in the vicinity.

I heard music and saw the contestants lined up and ready to take the stage, but I didn't see the costumed cowboys anywhere. As I slipped through them and rounded the stage, I heard Mary Ann's voice before I saw her downstage making sweeping arm gestures. *Oh no.*

The full view of the stage showed me what I was afraid to see. The cowboys and farmers were onstage dancing, including Heath. And he did *not* look happy about it. Dancing wasn't in the plan we'd concocted. Luckily, he had Archie, who was an enthusiastic dancer, to hide behind. It was a simple four-step, but getting a few gangly teen boys, a couple of twentysomethings, and some older gentlemen to be in sync apparently took quite a bit of effort on Mary Ann's part. Baz was on the lawn also taking in the show and, by the big grin on his face, he was clearly amused.

"Don't tell me that's who I think it is up there behind Archie," he said when I reached him.

"Okay then, I won't. But it is and he's going to kill me," I replied.

"So this was *your* idea?" Baz laughed, liking that even more.

"I figured the girls would be rehearsing first and he'd have time to hang out and eavesdrop. Chief Womack's about to join them too. This is a disaster. I need to get Heath off the stage without drawing attention to him."

"As much as I hate to stop this, leave it to me." Baz headed toward the stage and cut in the front of the line of contestants. He trotted up the stage steps. Once the dancers saw him onstage, they dropped off until none of them were following the beat anymore. Mary Ann's wildly swinging arms were the last to stop. The music cut out. Even though Baz was now right next to her, I could hear her yell, "What is it?"

I didn't hear what Baz said, but he was pointing to the lights at the back of the stage. She nodded and gestured for him to go. She picked up a megaphone that was at her feet. "Everyone off the stage. Five minutes. Five minutes only. Stand by, please."

Baz went to pretend to check on the lights and the cowboys clomped down the stage steps. Heath headed around the back, and I hurried to catch up to him.

"Heath!" I whispered loudly from behind him.

He slowed down so I could walk beside him.

"Sorry about that. I told Baz we needed to get you off the stage, so whatever he said to Mary Ann was just an excuse to stop the dance," I said.

"I'll have to thank him later," he replied.

I looked toward the tents. "Womack's here. Is that him walking this way? Head down."

Heath kept his head lowered, allowing the brim of his hat to cover his face, as we hurried toward the guys' tent. It was obvious Womack didn't want to see me any more than I wanted to see him, so we passed each other from afar without issue.

"I'm getting out of this costume," Heath said.

"Did you discover anything?" I asked.

"That square dancing is not my thing," he answered. He threw me a little grin to show me all was forgiven.

"I'll be waiting for you here. I have something I want you to look at."

I once again stood outside the guys' tent. Luckily, everyone else was at the stage, so we weren't interrupted. I saw Baz coming my way.

"Thank you so much," I told him. "You really came to the rescue."

"I told Mary Ann one of the spotlights looked like it needed tightening. After what happened to Nadine, I knew she'd have to take precautions."

Heath emerged from the tent, back in his regular clothes. "Smart thinking, Baz. You saved me."

"I'm glad you're both here. I've got a code that needs deciphering," I told them.

"Not another riddle," Baz moaned. He was surely recalling the ones from our last case that led us to the secret of a valuable blue cheese everyone was after.

"It's a code of some kind." I explained what happened with Fiona and Tabitha's mother, Lynette. "Mrs. Schultz and I obviously interrupted something between them, so this was Fiona's way of telling Lynette something without us knowing. Lynette must know what it means, so it shouldn't be that hard to figure out. Fiona was quick to want to get out of there once Chief

Womack showed up, which makes me certain that something's up with her and her Becky's Bakeware."

I showed them my phone. *B25@1.*

"'At one' could be a meeting time—one o'clock," Heath said.

"Ooh, I bet you're right. You're good at this," I said.

"It's almost like he's a detective or something," Baz quipped.

I stuck my tongue out at him, then went back to the numbers. "Do you have any thoughts about 'B twenty-five'?"

Heath stared at the phone and shook his head.

"Beats me," Baz said. "It sounds like a Bingo number."

"They do have Cow Chip Bingo here. I wonder if they're going to meet at the bingo tent at one o'clock to do whatever they need to do that we interrupted," I said.

Heath's glance swept the area, making me look around too. There was nobody nearby and the cars were far enough away where we couldn't be overheard. "We should stake it out," he said.

"That's a good idea! Archie will be done with rehearsal well before lunchtime. I'll leave him in charge of the booth, so we can scope it out. How about you, Baz?"

"Uh, I'm in," he said hesitantly.

I picked up on the uncertainty in his voice. "You don't have to if you've got something else going on."

"It's not that. This"—he waved his finger back and forth between me and Heath—"is just strange."

Heath and I smiled.

"I can't officially be on this case, so we've agreed to try to figure this one out together," Heath explained.

"So he's a part of Team Cheese now?" Baz asked me.

"He's got too many credentials for that," I said.

"Team Cheese?" Heath questioned.

"I'll explain later," I told him.

"I'm going to find Shep and see if he's heard anything, even though he's not supposed to. He always manages to be in the right place at the right time," Heath said.

"It's almost the opening hour. We'd better get to my booth and unload the cheese coolers," I said to Baz.

"Do you need my help?" Heath asked.

"No, we can handle it. I'd rather you get some information from Shep if you can. Meet you at the bingo tent at noon?"

"See you then. Take it easy, Baz," Heath said in parting.

"Uh, yeah, you too," Baz said, again with some hesitancy.

I allowed Heath to be out of earshot before speaking with Baz again. "What's the matter?"

"Nothing. That's just gonna take some getting used to."

"Why? You're friends with Shep and *he's* a cop."

"Yeah, but Shep's Shep. He wasn't interrogating me last year about a murder like the good detective was."

"Okay, but he's helped us a lot since then. I'm just relieved I don't have to keep anything from him."

Baz let go of his misgivings. "I'm glad things are good between you two again."

"Me too."

"So . . . how good are they?" Baz and his raised eyebrows wanted to know.

"Stoppp. We're just looking into this case together. That's all."

"Okay." He said it with a rise in his voice, the way I'd done after asking about him and Constance.

I knew I wasn't putting anything over on Baz, but I still glanced away to hide the smile that tugged at my lips whenever I thought about Heath. This case wasn't the only thing I hoped to get resolved soon.

Baz chucked me on the arm and I elbowed him back, our way of ending a conversation when one of us didn't want to get into details, namely me this time.

"Come on, let's get to your truck so we don't miss the opening *moo*," I said.

CHAPTER 23

The opening *moo* sounded just as we'd set the last cooler in my booth. Ready to open, I thanked Baz and agreed to meet him at the bingo tent at noon. The fields were quickly filling with people. I familiarized myself with where the grazing boxes were located within the coolers and hung up the new signs with today's selections.

About an hour into the morning, I spotted our mascot friend by way of her signature handstands, this time in a sheep costume that didn't hide her face. Archie was going to be sorry he was still at rehearsal. I waved to her, and she came over to the booth. I saw the face of a cute young woman, probably in her early twenties, with dark brown eyes, a wide nose, and cherub cheeks. Her wooly headpiece covered her entire head, ears, and neck. Although it was cooler today, it had to be hot under there.

She smiled shyly, then peered past me into the booth. I figured she was looking for Archie.

"Archie's still at the pageant dance rehearsal. He should be back soon, though. I'm Willa, by the way."

"Hi. I'm June."

"Nice to meet you and put a name to the . . . sheep.

Are you in the mood for some cheese? Archie made you a special grazing box, but if you don't like it, you can choose whichever you prefer."

"I'm sure I'll like it. I've never met a cheese I didn't like."

"A fellow soul sister of cheese. I knew I liked you." I brought out our Around the Campfire box and opened it for her.

She took off one of her *hooves* and picked up the Idiazabal, putting it up to her nose. "I love smoky cheese." She paid attention to the copper-colored rind and took a bite. "I've had this before. It's a Spanish cheese, right?"

"That's right. Idiazabal."

She nodded and went for the smoked Gouda next and pegged it as such.

"Wow, you really know your cheese," I said.

She smiled at the compliment, this time less self-consciously.

"Sheep don't have pockets, so I'm afraid I don't have any money on me—"

"No charge. I told you I'd bring you something. It's on us."

"Thanks!" She continued to nibble on the Gouda.

"Can I ask you something, June?"

She nodded.

"You said yesterday that you grew up here in Lockwood. Were you a Miss Dairy contestant when you were in high school?"

"My mother tried to make me, but I didn't want to. There's no way I would've won, anyway. This is really good, by the way," she said about the cheese.

I was glad she liked the cheese, but I wanted more info about the pageant. "Why would you say that? You have all the qualities of someone who could win, plus you know your dairy."

She looked down and shook her head, dismissing my words. "I wouldn't have won." She went back for the Spanish cheese. "Anyway, it was easy enough to get disqualified—I bought a pack of cigarettes and made sure Miss Hockenbaum found them on me. I don't even smoke. But it did the trick."

"Had other pageant contestants been disqualified before?" I asked.

"Oh, sure. Miss Hockenbaum was super strict about being—what did she call it?—morally upstanding." She rolled her eyes. "She wasn't afraid to disqualify contestants. But it worked out for me. I didn't plan on going to college anyway, so why go through the torture of the pageant?"

I filed what she said in the back of my mind. "Where do you work now?"

"I work in the office at the gas company. It's pretty boring, but only one other person works there, so nobody bothers me." She used her free hand to swipe the softened Moody Blue with the hearty fig bread and popped it in her mouth.

"If you're looking for something more interesting, I could use someone else to work at Curds and Whey. I'm opening a Cheeseboard Café in a couple of months in my shop, and I need more staff. Someone who knows about cheese like you do would be so helpful. Would you be interested?"

Archie strolled up to us, dressed in his Curds & Whey T-shirt and cargo shorts again. When he realized who the sheep might be, he broke out in a smile. "Hi! I'm Archie. Were you the milk carton yesterday?"

"Yeah, that's me, June. Hi." The shy smile was back.

"Are you on your lunch break or do you want to do some tricks together?" Before she could answer, he turned to me. "Did you bring my costume?"

"I did. I was just asking June if she'd be interested in working at Curds and Whey," I explained.

"That would be awesome!" He looked at June with a hopeful expression.

"I don't think I could. But thanks for asking. And thanks for the cheese." She grabbed her previously discarded hoof glove and quickly walked away, leaving the rest of the uneaten grazing box behind.

Archie's smile vanished. "Did I say something wrong?"

"Of course not," I assured him.

"I hope it wasn't me," Archie said again, still looking a bit distraught by June's sudden departure.

"It could've been me. Maybe she felt put on the spot with the job offer. It's too bad. She seemed like she'd be a good fit at the shop."

We all seemed to be getting along so well. Was she feeling shy around Archie or was there another reason she left?

CHAPTER 24

We left our questions about June, and Archie joined me in the booth. We managed a fairly steady stream of customers. When we finally had time to ourselves, I told him about the code Fiona had given to Tabitha's mother, Lynette. Archie was excited about our proposed stakeout, even though he couldn't accompany us. Hunger pangs alerted me that it was almost noon, the time we'd planned to do a fondue tasting. We hoped the gooey cheese setup would entice people to not only get a grazing box, but to take home one of the personal-sized fondue makers we were selling. Archie assembled the cast iron fondue pot, and I brought out a quick cheddar cheese sauce I'd made this morning that only needed to be heated up. I carefully lit the burner and scooped in the sauce, stirring until it warmed and adding more broth to thin it out to the right consistency. Archie cut several crusty sourdough loaves into chunks and filled a basket with them.

I tried a few bites for quality control, but also to quell my grumbling stomach—I hadn't eaten lunch. As soon as we put up a sign offering free fondue, festivalgoers began strolling closer to our booth.

"That wasn't very smart of me to do this tasting at lunchtime now that I have to leave," I said. "Maybe I'll just let Heath and Baz go without me."

"I can handle this. You have to go!" Archie said.

I knew he was right. Archie was a great salesman, chatting up everyone who came to dip their toothpick of bread into the cheesy sauce and making sure no one walked away dissatisfied.

Beyond the next batch of people who came to get a free sample of happiness on a stick, I saw a familiar person-shaped sheep doing gymnastics and waving people our way.

"June's back," I said happily. "See? I told you nothing was wrong." I acted more confident about that than I was. She *had* left abruptly.

"You'd better go. The stakeout's more important than free fondue," Archie said.

"Bite your tongue," I kidded. "But you're right. I don't want to be late. I've got my phone. Text me if you need me."

"Good luck!" he called after me.

I waved to June as I passed to go to the bingo tent, and she waved back. Maybe she'd been feeling particularly shy in front of Archie. I crossed my fingers that she'd go over to the booth while I was gone.

I made it to the bingo tent, and to my surprise there was only a smattering of people using the tables and chairs to eat or to rest their legs. Heath and Baz were already there.

"When's bingo starting?" I asked.

Baz pointed to the sign. "The next one's at three o'clock."

"Three? So there's no bingo at one o'clock?"

"Fiona may have known that and wanted someplace fairly private to do whatever transaction they plan to do," Heath said.

"Then why meet at Dairy Days at all? What has to happen this afternoon that can't wait?"

"Let's split up. We'll each take a corner," Heath said.

"What was I thinking? A stakeout with no snacks? That's not my usual MO," Baz groused.

"I hope you survive this one," I said sarcastically, patting him on the shoulder.

We went to our assigned corners. I tried to be inconspicuous by the folds of the tent while I kept my eyes peeled for Fiona or Lynette. I wasn't sure how we'd get close enough to hear or see what was going on without the shelter of a noisy crowd.

A. J. popped his head around the tent. "Who are you hiding from?"

"Jeez, A. J.!" I put my hand on my heart, annoyed once again by his ability to sneak up on me. Then again, that might be a useful skill right now. "Are you interested in helping me out? I'm on a stakeout."

He rubbed his palms together. "A stakeout? You bet! Who are we waiting for?"

"Fiona Carson."

"The judge Nadine tried to get rid of?"

"That's the one. She was wearing her Becky's Bakeware blazer, so she shouldn't be too hard to spot. And one of the pageant moms, Lynette. She's kind of short, brown hair, she was wearing a purple button-up shirt, untucked," I recalled from our brief encounter earlier.

"What makes you think they're coming here? And what will we be catching them doing?" he asked.

"Mrs. Schultz and I interrupted them at Fiona's car this morning. They covered it up by saying Lynette was buying some Becky's Bakeware Fiona was selling, but she didn't even seem to know what she was buying. She wanted her daughter, Tabitha, to drop out after Nadine was killed, but I think she's had a change of heart. My guess? Lynette may be making a payoff in exchange for Fiona to vote for Tabitha as Miss Dairy Princess."

"That might be worth putting Grace on hold," he said.

"You're meeting Grace Kelp?"

"She's covering the cow parade, or at least that's the excuse she used to get out of answering my questions. We need to follow up with the Tyrell thing. Let me see what time the parade starts." He pulled out a Dairy Days schedule. "It's in full swing right now behind barn D."

Barn D? I grabbed the schedule from A. J. and read it. *Cow Parade. Barn D.* "Does this mean there's a barn B too?"

"A, B, C, and D. Why?"

"The note for this meeting said B twenty-five. We thought it sounded like a bingo number, which is why we're here. But now I'm thinking it's Barn B."

"Stall twenty-five. What time?"

"I'm pretty sure one o'clock."

A. J. checked his phone. "We've got forty minutes. Let's go."

"Hold up. I'm here with Baz and Heath."

"I'll meet you there. You gotta get to a stakeout early." A. J. strode away in a hurry.

I left my tent corner and found Heath and told him about the barn theory.

"That sounds more likely," he agreed.

Baz saw us conversing and came over to check out what was going on.

"Do you mind staying here just in case?" Heath asked him.

"Sure, I can do that. But don't you think it'll look more natural if I'm eating, say, fries smothered in cheese sauce?"

I chuckled. I couldn't fault him. I'd have made him share it with me if I was staying. "You're right. I think the poutine truck is right next door."

"Three trucks down," he said, very familiar with the layout after his festival food spree yesterday.

"Text Willa if you happen to see them," Heath said.

He saluted Heath and then took off to grab some cheesy fries.

Heath and I started our trek across the festival grounds toward the barns for the real stakeout.

CHAPTER 25

The original barns that had been used on the working ranch when the museum was a family home had long since been demolished. They'd been rebuilt on the festival grounds as much larger concrete-slab buildings with stalls specifically for housing livestock during Dairy Days and other agricultural events. Now that I was looking for it, the large letter attached to the siding of each of them was obvious.

We entered Barn B and walked down the wide center aisle. A handful of families were admiring the woolly sheep in their pens to the left of us, but the building was otherwise fairly empty. To the right were rows of open stalls, where a few remaining cows were lazing. Other stalls were being raked out or provided with fresh straw, but most of the farmers had accompanied their cows to the parade behind Barn D, vacating their stalls. It made me think we were on the right track this time—if you wanted to meet someone privately, this would be a good time and place to do it.

I took a few steps into one of the rows and saw where each stall was numbered. It started with number one, so it wouldn't be hard to find twenty-five.

"I wonder where A. J. went off to. This might be

harder to stake out than the bingo tent. You can't see what's going on in any of these stalls unless you're in them yourself," I said.

Heath was silent as we walked through. I could see he was observing our surroundings, so I kept quiet.

We made our way to the row we figured stall twenty-five would be in. The stalls in this row were not in use. They'd been cleaned out with fresh beds of straw and more baled straw stacked in front of each. We walked down the row until we found stall twenty-five, the last one at the end. No sign yet of Fiona or Lynette. We still had some time before one o'clock, but if we didn't decide what to do, either one of them might see us.

"What do we do now? There's no one here to blend in with," I said.

With his hands on his hips, Heath stared into a stall. "How do you feel about straw?"

"I was afraid you'd say that."

We stepped inside the stall that abutted stall twenty-five. Heath and I stacked bales of straw inside it to conceal ourselves from anyone who walked past. I moved the bed of loose straw around, trying to make it comfortable to sit on, but it was prickly. At least it was clean . . . I hoped.

I sat down first, followed by Heath, who was forced to bend his long legs until his knees were up to his chest. We were scrunched in the corner that shared a wall with stall twenty-five. I was hyper aware of how close our bodies were to each other. The only other time I'd been this close to him was when we'd slow-danced together for mere minutes, but I'd only just met him then. I'd felt the same chemistry, but I'd been confused about any feelings beyond that. I wasn't confused anymore.

We adjusted ourselves, trying to offer a little more room. Minor repositioning didn't make much difference—we remained smushed against each other, shoulder to shoulder. I caught the scent of his cologne—citrus and wood.

"Should I move the bales?" he asked.

"No," I answered, probably too fast since I didn't mind the current situation. "We'd better not. They could come any minute."

He nodded and we sat in silence. I was sure he could hear my heart pounding. I had to think of something else besides being this close to Heath.

"I hope they come before the cows do," I said in a quiet voice. We were so close we didn't need to speak above a whisper. I checked the time on my phone.

"Do you have the ringer off?" he asked.

I hadn't thought to do it. I switched it off and saw the time. "We still have twenty minutes."

"Twenty whole minutes? Remind me not to take you on an overnight stakeout."

"You know me—I don't have patience for stakeouts. I prefer to dive in and ask questions."

"Do people usually answer them?"

"They do. Not always truthfully, but I usually find out something."

"So do they—they find out you're onto them. That's what's gotten you into trouble before," he said, now more serious.

"No worries this time. I've got you with me." I turned my face to his and smiled. "Thanks for doing this."

"Given that Womack's hands are tied until the festival is over, I can't sit on the sidelines, so I might as well sit in a cow stall instead."

"So sometimes there *are* circumstances where one

might have to investigate on their own?" He'd made it clear in the past that my sleuthing wasn't necessary, so I couldn't hide the smugness I felt pointing this out.

He pulled at the collar of his T-shirt. "This is a rare exception. I also know Chief Womack doesn't have the manpower during the festival to be going on a wild-goose chase like this."

"It's not so wild. To solve a case, you have to follow every lead, right?"

"I know you think all detective work should be chasing, but sometimes the best way to get it done is by staying put and thinking it through until you figure it out. You don't always have to have a confrontation with possible murderers."

"Believe me, I'd rather not," I said.

"Really?" He sounded like he didn't believe me.

I leaned away from him to get a better look at his eyes. He was serious. "I know it might not always seem like it. I've seen more than my fair share of dead bodies, so I know the reality of the risks I take. I just might not always think it through the way I should."

"It's more than just seeing a dead body to fully appreciate the risks. Death is all too real when it's someone you know getting hurt or worse. It's real when they don't come home." His words began to take on an urgency. "When you have to face day after day without them. When it's someone you love . . ." He trailed off, then cleared his throat. "Sorry."

"You don't have to be sorry." We were quiet and then I ventured, "You're thinking about your wife, aren't you?" I knew his wife had died, although we'd never discussed it in length. I'd seen her picture on a bookshelf in his home and her moody paintings hung on his walls, which must've been comforting reminders of her. He didn't answer right away, and I was afraid I'd touched on a subject that was taboo.

He picked up a strand of straw and rolled it between his fingers. I stared at my Keds.

"She died in a scuba diving accident," he eventually said.

I squeezed my eyes shut for a moment. I knew what this pain felt like. "How awful." I rested my hand on his arm. "I'm so sorry."

"The thing about it is"—his pause lingered for several long seconds before he finished—"she was on a trip to get away from me."

I whipped my head up in surprise. I looked back at my shoes, not wanting to make him feel self-conscious for sharing something so personal.

He must've felt okay about telling me because he continued. "She wanted to separate. I didn't. So she went on a girls' trip and that's when she had her accident and died."

This time I did look at him. "It's not your fault, you know."

"Hmm," he answered, apparently unconvinced.

"I know something about that feeling." Since he'd shared such a personal story, it was time I told him mine. "My younger brother died in a car accident the weekend before he graduated college." I stuck to staring at my shoes. I'd experienced his sympathetic gaze before, and I didn't trust myself to keep my emotions in check if I saw it this time.

"I had no idea. I'm so sorry," he said.

I nodded my acknowledgement. "So I *do* know how real it is. When someone I care about is in trouble, it's the reason I do whatever I can to protect them. For a long time after my brother's death, I made sure I didn't get too close to anybody. But when Archie, Mrs. Schultz, and Baz showed me so much loyalty the way my brother Grayson used to, I had to do what I would've done for him had I been able to—protect them. That's why I got involved in your cases. It was never because I didn't trust you or respect you."

We landed in silence again as he took in my words.

"Thanks for telling me that. It does explain some things about you," he eventually said.

"I'm also naturally stubborn, so . . ."

We laughed quietly, breaking the somber mood.

"Was this around the time your fiancé became your ex-fiancé?" he asked. I'd shared that story with him before we'd stopped speaking.

"The breakup was about a year before then," I said.

It still left a sour taste to even think about it. There were actually two breakups—one with my college sweetheart who was my fiancé and the other with my best friend, who he left me for. We were the three musketeers with plans to run a cheese shop together. While I was off putting in hours for my cheesemonger certification, they were falling in love behind my back. They even used the money from my returned engagement ring to open a chocolate shop in our hometown. It's one of the reasons you'll never see me serving chocolate fondue.

"That's a lot of loss in a relatively short period of time," Heath said.

I happily brought my thoughts to the present. "I think it's why I take a while to trust people, but I *do* trust you." I forced myself to look into his dark eyes, even though by doing so we were practically nose to nose. I wanted to fix what I'd broken months before. "Heath, I—"

He put his lips to my ear and whispered, "Shh."

I thought it was his way of telling me all was forgiven, but then I heard the footsteps he must've heard seconds before. She was early. We could hear the clacking of sandals pacing back and forth in front of our stall and stall twenty-five. We scooched down even farther to be sure we wouldn't be seen. Then more footsteps.

"Good, you're on time," a voice, possibly Fiona's, said.

"Your text was pretty adamant. What's with all the cloak-and-dagger? We were supposed to meet by your car," a second voice said. It must've been Lynette's.

"I don't like to leave a text trail, but this was an emergency. There were too many Nosey Nellys over there. Mary Ann's getting out of control, siccing her people on me. She's almost worse than Nadine, and if she convinces Tyrell to fire me as a judge, that won't help you at all, will it?" That was definitely Fiona.

"You *are* going to be a judge this year, aren't you? I'm not giving you this money for nothing."

"I told you, Tyrell reinstated me. Nadine was the problem."

"There was a lot of gossip that last year's winner didn't deserve the title. Of course, my daughter deserves to be crowned Miss Dairy Princess, but I don't want people questioning it afterward. Are you sure no one else knows about this?"

"Nadine was the only one who knew about last year's payoff."

"You're sure she didn't tell her cousin?"

"Mary Ann wouldn't keep it to herself now that Nadine's gone," Fiona said.

"What about Tyrell? Nadine must've told him why she wanted you gone after last season."

"He told me he didn't know why she wanted me out, that she just expected him to abide by her decision. Don't worry. Nobody suspects. If people ask, I tell them Nadine wasn't happy with the Becky's Bakeware perceived conflict of interest, which isn't a valid reason to take me off the judges' table. Now, do you want a guaranteed win for your daughter or not?"

"Of course I do. I just wanted to be sure everything was under control. How can you be sure the other judges will vote the right way?"

"It doesn't matter how they vote. I'm the head judge, the one who tallies the numbers."

There was a pause. And then, "Okay, then. Here."

"Say cheese!" A. J.'s voice broke in—it was one I knew well.

A flash went off. Heath and I scrambled to our feet and over the straw bales. I saw Fiona immediately, but instead of also seeing Lynette as I expected, I saw the back of Pageant Mom Barbie—a thin woman with a helmet of hair in a bright dress and heels, with a large handbag firmly tucked under her arm. She turned when she heard us. Yup—it was Barbie, Annabelle's mother.

"What do you think you're doing?" Fiona growled at A. J. "This is hardly the place for pictures. You're that Yarrow Glen reporter, aren't you? Shouldn't you be at the cow parade?" She attempted to stuff a wad of bills into her closed purse without looking at it, trying to keep her cool. Barbie, who stood with a muffin pan and flushed cheeks, appeared much less so.

"What's going on?" Barbie said, her pupils darting around to each of us.

"You tell me," I said.

"There's nothing wrong with buying Becky's Bakeware from Fiona. It's just a muffin pan."

"That's one expensive muffin pan. That's a lot of twenties," A. J. commented, stretching his neck to see the packet of new bills visible in Fiona's hand.

Fiona finally looked down at her purse and realized it was zipped closed. "She's got a lot more bakeware coming," she explained, unzipping her purse and cramming the cash inside, even though it was too late.

Heath stepped forward, taking over. "Maybe I should introduce myself. I'm Detective Heath of the Yarrow Glen Police Department. We heard everything."

Barbie's eyes widened. I could practically see her trying to remember what incriminating things she'd just said.

"There was nothing to hear, Detective," Fiona stated, still playing it cool.

A. J. stuck his hand in his bag and pulled out his voice recorder. "Should I play it back?"

"This is a sting operation! I thought you said nobody suspected you!" Barbie cried.

"Barbie!" Fiona shot back.

"Obviously they were onto you." Barbie turned her back on Fiona. "She said if I gave her money, she'd guarantee my daughter would win the pageant. *She's* the criminal, not me."

"Isn't that your money in her purse?" A. J. pointed out.

"Yes, but . . . but . . . Please, I'll cooperate. Don't blame this on Annabelle. She knows nothing about it."

"Barbie, shut up!" Fiona barked.

"You've ruined everything, Fiona! My daughter

won't amount to anything because of you!" Barbie's eyes welled with tears as her cheeks turned splotchy red.

"You two had better come with me to see Chief Womack," Heath said calmly.

"I was selling her Becky's Bakeware, nothing more. I'm the number one Becky in the Valley," Fiona contended as Heath led her and Barbie out of the barn.

A. J. smiled broadly. "There it is! Fiona did it! Another case closed. I gotta get back and start prepping for my podcast. Who should I interview first?" A. J. asked, but he wasn't looking at me—I think he was consulting himself.

"This doesn't prove anything except that the pageant's been rigged for who knows how many years," I said.

"Isn't it obvious? Nadine was going to keep Fiona from continuing her money-making scheme, so Fiona killed her."

If I'd learned anything from Detective Heath, it was to not jump to conclusions. "All we know for sure is that she was making extra money to guarantee a pageant winner. Nadine somehow found out and was going to end it. Lucky you had your recorder, or they might've not copped to any of it. You'd better let Chief Womack have that."

"This?" He showed me the mini recorder. "There's nothing on it. The batteries ran out this morning. But it served its purpose to use as a bluff." He laughed. "I got a good picture, though. They were right in the middle of the cash hand-off. I'm going over now to bring him the photo and get a statement for the paper. Do you think he'll agree to be interviewed for my podcast? It may not be a murder, but a pageant judge taking money to fix the outcome is still a crime when there's a fifteen-

thousand-dollar scholarship at stake. I'll call the epi-
sode 'Becky's Bribes.' You don't think the bakeware
company will sue me, do you?" A. J. was deep in
thought with his big podcast plans as he walked away.

CHAPTER 26

I walked through the barn, deep in my own thoughts. If Fiona wouldn't even cop to soliciting a bribe, she wasn't going to confess to murder. If she was the killer, we had to find another way to prove it.

Once outside, a parade of cows caught my attention: black-and-white Holsteins and brown Guernseys, brushed and groomed until their coats shined, some with ribbons on their harnesses. Their proud owners were leading them back to the barns.

The cow parade must've been over, and it reminded me that A. J. and I had dismissed the idea of speaking with Grace Kelp. If there was more dirt on Fiona, Grace might be the one who knew about it.

I made my way to the paddock behind Barn D and found Grace leaning against the barn, focused intently on the viewfinder on the back of her camera. She looked like a farmer herself in bootcut jeans, cowboy boots, and a scoop-neck shirt.

"Hi, Grace," I said.

Her face popped up to look at me. "Hi."

"Willa Bauer?" I reminded her.

"I remember. We met yesterday through A. J."

"That's right. I heard you were covering the cow parade."

She pointed the viewfinder my way so I could see the photo in the screen. "A camera full of cow photos. Somehow, I didn't think this would be my lot in life, but here we are." She gave me a resigned smile.

"A. J. told me about that article you wrote last year for *All Things Sonoma*. That's a big deal."

"I thought it would be. But then I was blackballed in Lockwood, and the magazine was sold and then practically went under, so it didn't exactly help my career, to say the least."

I knew all too well that the wealthy Sonoma family who'd bought the magazine was still trying to recover from a scandal last winter.

"Maybe you should branch out. Work in a bigger town or a city," I suggested.

"I can't. My ex and I share custody of our daughter, so I have to stay here. I thought by now the fury would die out about the pageant article, so I was surprised by Mary Ann's accusation. I really hope it doesn't start the whole thing up again."

"Why speak out against it? I heard you won the pageant when you were in it."

"When I was a high school senior. Nothing like reinforcing to young women who are about to go out into the world that how they look is their most important asset. I'm more than my looks and I have to work hard to prove it. All these girls are more than that."

"For what it's worth, I agree with you about pageants."

Grace leaned in. "Don't say that too loudly around here; you'll be run out of Lockwood. It's just a stupid pageant. You'd think I'd poisoned the town's water supply."

"Can I ask, then, how did you keep your job?"

She paused and went back to looking at the photos on her camera's screen and said casually, "A friend helped me out."

"Tyrell?"

Her attention left the camera entirely and she let it dangle from her neck. "What makes you say that?"

"I saw you two together. You looked . . . close. Is he your ex?"

She sighed and turned away for a moment, seeming to decide what to divulge. "No, he's not my ex-husband. He's my boyfriend. It's only Tyrell's third year at this job, so he was afraid he'd get blowback if people knew we were dating because of the whole pageant thing. We're going to come out of the shadows when Dairy Days is over. People can take the year to get used to it, or better yet, get over it."

That seemed like an honest explanation. I liked Grace, so I went with my instincts. "There's a much bigger scandal they're going to be talking about, and you can be the one to break it."

"Oh?" She seemed to brighten.

"Fiona's speaking with Chief Womack right now about taking money in exchange for fixing the outcome of the pageant in a contestant's favor."

A severe line appeared between her brows. "What? Oh no. How did he find out?"

I thought this development would thrill her, but she was clearly upset.

"Wait, you knew? Did you see it happen last year when you were researching your story?" I asked.

"No, I would've put it in there."

"How did you find out?"

She hesitated before saying, "Someone told me about it just a couple of weeks ago."

"Tyrell?"

She pressed her lips together. For me, that was as good as an admission.

"So Tyrell *did* know what Fiona was doing," I confirmed.

After what looked like a little more internal wrestling, she finally said, "Nadine told him. She knew last year's winner didn't do well enough to be Miss Dairy Princess. She eventually got the truth out of the girl, but if Nadine told anybody, the pageant would be ruined. They had no idea how many years it had been going on. I can tell you it didn't happen the year *I* won, so it must've started sometime in the last ten years. The implications of a cheating scandal with all that scholarship money involved . . . whoo! That's a lot to contend with. The sponsor could pull out and there's no way they'd get another. Or worse, the town could be sued. But Nadine didn't want to compromise the pageant by letting it continue being a sham. You've got to give Nadine credit—she believed in the pageant."

"So she wanted Fiona out as a pageant judge?"

"Yeah. She confided in Tyrell and told him it was the only way she'd feel okay about continuing with the pageant and keeping the big secret. He didn't want to rock the boat that much. He thought if they let Fiona know they were on to her and demoted her from head judge, it would be enough to make her stop. Nadine wasn't satisfied with that solution. She didn't want Fiona to have anything to do with the pageant. Tyrell had to be the one to tell Fiona she was out, but he didn't want to admit he knew about the scandal. He hoped it would

all go away with Fiona. But wait, you said Chief Womack knows?"

"Yeah. We caught Fiona taking money from one of
the pageant moms who confessed."

"Oh no." Grace turned to leave in a hurry.

I caught her by the arm. "Grace, hold on!"

"I have to get to Tyrell. He's got to do damage control. If this gets out, the pageant is doomed. Between
this and what happened to Nadine, he's going to lose
his job." She shook off my hand and left me staring
after her.

The last thing I expected was for my news to worry
her. She seemed to really care about Tyrell and his
position, which shot down her motive to have killed
Nadine. But it still didn't indict or clear Fiona, it only
confirmed *her* possible motive. I wished we'd overheard something more conclusive about Nadine's
murder. Who else would know something more about
Fiona?

I pulled my phone out to see how long I'd been gone
from my booth. It was almost one fifteen. One o'clock!
Catching Barbie had made me forget that Fiona was
supposed to be meeting *Lynette* at one. Fiona had ar-
ranged to meet Barbie *before* one o'clock. Had Fiona
been promising *every* mom who was willing to pay up
that her daughter would win? I ran to Barn B, keeping
my fingers crossed that Lynette would still be waiting
for Fiona.

CHAPTER 27

Once at the barn, I hurried down the aisle, peeking in each row as I passed until I got to the one that held stall twenty-five. I was relieved to see that the stalls were still just as empty as before. Lynette stood in front of the appointed stall with two of the colorful plastic containers Fiona had given her earlier. Her arms were wrapped around them, as if protecting a prized possession. My guess—a bunch of money. She kept both hands on them as she checked the smartwatch on her wrist, just before turning at the sound of my footsteps. The surprise that it was me and not Fiona was apparent on her face.

"Hello again," I said, trying to act as if I'd just happened to run into her. It was hard to appear casual when I was still breathing heavily from the run over.

"Hello." She pressed the containers closer to her body, as if trying to hide their existence. Apparently, both of us were lousy at pretense. "I think I got my signals crossed. I need to get back to the rehearsal," she said.

"You were planning to meet Fiona here, weren't you?" I asked before she could take off.

"No. I—" She looked down at the containers in her

arms. My presumption seemed to be correct—they didn't appear as empty as when Fiona had given them to her. "As a matter of fact, we had agreed to meet here so I could return this bakeware I'd bought. The lids don't fit right."

"It's no wonder, with all that money you've got stuffed in there."

It was just a guess, but her eyes widened, telling me I was right.

"Wh-what do you mean? I don't know what you're talking about." She began again to walk past me.

"You should know that Fiona is with Chief Womack right now."

She stopped without turning around.

I hurried my words to keep her from leaving. "She was caught taking money from Barbie in exchange for making Annabelle the winner of this year's pageant."

She whipped around to face me. "What?"

"Apparently Fiona was making a lot of promises." I wondered how many of the pageant moms would show up at the barn today intending to see Fiona with their Becky's Bakeware filled with cash. "I'm afraid your daughter will just have to win on her own merits," I finished.

A humorless laugh escaped her. "You think this is so Tabitha would win? This was supposed to make sure she *wouldn't*. The last thing I want is for Tabitha to become Miss Dairy Princess." Lynette stared at the containers, shaking her head. She said to herself, "I can't believe Fiona would've taken money from me when she knew another girl was going to win anyway."

"She's obviously not an honest person." That seemed like something I shouldn't have had to point out.

"I know, but all this time she knew how worried I was. She kept pretending like she cared so much about Tabby, but at the same time, upping her price."

"Why are you so worried your daughter will win?"

"Because she will! Nadine favored her. She made sure Tabby had the prettiest costume and she put her in the very middle of all the girls on stage so all eyes would be on her. You've seen my Tabby. She's the prettiest and she's smart and everyone likes her. She attracts people to her. She always has." Lynette's voice became shaky. "Ever since she was a baby, everyone loved her. She had the biggest blue eyes and a full head of curly red hair. People would comment on it all the time. Even back then, Nadine told me that when Tabitha was old enough to vie for Miss Dairy, she was sure to win. She said she'd never seen a more beautiful baby." She began to tremble.

"Lynette, are you all right? Maybe you should sit down. Here." I steered her to a straw bale and made sure she took a seat on it.

She was crying now and rapidly wiping her tears. "I'm sorry. I know she's not a baby anymore, but if she leaves me for good, I don't think I could stand the worry."

"I heard what happened when your daughter was younger," I said gently.

"She went missing for an entire day because I left her alone for a handful of minutes." Lynette's eyes welled with fresh tears, and she looked off in the distance, likely seeing the memory play like a movie before her. "I was expecting a friend for lunch, and I just went inside to make lemonade. Tabby was so happy playing in her sandbox. I didn't think she'd even notice

I was gone—she was such an independent toddler. It was just for a few minutes, but it was like she'd vanished into thin air."

My heart was heavy for her. "I'm so sorry."

"It was the worst nine and a half hours of my life. I imagined the absolute worst things. Did she wander off? Was she taken? Was someone hurting her? I could barely breathe. The police were so good—they were on it right away. The whole community came together to look for my Tabby. I didn't hold out any hope, but then . . ."

"They found her," I reminded Lynette.

She nodded and cried some more, as if it were happening again right at that moment. I sat down on the straw bale next to her, put my arm around her and squeezed. "They found her," I said again.

"It was a miracle. Whoever took her had a change of heart and called the police anonymously. They left her in the park." She'd set the containers on the nearby straw bale and taken a tissue from her purse. She dabbed at her cheeks and then her nose. The tiniest of smiles shone underneath the tissue. "There wasn't a scratch on her. She was smiling. Her eyes were just as bright as they'd always been. My husband and I didn't see any difference in her. The doctors assured us she was perfectly fine." Lynette blew her nose. "My therapist tells me to remember that last part. But whenever she goes to school or wants to meet her friends at the mall, all my body remembers is that first part—the panic." She shook her head and gathered herself. "I'm suffocating her. I know I am. I've done it her whole life. I can't help it because I suffocate without her."

It was hard to hear about the pain she lived with every day because of one day so long ago. "That's why you don't want her to win the scholarship money. You don't want her to leave home."

"I know she will anyway. I know she has to. Just not now. Not yet. Maybe I'll be ready when she's older." Lynette wiped her eyes and blew her nose. When she'd collected herself, she stood. "So Fiona's been caught, huh?"

"Yes."

"Where does that leave the pageant?"

"I'm not sure."

Another small smile crossed her lips. "Maybe I've gotten lucky after all." She scooped up the cash-filled containers and walked away.

I breathed in deeply and exhaled to rid myself of Lynette's anxiety from her horrible experience that still clung to me like a sickening perfume. My nostrils filled with the stink of cows and hay. I stood to leave and checked my phone. There was a text from Archie that we were almost sold out of grazing boxes. I texted him back that I was on my way.

CHAPTER 28

The sun still held some of its summer strength, so I found myself too warm by the time I reached my booth. To my surprise, the only person there was Baz.

"Hey, Baz. Where's Archie?"

"He and June are carrying one of the empty coolers to my truck. I told them I'd watch the booth."

"June's here?"

"Yeah. I got the impression she'd been here a while," he said.

That made me happy. She must've reconsidered whatever had made her run off before.

"So what happened? Give me the details," Baz said.

I spotted June and Archie coming back. June was still in her sheep costume. "I'll tell you later. We ought to have a Team Cheese meeting. Where's Mrs. Schultz?"

"Still at rehearsal, I guess."

Chief Womack must not have informed Mary Ann yet about what had happened.

Archie and June said hi. Archie was beaming and June looked much more relaxed than she had earlier, although her face looked red. She hadn't even taken off the headpiece or gloves.

"June, you must be boiling in that costume. You should go sit in the shade. You don't need to be helping us while you're wearing that," I said.

"That's what I tried to tell her," Archie said.

"I'm fine. I'm used to it," she replied.

"Are you sure?" Archie asked.

"I'm sure, I'm sure! Look, I can still do handstands."

Behind our booth she did a cartwheel that led into a handstand. Suddenly, she crumpled to the ground, completely still.

"June!" Archie yelled.

We ran over to her and turned her on her back. Her eyes were closed, and her face had turned a ghostly pale.

"June! June!" Archie attempted to wake her.

"We have to get this costume off her!" I said.

Baz and Archie rolled her onto her side, as her eyes fluttered open.

"June, we're getting you out of this costume. You've fainted," I said.

I felt around the back of the costume to find a zipper. I finally found it and hurried to unzip it. I removed the headpiece and then began to peel off the costume from her upper body. She was wearing a tank top and shorts underneath that were soaked in sweat.

"There's melted ice in the coolers," Archie said, thinking fast. He sprang off the ground and ran back to the booth.

Baz continued to hold her upright as I took out her right arm and then her left. We laid her down on her back.

"I'm okay," she said groggily, trying to pull her costume back on. She was obviously delirious.

"June, you're overheated. You need to keep the costume off," I said.

"I've got a drink with electrolytes in my truck," Baz said, running off.

Archie returned with a wet a towel and gently placed it around the back of her neck.

Her eyes were now fully open.

"Can you hear me?" I asked.

"Yes," she answered.

Baz came back with the drink, and we carefully sat her up so she could sip it.

She looked down at herself, now out of her mascot costume to her waist.

"We had to cool you off," I explained.

She flicked off her sneakers and took her legs out of the rest of it.

"How are you feeling?" I asked.

"Embarrassed," she answered.

"Don't be. We're just glad you're all right," Archie said.

"I'm fine," she said, struggling to get on her feet.

"Whoa. Slow down," I told her. "You need to stay in the shade for a while and drink this." I handed her Baz's drink bottle. "Or better yet, Baz, turn the AC on in your truck and we'll let her sit in there."

Baz nodded and trotted off to his truck.

"You should've gotten out of that stupid costume hours ago," Archie said.

She looked down at her left arm and tried to cover it with her hand. It had barely registered when I was removing it from her costume that the skin on most of her left arm from her wrist to her shoulder was raised and jagged. It continued up her neck and ended just below her left ear.

"I didn't want you to see." She directed this to Archie.

"See what?" he said.

She rolled her eyes and took her hand away, fully exposing her scarred arm. "This. Obviously, you noticed it. How can you not?"

"I did, but I was more concerned with you waking up and being okay. Besides, like, so what?" Archie said.

"So what? I'm Freddie Krueger. The Joker. I've been called them all—every freak out there."

"Your scars don't make you look like a freak," I said gently.

"That's not what the movies tell people," she replied.

"Do you think *I'm* a freak?" Archie asked her, pointing to the port-wine stain on his cheek, an irregular red birthmark about the size of a half dollar.

I'd stopped noticing it by about the third day we worked together. It was just a part of Archie, like his freckles and his contagious smile. He'd simply explain it to customers who were forward enough to ask.

"Of course not," June said. "It's just a birthmark on your face. Besides, it doesn't seem to bother you at all. You're confident and funny and smart, and you know everything about cheese."

"You're all those things too, and you're a good acrobat," he countered.

She looked down at the costume strewn around her. "I'm only confident when I can hide."

"That's dumb. I mean, I'm sorry, but it doesn't change who you are. You think my birthmark never bothered me? I got called nicknames too, when I was younger. But my mom always said that this birthmark was God's stamp of approval before she gave birth to me. How can that be a bad thing? We're all made to be different but just as perfect, no matter what. That includes you, June."

"That's a nice thought, Archie, but I wasn't born this way." June took another sip of the drink. "This happened in the fire at the historical society museum."

I crept back into the conversation. "You were one of the kids trapped in the widow's peak?"

She nodded and took another sip before telling us the story. "I was only seven. My big brother was twelve. We used to walk to these grounds from our house and play out by the barns. We were on our way home when we saw a light on inside through one of the kitchen windows. The museum was supposed to be closed, so we got closer. We'd heard about the older kids finding a way to get in and climb up to the widow's walk. We looked through the windows, but we didn't see any kids. My brother tried the side door, and it was unlocked, so he wanted to go in. I was afraid someone would think it was us who'd broken in, but my brother said since it wasn't us, it was okay. He wanted to climb up the widow's peak like the older kids. I was scared, but I went inside with him." June began pulling fistfuls of grass from the ground. "The sky looked so cool from up there. I remember all the stars. I don't know how long we were up there. Next thing we knew, we smelled smoke, and we ran downstairs, but the room was really smoky and hot, and we saw flames. We couldn't get out the door."

"You must've been really scared," Archie said.

"I was. I'm sure my brother was too, but he acted brave for me."

"How did you get out?" he asked.

"I don't remember. We passed out from the smoke, but when we woke up, we were outside with the firefighters and the police, and then we were brought to the hospital."

"How's your brother?" I asked, my throat constricting with the possibility of the same fate as my own.

"He's fine. He's got a burn on the back of his shoulder. They said they found him trying to shield me."

I turned away so June couldn't see me tear up. An older sibling protecting his younger one, something I wish I could've done for my own brother.

"Thank goodness you both survived," Archie said.

June nodded. "At first we were in a lot of trouble, though. The police thought we'd started the fire, but the fire department investigated and found it was an electrical fire that started at one of the outlets that was activated with the light switch. Old house."

"That must've been really hard on you and your family—to be burned and then also suspected of setting the fire? I'm sorry that happened to you," Archie said. He put a hand on her arm, the one with the scar. She flinched at first, but then relaxed and allowed it to stay.

"Thanks, Archie. I'm feeling better already." She smiled and took a longer sip of her drink.

"Good. Let's sit in Baz's truck and I'll get you another drink," he said.

He took June by her hand and helped her to her feet. They walked together to Baz's truck.

CHAPTER 29

Archie stayed with June in the cooled cab of the truck. I didn't care that we still had a few more grazing boxes to sell—I'd had enough for today. Baz and I finished lugging the rest of the coolers and supplies to his truck. I wanted to let Mrs. Schultz in on what had happened, so I told them to go on without me and I'd find my own ride home.

I walked across the grounds, wondering what the mood would be like. I assumed everyone would be packing up, having been informed about what had happened with Fiona. When I got to the stage, I was surprised that rehearsal was still going on. I watched Mary Ann take the girls through their pageant paces, as one by one they walked upstage to introduce themselves, then went back in line. I didn't see Annabelle.

On my way to the tent to find Mrs. Schultz, I discovered her waiting behind the stage for the girls to make their exit. She was surprised to see me. Since we were alone, I gave her the short version of what happened between Fiona and Barbie.

"Oh, no. Someone needs to tell Annabelle, and it shouldn't be the police," Mrs. Schultz said.

"Annabelle's not at the station?"

"She wasn't feeling well, so she's sitting by the tent with Beatrice."

"You're right, she should be told. Will you come with me to soften the blow?" I asked.

She glanced back at the stage, but then made her decision to leave her post. We walked toward the tent where Beatrice was sitting with Annabelle under the shade of a tree. Annabelle was sipping a bottle of water.

"How are you feeling?" Mrs. Schultz asked her.

The girl allowed a bit of a smile. "Better, thanks. I'm glad my mother wasn't here. She would've made me stay onstage."

Mrs. Schultz and I looked at each other, then she spoke. "Annabelle, I don't think your mother will be returning to the pageant."

Annabelle sat up straighter, her face going from sickly to worried. "Why not? Is she okay?"

"Yes, she's fine," Mrs. Schultz said, quickly reassuring her.

"What's going on?" Beatrice asked. She got to her feet and helped Annabelle stand too.

I decided to be the bearer of the bad news so Mrs. Schultz could focus on comforting the girl. "Annabelle, the police discovered that your mom was paying off Fiona Carson to ensure that you won the pageant."

"What?" Annabelle's hands went to her stomach, as if she was feeling sick again. "How could she?" Shock slid into anger. "I'm not doing what she wants! I'm not! No matter what she says, I'm not giving it up!" Annabelle's voice was shaky, but she didn't cry.

I was confused but said nothing while Beatrice and Mrs. Schultz flanked her and tried to soothe her with comforting words. When she'd calmed down, I said,

"Should we call someone to come get you? Or do you want us to bring you over to Chief Womack's office at the carriage house? I'm pretty sure that's where they are."

Annabelle's mouth tightened and she vehemently shook her head. Her stiff hair moved as a single unit. "I don't want to see her. She thinks winning the pageant will get me to change my mind about keeping my baby, but it won't."

Her baby?

Although I didn't ask aloud, she explained anyway. "She thinks if I keep my baby, my life will be ruined. She wants me to give it up for adoption and go to college, but I'm not giving it up. I can do both things if she'd just show a little support. Whatever money she bribed Fiona with could've been spent on her future grandchild!" Her hand went back to her stomach. I now saw it as the protective gesture it was.

"Do you want me to drive you home?" Beatrice asked her.

"No. I'm going to call my boyfriend. He'll come get me. I need to change out of this stupid dress. Thanks for keeping my secret," she said to Beatrice, "but I don't want it to be a secret anymore. I'm not going to be ashamed." She started to walk to the tent, then turned. "And you can tell Mary Ann that I'm not coming back." She continued to stomp toward the changing tent as I continued to process this news.

When Annabelle had gone, I asked Beatrice, "You knew she was pregnant?"

"I had to keep taking out the seams at the waist of her costumes, so I figured as much. There were a few times she'd get nauseated during these past weeks of rehearsals, so I made sure she had crackers and water. It was unspoken," Beatrice said.

What I knew of Beatrice was that she had an eye for cool vintage stuff, she was an excellent seamstress, and she liked to unapologetically stick her nose in your business. What I didn't know was that even if she knew your business, she could keep your sensitive secrets.

"Poor girl. She's going to need her parents' support," Mrs. Schultz said.

"Maybe Barbie getting caught will turn things around for them." I hoped, anyway.

"Do you think the pageant will go on?" Beatrice asked.

I looked toward the stage where Mary Ann's commands to the contestants could be heard. "I don't know if this is something that can be kept quiet, especially since I can guarantee this wasn't the first time Fiona's taken money in exchange for a pageant winner. With a scholarship as the prize, it's a serious crime."

"More serious than murder?" Beatrice said, her penciled-in eyebrows raised.

We left that unspoken as well.

CHAPTER 30

I walked away from the stage until I found a spot where my phone had bars so I could get in touch with Heath. I saw a text from him, so we agreed to meet outside the historical society museum. He was leaning, ankles crossed, against his car parked in a dirt patch where Mrs. Schultz's Fiat had been last night. A leather jacket and a cigarette hanging out of his mouth would be all that he'd need to look like one of those old movie stars in their heyday. He already had the chiseled jawline, the thick head of hair, and the cool, enigmatic demeanor. He smiled when he saw me, which awakened a migration of butterflies in my stomach.

"How'd it go with Chief Womack?" I asked. Getting right down to business was the best way to push down my attraction for him.

"I don't think Fiona's going to veer from her story of simply selling Becky's Bakeware," he said.

"Will it help if I talk to him too?"

"After I gave my statement, he said he'd contact us."

"Don't call me, I'll call you, huh?"

"He's interviewing them separately now," he replied without casting judgment.

Heath wasn't going to talk critically about how a

fellow police officer, much less a police chief, was handling a case, so I moved on to the new information I had and told him about Annabelle's pregnancy.

"It could be an even stronger motive for Barbie to be the culprit. If Beatrice figured out that Annabelle was pregnant, then maybe Nadine had too, and was ready to disqualify her," I finished.

He stared at me, one eyebrow raised.

"What? You think it's a reach?" I said, trying to read his reaction.

"Not at all. I think you're not bad at this," he said.

I laughed, relieved. "*Not bad*, huh? Maybe I'll even work my way up to *pretty good*."

"I'd rather you not work your way to anything involving more homicide investigations."

"Back to that again, are we? You've admitted that there are times when you have to investigate, even without a badge. You can't walk your way back from that, Detective," I said lightly.

He looked away with a smile on his face, accepting the outcome. "I'll let Chief Womack know about Annabelle," he said, making no further admissions.

"You should probably let him know about Tabitha's mother too."

Heath nodded with interest as I filled him in on my encounter at the barn with Lynette.

"If Lynette's willing to admit to what was about to go down between her and Fiona, it makes a much stronger case against Fiona," he said.

"So you think Fiona killed Nadine?" I asked.

"I was talking about the bribery case. First things first."

I set aside his response. "But who do you think murdered her? Fiona or Barbie?"

He went back to leaning on the side of his car. "Why not Lynette? She seems to be operating on a high anxiety level."

"True. I guess I have to take my own emotions out of it. If she'd already made her deal with Fiona and then she overheard that Nadine was going to get rid of Fiona as a judge, maybe she panicked. Murder's not a normal reaction to not wanting your daughter to win a pageant, but like you said, she's high anxiety. It could've happened on impulse. She did say Nadine favored Tabitha."

"She *favored* her?" The crease between his eyes showed his confusion.

"Yeah. She said Nadine gave Tabitha the most flattering costumes and made sure she was center stage. Most of the moms had the opposite complaint about their daughters."

"That seems out of character from everything we've learned about Nadine, doesn't it? She cared about the pageant's integrity—isn't that what everyone said, including Mary Ann, the person who supposedly knew her best?"

I hadn't considered that. "You're right. Maybe it was Lynette's fear talking. It could've just been her perception that Nadine favored Tabitha because Lynette was so afraid she'd win. Every mother thought their daughter was the most deserving to be Miss Dairy Princess. Lynette was probably no exception."

Heath nodded, but I could tell he wasn't dismissing the comment.

"I'd better get to Womack and give him this new information," he said, pushing himself off the car.

"Do you think it'll help prove one of them killed Nadine?" I asked.

"As it stands, it's all circumstantial."

"But the pieces are adding up, aren't they? What else can we do to prove one of them committed murder?"

"We continue the work. I'm going back to the station to follow up on some open leads. Do you need a lift home?" He opened the passenger-side door, and I got in. He started up the car and we drove to the parking lot near Chief Womack's temporary office at the carriage house.

As I unbuckled my seat belt, he put a hand out to stop me from getting out of the car.

"You can wait here, I'll just be a minute," he said.

"I just want to make sure Chief Womack's connecting the dots, that's all."

"Willa, he's not going to be receptive to your input in the middle of interviews. Let me just give him the information he needs, okay?"

Heath got out of the car, and I begrudgingly stayed put. I didn't have Heath's confidence in Lockwood's chief of police. There was, after all, still that issue of his wife who seemed to have vanished.

CHAPTER 31

It felt good to be back in the Curds & Whey kitchenette again. We still had a loaf of sourdough from ones we'd gotten for the festival fondue sampling and a shop full of cheese, so grilled cheese sandwiches were on the menu. Baz handed me thick, hearty slices of the sourdough, which got a sweep of butter before they hit the warmed skillet. Then I layered Archie's thin slices of Shelburne Farms Two-Year Cheddar, Alpha Tolman, and Whitney—all classic cheeses that melted beautifully to produce a gooey grilled cheese.

Archie's phone dinged with a text. A smile crossed his face when he read it. "It's June. She wanted to thank us again."

"You exchanged phone numbers! Good. Let her know we're glad she's okay," I said.

He texted her a message while I topped the sandwiches with another thick slice of buttered sourdough.

"You know, Archie, I have to say I really liked the way you spoke with June. You made her feel better when she was in a very vulnerable situation," I said.

He put his hands over his face. "I can't believe I quoted my mother. Don't ever tell her! I'll never hear the end of it."

The three of us laughed. At twenty, I was also not ready to admit to my parents that they were right about some things, but now I often found myself following their wise words. Archie had a few years to go before he'd have that realization.

Mrs. Schultz arrived just as the grilled cheese sandwiches were ready to be taken off the skillet, having turned a golden brown.

"Sorry I'm late. Beatrice and I wanted to organize the tent since everything will probably be going back to her shop as soon as the scandal breaks," she said as she joined us in the kitchenette.

"How did Mary Ann take the news about Fiona?" I asked.

"I don't know. We were going to tell her after the rehearsal broke up, but one of the security officers told her Chief Womack wanted to talk to her and she was headed over there. I feel cowardly to say it, but we decided to let him do the dirty work." Mrs. Schultz had a sheepish look on her face.

"I don't blame you. They seem pretty close. The news will go down better coming from him." I cut the sandwiches diagonally and Archie put one in front of each of us as we gathered at the table.

"Better to let him explain it, anyway. He's the one with the answers," Baz said.

"Speaking of answers, let's call this Team Cheese meeting to order. Tell us everything, Willa," Archie said as soon as he sat down.

I skipped conveying the personal talk with Heath and went straight to telling them what Heath, A. J., and I had overheard from Fiona and Barbie at the barn.

"Do you think Fiona killed Nadine just to stay on as a pageant judge? How much money are we talking about here?" Baz asked. He took his first bite and strings of cheese clung to the sandwich like a zipline.

"If they needed the scholarship money for help with college, they couldn't have been offering up that much. But Fiona also planned to take money from Lynette to ensure her daughter *didn't* win."

"She was taking money from two of the moms?" Archie said. He shook his head in disbelief.

"And the other mothers were buying plenty of Becky's Bakeware hoping to get in her good graces too," Mrs. Schultz added. "Maybe that contributed to her being the number one Becky in Sonoma Valley."

"It was a lucrative setup, but enough to kill for?" Baz asked, obviously skeptical.

"Remember, it was her reputation too. Being the number one Becky seems to be her identity," Mrs. Schultz pointed out.

I was convinced it was one of them after it all went down, but after having time to think it through, Baz's skepticism had started to rub off on me. "I know Mary Ann said Nadine would do what she had to in order to uphold the integrity of the pageant, but would Nadine really have blown the whistle on Fiona? If that got out, Nadine's legacy would be ruined. It would harm her just as much as Fiona, maybe more."

Archie finished chewing before saying, "It seems like Fiona had options to remain pageant judge other than killing Nadine. Unless it was for revenge," he added.

"And what about the note? Fiona and Nadine had just had it out in public. Nadine wouldn't have gone to the museum to meet her right after they'd just argued about it," I said.

"It doesn't sound like you really think Fiona's the one who murdered Nadine," Baz said.

I had to admit that I wasn't so sure anymore. "I think we still have to look at the others." The satisfying sandwich was helping to turn the gears of my brain as I tried to bring this fuzzy mystery into focus. I repeated a theory I'd told Heath earlier. "For all we know, it could've been Barbie. Our mascot friend, June, said Nadine would disqualify any candidate for moral impropriety. What if Nadine had found out that Annabelle was pregnant? If she was going to disqualify her, and Barbie had gotten wind of it, then maybe *she* murdered Nadine."

They considered this.

"Would Barbie take the risk that the pageant would go on without Nadine? And would she risk it again by trying to harm Mary Ann? We can't forget what happened to me in the prop room," Mrs. Schultz said.

"You could be right. I don't know," I replied. There were too many options. "Let's look at the three incidents: Nadine falling through the open trapdoor, Nadine getting killed in the museum, and the cabinet falling over in the prop room. If we could narrow it down to who was at all three scenes, that would help—but that's impossible to say for sure."

"And we don't even know for a fact that Nadine's broken foot or what happened to you in the prop room was intentional," Baz said, finishing his sandwich already.

Mrs. Schultz gave him the other half of hers. "The sandwich is delicious, but with the pageant likely to be canceled, I don't have much of an appetite."

"I'm sorry, Mrs. Schultz. Maybe we should just call it a day. It's been a hard weekend," I said. I was sitting next to her, so I wrapped my arm around her shoulders in a hug.

"Are you kidding? Figuring out who murdered Nadine would be the only silver lining to this whole thing. We've got to talk it through." She banged the table a single time with her fist.

Archie smiled. "Nothing takes down Team Cheese."

I looked at my three friends, who all seemed resolute. "If you insist." I went back to the case. "Since we don't know who it is, let's try to narrow it down to who it's *not*," I said. I went on to tell them about my conversation with Grace Kelp and how she's been secretly dating the festival director, Tyrell.

"You said Tyrell kept what Fiona's been doing a secret, because he's trying to keep his job. None of what happened makes his job easier. So, I vote that he didn't kill Nadine," Archie said.

Nods went around the table.

"I agree. And I don't think Grace Kelp would do anything to jeopardize Tyrell's job either. I could see how upset she was that Fiona's secret dealings were discovered. I think she loves Tyrell," I said.

Everyone agreed with me.

"Two down. Where does that leave us? Who's left as a suspect? Mary Ann?" Baz asked.

Mrs. Schultz got up from the table to wash her hands and spoke up. "If it's Mary Ann, then that means she was targeting me last night at the historical society museum, but I don't believe that. We've been on good terms since that first outburst. I don't see the motive."

"What about an inheritance?" Archie asked.

"We talked to A. J. last night about that," Baz answered. He relayed what A. J. had told us at The Cellar about Nadine's finances.

"So we can cross inheritance off the list of motives," Archie said.

"After all Mayor Sonny did to keep Nadine's murder under wraps, it looks like the pageant's going to end abruptly anyway. I can't see it continuing once what Fiona's done makes its way around," I said.

Mrs. Schultz shook her head. "I feel terrible for the girls."

"I'm sorry for you too, Mrs. Schultz. You put a lot of work into this," I said.

"I was just getting the hang of that stupid dance," Archie said, popping the last bite of the sandwich into his mouth.

"I know one mom who's going to be happy about it. I didn't tell you yet what happened when I went back to the barn." I told them the rest of the story about my meeting with Lynette and all she'd told me about Tabitha's disappearance when she was a toddler. "It certainly explains her behavior."

"If she didn't want her daughter to compete and she didn't feel she could forbid it, why wouldn't she have planted something to have her disqualified?" Baz said. I'd told him earlier about June disqualifying herself the year she was supposed to be in the pageant.

"She was protective of Tabitha in every way. She'd have had to do something that could be damaging to her daughter's reputation, and I couldn't see her doing that," Mrs. Schultz said.

"So is Lynette a suspect too?" Archie asked.

"Detective Heath still has her on the list, but she's not at the top of mine," I said.

Mrs. Schultz nodded in agreement.

"So, we're out of suspects?" Archie asked us.

We looked at one another without more names volunteered. I wasn't ready to give in, though.

I wiped my hands on my napkin, having finished my

sandwich too. "Archie and I must've been there mere minutes after Nadine was killed. That's risky. It feels like whoever was meeting her there decided at the last minute to kill her and found a sloppy way to cover it up." Then I remembered something we'd forgotten. "Do you think that announcement she was going to make when we got there on Friday had anything to do with her death?"

"We'll never know, will we?" Baz said. He swept his bangs from his eyes. "I wonder what she was going to say."

"Mary Ann said she thought Nadine might be announcing that Fiona would no longer be the pageant judge," I said.

"That makes the case for a last-minute murder," Baz said.

"I'm putting Fiona at the top of the list again," Archie agreed.

Mrs. Schultz sighed. "The festival will be over tomorrow afternoon and then the Lockwood police can really investigate. Hopefully they'll see something we missed."

"Does Detective Heath have a theory?" Archie asked.

"He likes to get all the information first, so he won't say. I'm not sure if anything will come of it, but he thought it was odd when I told him Lynette said Nadine favored her daughter, Tabitha. Do you think that's true, Mrs. Schultz? Did Nadine favor Tabitha?"

"Some of the mothers thought so, I know that much." Mrs. Schultz rubbed her scarf between her fingers, a sure sign she was in thinking mode. "Come to think of it, Nadine told Beatrice to make sure Tabitha got a certain milkmaid dress, which happened to be our newest one. I guess she could've been."

"Why would she do that? Heath said it would've been out of character for Nadine, and he's right," I said. "You, Mary Ann, and even Grace said everything concerning the pageant had to be fair and aboveboard. What would make Nadine go against her code of ethics for Tabitha?"

Mrs. Schultz didn't have an answer.

Archie pushed his crumb-filled plate away and rested his forearms on the table, sulking. "Two days of investigating and we have more questions than answers. Let's hope one of them confesses."

"What's your bet, Arch? Is it Fiona or one of the moms?" Baz asked.

Archie shrugged. "I don't know. What's a good reason to kill someone? Not because of a beauty pageant, that's for sure."

Mrs. Schultz, her scarf still between her fingers, said, "I hope it's not one of the pageant moms. I hate to think of the possibility that either of those innocent babies, for completely different reasons, may have put this drastic event in motion."

"Those innocent babies?" Archie asked.

"Annabelle's unborn child and baby Tabitha. Barbie wants Annabelle to give up her baby for adoption, so she did everything to push her daughter toward college instead of teenage motherhood. As far as Lynette goes, she still hasn't fully dealt with the emotions of her two-year-old daughter's disappearance after all these years, so she did everything to keep Tabitha near her."

"Did doing everything they could include one of them murdering Nadine?" Baz wondered.

I considered what Mrs. Schultz just said. "I was so

caught up in Lynette's emotions that I wasn't thinking about what happened to Tabitha all those years ago as its own case."

"What do you mean?" Baz asked.

"When Beatrice first told me about it, it sounded like Tabitha wandered into the woods from her backyard. But Lynette's details made it clear it had to be a kidnapping. Did they ever find who did it?"

"It was a cold case, as far as I remember," Mrs. Schultz said.

Archie had taken out his phone and was tapping it. "What's her last name?"

"Finley," Mrs. Schultz provided.

He added it to his internet search. "Here it is." He read silently while scrolling. "It looks like it was never solved, like Mrs. Schultz said."

"What are you thinking, Wil?" Baz asked.

"Lynette said that whoever took Tabitha left her safely in the park and called the police anonymously to let them know," I relayed. "She was completely unharmed, happy even, which meant she'd been taken good care of. That doesn't sound like your average child abductor, does it?"

"Are we trying to solve a cold case now or does this have something to do with Nadine's murder?" Archie asked.

"Bear with me, Archie." My mind was racing to fill in the blanks from what I knew.

"It sounds like it could be someone who wanted a child but had a change of heart?" Mrs. Schultz considered.

"Exactly what I was thinking. Nadine considered the pageant girls like her children because she didn't have any. Lynette told me Nadine said Tabitha was the most beautiful baby she'd ever seen. And Nadine favored Tabitha at the pageant, something very out of character for her."

"Are you saying you think Nadine kidnapped Tabitha all those years ago?" Baz said.

"Doesn't it make sense?"

"Oh, Willa. You've jumped to conclusions before, but this is a monumental leap." Mrs. Schultz was not convinced.

"There's no way she could've gotten away with it unless she was planning to leave town," Archie said, just as skeptical as the others.

"I agree. Lynette said Tabitha had big blue eyes and lots of curly red hair—she would've been recognizable anywhere if there was an Amber Alert for a baby, which is why I think she was taken impulsively and then returned once she thought it through."

"And then she made that anonymous call so the baby wouldn't get hurt." Archie started to buy into my theory.

"Maybe this is the missing piece of the puzzle, the strong motive we've been looking for," I said, not ready to give up on it.

Baz slowly nodded. "If Lynette somehow found out after all these years . . ."

"She's been reliving that nightmare every day since it happened," Mrs. Schultz said, now on board with the possibility.

"That would certainly be something someone might kill for," I said.

Mrs. Schultz drank her water, reconsidering. "I don't know, Willa. It still seems like a wild theory."

"Willa's wild theories have been right before," Archie chimed in, now excited at the possibility that we finally had an answer.

"They've also been wrong. I'm going to run it past Detective Heath and see what he thinks." My excitement had been equal to Archie's, but I also had to heed Mrs. Schultz's caution.

"Ah, ma-an," Archie moaned.

"I think that's prudent," Mrs. Schultz said.

"I think this wraps up our meeting. We've got a half a day of Dairy Days tomorrow." I stood and cleared the plates.

"More grazing boxes. I forgot." Archie pulled himself up from the table.

We'd agreed earlier to assemble everything but the cheese tonight, but now that didn't sound like such a great idea.

"You know what? I know we left the festival a little early, but I feel like it's been a long day. We won't need to go to the festival early if Archie's not going to have rehearsal. Who's for doing everything in the morning again, instead of tonight?"

"Me!" Archie raised his hand.

"Me too," Mrs. Schultz said. The energy of the stage had finally worn off and I imagined she was feeling sad about the outcome of all her labor.

"Go home and get some rest," I told them.

"Mrs. Schultz, let me give you a lift home," Baz said.

"Thank you, Basil," she replied, using his given name.

I made them leave the dishes to me. They headed out the door, Archie to his shared apartment over The Kick Stand bicycle shop, and Baz and Mrs. Schultz in Baz's truck.

CHAPTER 32

Once everyone had gone, I called Heath. He answered right away.

"Want to hear my latest theory?" I asked, leaning against the marble island.

I was met with laughter on the other end. "Hit me."

I told him about the possibility of Nadine having a momentary lapse in judgment and taking Lynette's baby. "Maybe *she* was the friend Lynette was having over and she saw Tabitha there all by herself in the backyard." Saying it to someone like Detective Heath made it feel far-fetched. "I don't know, it's probably silly."

"It's worth considering every theory. You said Nadine favored Tabitha, right? This could explain why."

"Maybe it does."

"I want to see what Womack got out of the interviews with Fiona, Barbie, and Lynette, and I know he won't be calling me up to consult with me about it. This will give me an excuse to talk to him," he said.

"You're going back to talk to him?"

"He said he was going to be at his carriage house office tonight if I had anything further to contribute to my statement."

"Why wouldn't he be doing the interviews at the Lockwood police station?"

"Who knows? They're probably still trying to keep everything on the down-low, which might not happen if they parade the women into the police station before someone's arrested."

"Oh, great. So they're going to try to suppress this too?"

"Dairy Days is over tomorrow afternoon, so they won't have any more excuses," Heath assured me.

"Well, be careful. You know I still don't fully trust Chief Womack. We still don't know what happened to his wife."

"Actually, I do. That was one of the leads I was chasing this evening."

His statement propelled me off the kitchenette's island. I paced in front of it. "What did you find out?"

"She's been living in San Diego for the past thirteen years."

I wasn't expecting her to be alive. "So she didn't fall off the face of the earth. That's good. You're sure it's her?"

"She's at the same address as her parents, so unless they're also covering up her death, which I highly doubt, it seems to be her."

"Why would a grown woman leave her husband to go live with her parents? And why aren't they divorced?" This explanation didn't wrap it up into a neat bow the way I'd wanted.

"Maybe one of her parents needs full-time care? I didn't look into it any further. She's alive. He didn't kill her. That's all we needed to know right now," Heath said.

I sighed, giving in. "You're right. You and Mary Ann

and even Mrs. Schultz keep telling me what a good guy Chief Womack is. I'm not sure why I had such a different view on him."

"I'll be heading out shortly to talk to him," Heath said.

"Thanks. You'll let me know?"

"Of course. I'll call you later."

"You could always stop by," I added quickly without thinking. Or maybe I *was* thinking and that's why I said it so quickly. "I mean, I'm not going anywhere, so I'll be around." I winced to shield myself from a possible rejection.

"Okay then. I'll be by later," he said breezily.

"Okay then," I repeated.

"See you later."

He hung up and I happily shimmied to the sink to do the dishes.

My mind played over my conversation with Heath as I washed and dried the dishes. I thought my feeling about Chief Womack was a gut instinct, but maybe it was just because of the way he treated Mrs. Schultz after Nadine's murder. And he did things so differently than Heath did, which I didn't approve of. Was it really my place to approve of the way a chief of police handled a case? I'd have to accept I was wrong about him. After all, he was a hero—he'd saved June and her brother from that fire.

Who else would have answers? I looked at the clock. It was still early. I wondered if Beatrice would mind a visit.

CHAPTER 33

To my relief, Beatrice seemed happy to see me.

She allowed me into the closed thrift shop and said in my ear, "Mary Ann's here and she knows what Fiona did."

Ah. Now I understood why I was a welcome visitor. I followed her and Sweet Potato upstairs to her cozy kitchen where Mary Ann was seated at Beatrice's small round table, miserably hunched over a mug of tea. She noted my presence but didn't greet me.

"Can I get you a drink?" Beatrice asked, opening the cabinet that I knew contained her rum.

"No, thank you. Thanks for letting me barge in."

"It's not like we were doing anything important. The pageant's ruined," Mary Ann groused. "I knew Nadine had a good reason to get rid of Fiona."

Beatrice rubbed Mary Ann's back and joined us at the Formica table.

"Tyrell should've abided by Nadine's wishes; then at least we'd have the pageant. I could continue Nadine's legacy," Mary Ann continued.

"You planned to stay on in Lockwood?" I asked, surprised.

"Oh, I don't know, but I considered it. Who else

could I entrust to continue what Nadine started? Now I'm not sure what to do with myself." She worked the tissue in her hands. "I know that sounds silly, but I've never gotten through anything without Deeni. *She* would know what to do, but she's not here to tell me. She never let me make an important decision alone. She was ten years older than me—I looked up to her. When I wanted to marry one of my horrible boyfriends, she was the one who talked sense into me. She was there for every breakup and to assure me how much better off I was on my own without a husband or children." She shook her head, possibly thinking about the turn of events. "But now I'm forty-four and alone and I don't have Deeni either. Maybe I *will* move to Lockwood. Once Fiona's out of the picture, I can give the pageant a whole new life."

"I hate to say it, but I think Fiona put a black stain on Miss Dairy forever. You have to face it, Mary Ann, the pageant's days are done and gone," Beatrice said without beating around the bush.

"How could you say that, Beatrice? You've been with Miss Dairy for years! How could you be willing to give in so easily?"

"It's not that I don't care, but you have to keep up with the times. Grace Kelp had a point—maybe pageants *should* go by the wayside." Beatrice wasn't backing down from her stance.

"Don't you dare mention Grace Kelp's name at a time like this. Nadine built a pageant that will withstand the test of time *and* Fiona's scandal. I'm not going to let that *Number One Becky* get away with ruining everything."

"Let's hope she confesses. The chief's got bigger fish to fry—he still has to find who killed Nadine,"

Beatrice said. Sweet Potato jumped in her lap and she absently petted her.

Mary Ann's anger melted away. "I've been hoping Pete would prove what happened to Nadine was an accident. Willa, you said you found my cousin, and you and Mrs. Schultz were in Pete's office. You must know more about this. What do you think?"

I had no desire to be in the hot seat. "I'm no expert."

"Now come on, Willa. You've played Jessica Fletcher enough to have an opinion," Beatrice prodded.

Gee thanks, Beatrice.

"Please, be honest with me. I want to know," Mary Ann pleaded.

I wrestled with what to say to her. I'd have liked to allay her fears and lie to her the way Chief Womack lied to the pageant moms and daughters. But Dairy Days would be over tomorrow, and the full investigation would begin. Mary Ann needed to be prepared for it. I said as prudently as I could, "I tend to believe Chief Womack that there's enough evidence for it to be investigated as a homicide."

Mary Ann squeezed her eyes shut for a moment, enduring the bad news again.

"I'm sorry," I said.

"No, I wanted you to be honest."

"Who do you think it is?" Beatrice wasn't done poking.

"That, I don't know. I really don't," I said honestly. I had my suspicions, but I wasn't going to share them.

"Fiona," Mary Ann stated.

"You think your instincts were right about her?" Beatrice asked Mary Ann. "It's possible. Nadine was onto her, wasn't she? That's why she dismissed her as a judge."

"It had to be the reason Deeni was murdered. Does anybody know where Fiona was when Nadine was killed?" Mary Ann asked.

"She left the pageant area just before Nadine went to the museum and . . . and we found her," I provided.

"She was at the pageant area on Friday?"

"I saw her too. She usually uses any excuse to pass out her latest Becky's Bakeware brochures, but she went right past the tent. She looked like she was on a mission," Beatrice said.

"Yes, she was arguing with Nadine. Tyrell must've just told Fiona about Nadine wanting to kick her off the pageant judging," I added.

"So it has to be her!" Mary Ann sat up, looking energized for the first time this evening.

"You accused her of it yesterday," Beatrice reminded her.

"That's just because I was mad that Tyrell was allowing her to stay on as a judge . . ." Her words and her gaze trailed off.

"Mary Ann, are you okay?" I asked.

She blinked and looked at us, seeming to come out of her trance. "We have to tell Pete. You two should come with me. He should hear it from you."

The last thing I wanted was for Chief Womack to know I was talking to Mary Ann about the murder of her cousin. Besides, I wasn't convinced it was Fiona. "I don't think that's a good idea," I said.

"Why not? Beatrice?"

Beatrice put her hands up. "I don't like getting involved with the police."

Thank goodness.

Mary Ann's mouth pursed. "Thanks for nothing!" Her chair screeched against the hardwood floor as she stood, scaring Sweet Potato. The cat ran to the corner, the fur on her tail puffed up.

"Mary Ann—" Beatrice began.

But Mary Ann was halfway down the stairs before Beatrice could finish. We heard the cuckoo clock announce her departure.

"Oh dear," Beatrice mumbled before taking another swig of her drink. "It's okay, Sweet Potato. Come here, girl."

The cat hesitantly walked back to the table and jumped in Beatrice's lap again. She gave me a wary look.

"I shouldn't have said anything," I said.

"You didn't say half of what you think. You and Mrs. Schultz have been nosing around since it happened. You can tell me. Do you think it's Fiona?"

I put my hands up in surrender. "I know nothing. Really."

"But what's your guess? You think it was Barbie making sure Fiona would still be a judge?"

I'd underestimated Beatrice again. She'd been coming to similar conclusions as Team Cheese had.

She continued speculating. "Or Lynette just trying to sabotage the pageant altogether? She hasn't been quite right since what happened with Tabitha."

"What else do you know about that? When you first told me about it, I took it that she had just wandered off. But that's not what happened, is it? She was kidnapped."

"We don't like to use the word *kidnap* when we talk about that day." She pet Sweet Potato until the cat finally settled in her lap. "Lynette and her husband and Tabitha lived on Mason Road. Theirs was the only house on that road back then. It backed up to the woods, which is why everyone was there searching them—we thought she'd wandered off. But she was found that night three miles from the house in the park in the middle of town."

"So what do you think happened?"

"I'll tell you what happened. Someone took the toddler for nine hours, changed their mind, stuck her in the park, and made a phone call to the police. They got her back as good as new, and they never figured out who did it, so Lockwood rewrote history. Any time it's talked about, we conveniently skip the word *kidnap*. She went missing and she was found. End of story."

My eyebrows went up in surprise, but somehow, I wasn't surprised. Conveniently covering up crimes in Lockwood instead of solving them hadn't started with Mayor Sonny.

"I know, it's a little Stepford-ish, isn't it? Lockwood is my ex-husband's hometown, so I assimilated, but it's one of the reasons I moved out of town when we got divorced. Hold on."

She got up, placing Sweet Potato on the table, and left the room. I twiddled my thumbs and stared at the cat, hoping for some guidance. She allowed head scrunches until Beatrice returned and then jumped off the table. Beatrice plopped a folded newspaper in front of me.

"I keep copies of the important ones. You won't find the full story in the online version anymore."

I looked at the newspaper in front of me with the headline about Tabitha's disappearance and recovery. I lifted it to unfold and read it, and realized there was another newspaper underneath. This headline read "Police Sergeant Womack Saves Child, Hailed a Hero."

I read the initial paragraph under the second paper's headline, expecting to read about the museum fire, but instead it was about Tabitha.

Beatrice noticed the second newspaper. "Oh, did I grab two by mistake?"

"I saw this headline at the museum. Somehow, I connected it with the fire. I thought he'd saved those two children who were trapped," I said.

"No, the fire department got the children out. Pete Womack was the one who took the anonymous call and found Tabitha in the park by herself. It was lucky because they were just about to call off the search in the woods where the rest of us were."

I forced myself to slow down as I raced through the article, absorbing the details of Tabitha's rescue. Womack got the call, not a dispatcher. Womack went out there alone.

Alone? That could've been dangerous. The kidnapper could've still been there.

He was minutes away from the park and didn't want to waste any time, he explained in the paper.

"So Chief Womack was the hero," I repeated to myself.

"He was the sergeant in charge of the investigation back then."

"That's right. The youngest to be promoted," I said, recalling what Heath had told me.

My thoughts took over. What if that phone call wasn't so anonymous? What if Nadine *did* take the baby? Maybe all this time, Womack covered up for Nadine. It served him well too—he got a big promotion, and he was Lockwood's hero. But something changed all these years later. Tabitha was forefront in their minds now that she was in the pageant. Did Nadine's conscience get the best of her? Was she going to tell the truth after all these years? Doing so would ruin Chief Womack too. Maybe she told him she planned to tell the truth and he killed her before she could tell anyone. Is that what that private meeting in that note we found was all about?

"What's going on in that Miss Marple mind of yours, Willa Bauer?" Beatrice said.

I pulled myself out of my web of theories and noticed her peering at me from across the small table.

"What do *you* remember about that day, Beatrice?"

"I remember that day very well. I was searching through my attic—this is when all my thrifting was just a hobby and I kept everything in my house. It was months before the pageant, but Nadine worked all year long collecting props and costumes. We were in my attic when we heard the news. We spent the rest of the afternoon with everybody else in the woods looking for Tabitha."

"You were with Nadine the whole day?" I sat back, dejected. If I were a drinker, I'd have taken a swig of Beatrice's rum tea right then. What I desperately needed was some cheese. "So Nadine was helping to search for Tabitha and Chief Womack was the hero." *Boy, Willa, your sleuthing skills have not improved.*

"Yeah, Pete Womack was definitely a hero. The poor man was up to his neck in casseroles that summer, between delivering Tabitha back to Lynette, and his wife, Sophie, leaving him."

"Was that when she left?"

"Just a couple days later, as I recall. I remember because he suddenly became the most popular guy in town. A guy who saves a baby, and then his wife leaves him for no good reason? If I hadn't been married, I might've been gaga for him too."

Was the timing coincidence or was it all connected somehow? "Mary Ann said his wife left and nobody heard from her after that. Is that true?"

"Pretty much. She just skipped town. There were rumors that she left him for someone else. Personally? I think after what happened to Lynette, it pushed her over the edge. She was good friends with her, and maybe she felt some guilt over it."

"Why would Chief Womack's wife feel guilty?" I asked.

"She was the friend who was supposed to go over to Lynette's house that day—the reason Lynette went inside to prepare drinks and left Tabitha in the yard by herself. Sophie's mental health was fragile, so feeling in any way responsible could've put it over the top. Once the rumors started, Dori, the pharmacist, let it slip that Sophie used to be on medication for depression, so that's the theory I came to as to why she left him. But maybe he just wasn't as good of a husband as he is a police officer."

"Did his wife search the woods with you?"

Beatrice shook her head. "She couldn't handle it. Nadine left the search a little early because she was worried about her. Nobody had seen Sophie all day."

My mind revved up with a new theory. "I need to get going. Thanks for all the information."

I tried to remain calm as she followed me down the stairs so I wouldn't get more questions from her. But my mind was screaming, *Chief Womack's wife took the baby and he knew it!* I said another quick goodbye and left out the front door, with Beatrice locking it behind me to the sounds of the cuckoo clock. I bolted down the block to my building with this new information implicating Chief Womack loud and large in my head. If Nadine knew his wife took the baby, she might've been holding this over his head for the last fifteen years. That note we found said she wanted to meet in private. It had to be with Womack. He couldn't let her clear her conscience after all these years, so he killed her.

I had to call Heath, but I didn't want to do it in front of Bea's Hive where she might overhear. Once I reached my building, I ran through the alley. When I got to the stairs behind my shop leading up to my apartment, I pulled out my phone. I tapped Heath's name and listened to it ring as I ascended the exterior steps.

"Pick up. Pick up," I pleaded as it continued to ring. I got to the small deck outside my door and reached into my pocket for my house key. My call went to voicemail. *Darn it!* I waited for the beep.

"Heath, it's me. Are you still with Chief Womack? Don't talk to him about Tabitha. I think his wife was the one who kidnapped her as a baby, and he and Nadine both knew it. If she was ready to spill their secret, that's his motive for murder." I pressed end and willed him to listen to my voicemail ASAP. If he asked too many questions about the kidnapping, Chief Womack could feel cornered. Heath could be in danger.

CHAPTER 34

I threw my legs over the low railing between my deck and Baz's adjoining one and pounded on his apartment door just as I saw his truck pulling into the lot behind the building. I ran down the steps and to his pickup as he parked.

I ignored his surprise at my appearance at the driver's-side window. "We've got to get to the carriage house where Chief Womack is and see if Heath's still there. He might be in danger. I'm getting in." I raced around the truck and hopped in.

Baz did a quick three-point turn and headed out of the narrow lot the way he'd come in.

"What happened? What did you find out?" he asked.

"Nadine didn't take Lynette's baby—Beatrice was with her that whole day. I think it was Chief Womack's wife who kidnapped Tabitha, and he knew about it. He made sure the baby was returned to Lynette and then sent his wife away so nobody would know, leaving him to look like the hero and be in line for a big promotion. Nadine either knew all along or she somehow found out, and seeing how wrecked Lynette still was about it, maybe she decided to clear her conscience. She could've given Womack a chance to tell everyone first. Instead, he killed her."

"So *Chief Womack* killed Nadine?" Baz took his eyes off the road for a second to look at me.

"I think so. That note we found said 'you can't ignore this,' so she must've already talked with him once about it. I think he was the one who rigged the trapdoor in the stage floor, trying to make it look like an accident. A broken foot didn't deter her, though. She wanted to meet him to talk about it again. That must've been what the note was about."

"But why would she write him a note?" Baz asked, pushing the speed limit.

"Mrs. Schultz said she wrote notes all the time. Maybe he refused to speak to her about it. What was she to do? Go to the police, which he was in charge of? Besides, she was best friends with Sophie. Turning in his wife would hurt Sophie as much as Chief Womack. She probably wanted to give him a chance to come clean."

"Instead, she shows up to talk it through and he kills her," Baz concluded.

"I'm afraid that's what happened," I said, feeling quite certain about it now that I'd explained the whole thing aloud to Baz.

"Do you think that's why he tried to kill Mary Ann too, when he thought it was her in the museum with you last night?"

"He knew it wasn't Mary Ann in the kitchen. I think he was the one who called her to tell her she was expected early to the funeral home so she would leave. It was me and Mrs. Schultz he was after. We'd given him the note and told him we thought it was tied to the murder. And it was! It was the note Nadine had written him, wanting to talk about Sophie kidnapping Tabitha fifteen years ago. He told us not to tell anyone about the note. He must've wanted it to stay buried and the only way for that to happen was to get us out of the picture. He had no idea you, Archie, and Heath knew about the note too."

Baz nodded. "Okay, so if that's what happened, I don't think confronting Womack is a great idea."

"We're not going to confront him. I want to make sure Heath is okay. He said he was going to talk to Womack about the kidnapping when we thought it was Lynette who killed Nadine. If Heath starts asking questions, Womack could do something to Heath." I checked my phone again. Still nothing from Heath. "I can't get in touch with Heath."

Baz said to his car's Bluetooth, "Call Shep."

We heard it ring, and relief poured out when Shep's voice came over the car's speaker. In a rush of words, we both explained our concerns about Heath meeting with Chief Womack.

"Don't do anything. I'll check it out," Shep said.

"We're pulling into the historical society museum parking lot," I said. "Heath's car is here." I recognized it right away.

"Stay in your car. I'll be there soon with backup," Shep reiterated.

"Don't call it in. Womack could overhear!" I said.

"All right, you're right. Just don't do anything." Shep disconnected.

Baz turned off the truck and we sat in the car. Baz's jiggling leg matched how I felt. The car's ceiling light faded, then extinguished.

"How long do you think it'll take Shep to get here?" Baz asked.

"Too long." I was out of patience. I opened the car door.

"Willa," Baz warned.

I ignored him and got out. Baz reluctantly followed.

"I just want to try to see where he is, make sure he's all right and if he is, then we'll make an excuse why we're there and get him out," I said.

We quietly crossed under the night sky to the front door of the carriage house. The windows were dark.

"Nobody's here?" I said, confused. Feeling braver, I tried the front door, but it was locked. I cupped my hands around the front window, but the still shadows confirmed no one was inside. "But Heath's car is here. He must be somewhere."

"It looks like there's a light on in the museum," Baz said. He'd left the stoop of the carriage house and was standing on the grass looking toward the large Victorian home.

We started toward it when an acrid smell hit my senses. "Do you smell that?"

"Yeah, it smells like . . ."

"Smoke! Is the museum on fire?"

We ran toward it. Black smoke was billowing out the back.

"What room is the smoke coming out of? Is that a window?" Baz asked. He used his phone's flashlight to try to illuminate the house as we approached, but with black smoke in the air, it offered little help.

I was confused by darkness and adrenaline, but then it hit me. "I think it's that milk delivery door in the records room. Someone got it open. Heath? Heath!" I called, looking around the ground, hoping maybe Heath had crawled out of the fire through the small door.

The stinging smoke was hitting my eyes now. I waved

my arm to try to dispel it so I could go through the small door, but the smoke grabbed me by the throat, and I started to cough. Baz and I were forced to step away.

"There aren't any windows in that room. If Heath's in there, he's in trouble!" I said, already making my way to the front of the house.

Our coughing subsided and we ran the rest of the way. The door was open and the lights were on. We couldn't see any visible smoke from the front of the house. I stepped across the threshold, but Baz held me back.

"Wil, we gotta be careful. Womack could be in there," he warned.

"If he trapped Heath in that room, he's probably long gone by now. We have to get Heath out."

I continued beyond the front door. The front entry hall smelled of smoke, but it only lightly clouded the air. The fire must've been contained at the back of the house.

We continued in silence and peered around the doorway that led into the hallway and the large parlor where I'd read all the headlines on the walls the first time I'd been here. Some light streamed in from the entry hall, but it was otherwise dark and shadowy. I had to allow a few excruciating moments for my eyes to better adjust before moving toward the back of the house where Heath must've been trapped. Through the far doorway, I saw movement in the dining room. My feet stopped as my heart caught in my throat, causing Baz to knock into me. I saw the back of a man dragging a body. Before I could think, I looked around for a weapon and grabbed the first thing I saw—a stoneware milk jug from the floor. I picked it up it and ran toward him, my adrenaline overtaking any sense of risk. As I closed in on him, I swung the jug behind me like a batter winding up to hit a home run.

"Willa!" Baz's voice rang out from behind me, just as I recognized who I was about to hit. Luckily, I was able to stop myself before I connected with my intended target.

"Heath! You're okay!" I cried.

He turned, surprise overtaking him. "Willa! Baz! Help me carry him out!" Heath shouted, his voice straining with effort. The body he was dragging was that of Chief Womack.

I ignored the stronger stench of this room and the sting of the smoke pricking my eyes. Baz and I each grabbed an ankle and lifted him as much as we could.

"Isn't there a back door somewhere?" I asked.

"I tried it. It won't open," Heath replied, getting a better grip under Womack's arms.

"What happened?" Baz asked.

"He was overcome with smoke from the fire in the records room," Heath said. "We put it out, but everything that caught fire in there is still putting out a lot of smoke. I don't know why the smoke alarms aren't going off. My phone is useless and he's not wearing his radio."

We clumsily made our way toward the front of the house, the smoke lessening with each step we took. Heath had to stop twice when his coughing overtook him. There was enough light for me to notice the soot on his face and hands.

"Baz and I will get him. You should get away from the smoke," I told Heath.

He shook his head and continued. My breathing was also becoming more labored, whether from the exertion or the lingering smoke that couldn't find an easy escape from the house, I wasn't sure. We managed to make it through the parlor and across the threshold of the front hall when Womack started to rouse. His sporadic movements made it impossible to keep ahold of him and we had to drop his ankles. Heath more carefully placed him on the floor in the middle of the entry hall. We'd almost made it out. He began to cough as he awakened.

"Be careful, Heath. He could dangerous. Should we take his gun?" I saw it secured in its holster at his hip.

Heath coughed into the sleeve of his jacket before he spoke, blinking away tears that eked from his reddened eyes. "He came here to put out the fire."

"Are you sure he didn't set it?" Baz asked. He took a seat on the floor against the wall to rest.

"I was trapped in the back of the room with the fire blocking the doorway," Heath explained. "There was a small wooden door—it was my only way out, so I used my gun to shoot it open at the same time someone burst into the room and started to put out the fire."

Chief Womack's coughing subsided, and Heath helped him sit up. "That was me. I'm glad you're okay. I grabbed an extinguisher when I saw the smoke, but the door was locked. I used it to bust it open. I started to put the fire out, but the smoke must've gotten to me. I'm sorry I couldn't get past it to get to you," he said to Heath.

"You were trying to save him?" I was having a hard time making sense of it.

"I couldn't get near the door either—the smoke was too much. That's why I left the house through that small door and then came back in through the front. I'm glad I did—I saw him passed out. I used the extinguisher to finish putting out the fire and then started dragging him out of the room," Heath explained again.

Chief Womack's coughing started up again and he laid back down.

We need to get outside," Heath said. He was now leaning against the stairway railing, rubbing his eyes, which were squeezed shut. "I can't see anymore. My eyes are stinging too bad."

I went over to Heath to lead him out of the house when Mary Ann appeared in the doorway.

Before I could ask her to help us, she ran to Chief Womack on the floor and knelt over him. "Pete!"

"No!" Heath yelled at the sound of her voice, confusing me.

Mary Ann popped off the floor, holding Chief Womack's gun. She pointed it back and forth between me, Heath, and Baz, who'd risen to his feet. We instinctively put our hands up.

Chief Womack pulled himself to a seated position. "Mary Ann. What are you doing?"

"She's the one who tried to kill me," Heath said. He kept wiping his eyes repeatedly, trying to keep them open.

"Mary Ann?" I repeated, barely able to believe it.

Chief Womack began to cough again.

"You need to help Pete. Get him out in the fresh air," Mary Ann commanded.

"I'm not going anywhere. Tell me why you're doing this," Chief Womack managed to say with effort.

"Don't you know? I'm doing it for you! That detective knows things. I came to your office to see you and I heard him asking you questions."

"You came to convince him that Fiona killed Nadine,

but instead you overheard them talking about Tabitha's kidnapping," I said, taking an educated guess.

Mary Ann turned the gun on me. I took a step back. She returned talking directly to Chief Womack. "When he left your office and I told him there was evidence against you here at the house, he believed me. He thought you were a killer, Pete! So I had to go through with it. He would've ruined you, just like Nadine was going to do. I couldn't let that happen!"

It was all clicking into place. "You killed Nadine, didn't you?" I said to Mary Ann.

"You killed Nadine?" Chief Womack's voice held equal parts surprise and sorrow.

"She was going to confess that she knew Sophie kidnapped Tabitha! It would've incriminated you, Pete!" Mary Ann cried.

Chief Womack shook his head. "I know, Mary Ann. I asked her to keep that secret for almost fifteen years. I understood why she couldn't keep it anymore."

"No, you don't. You think it's because she was wracked with guilt about Lynette. That's not why she was doing it. She didn't have a sudden change of heart over guilt. It was because she saw you and me getting closer."

"You're in love with him, aren't you, Mary Ann?" I hoped admitting this would allow her softer side to prevail and maybe she'd listen to Chief Womack.

There was a long pause where we waited for her to speak. "You might not understand any of this, Willa, but Pete does. He understands doing anything for the person you love, don't you, Pete? But Nadine . . ." Any vulnerability I'd hoped to capitalize on vanished the moment she said her cousin's name. "She could never understand. I told her I wanted to move here perma-

nently. As soon as I told her it was because of my feelings for you, she said you weren't the man I thought you
were. That's when she told me about Tabitha's kidnapping. She never wanted happiness for me. She thought
it would change my mind about you, but that just made
you even better in my eyes. Getting help for your wife
was so loving. She would've been in prison otherwise."
Mary Ann shook her head slowly, her mouth tightening. "Nadine kept that secret all these years, why did
she have to tell it? Why now? It was because she didn't
want me to be happy. She always talked me out of any
guy I was dating. Talked me out of marriage. Children.
She had a life of loneliness, and what would she do if
her cousin—who came every time she called—had a
family and a life?"

Wow, she told that story differently at Beatrice's.

"We can start another fire, Pete, and lock them in. I
already barricaded the back door," she said.

"Mary Ann, this isn't the way. Give me the gun
and we'll talk about it. We'll talk about our future together," Womack said, playing along.

"There won't be a future if anyone who knows your
secret is alive. I don't want to shoot them—it's your gun
and there'll be too many questions—so please, Pete,
cooperate!" I could tell the lingering smoke in the air
was getting to Mary Ann too. She kept rapidly squeez-
ing her eyes shut. She held her arm up to her mouth and
coughed, then used the back of her hand to wipe her
eyes.

Maybe if we kept her talking, she'd become more in-
capacitated.

"You orchestrated that first accident, didn't you?
When Nadine fell through the trapdoor on stage and
broke her foot?" I said to Mary Ann.

She answered my question but spoke once again to Chief Womack. "I thought by getting her away from the pageant and Lynette, she'd come to her senses. When you came to her rescue, I thought that would be enough to convince her not to ruin your life." Her face changed, transforming into resentment. "But nothing was going to change her mind about confessing, because the person Nadine really wanted to hurt was me. I found a note she was intending to give you and it proved to me she wasn't going to let this go. She was determined to keep me and you from being together."

I filled in the pieces as I'd determined them. "So you lured her into the records room of the museum."

"It wasn't hard. I told her that Pete wanted to meet her there. Nadine was always making me go to the museum after hours to bring back something, so I was able to set it all up the night before to make the shelf top-heavy enough to tip it over. The hardest part was to get to the museum before her—she'd rarely let me out of her sight. She must've really wanted to talk to you, Pete, because she didn't ask questions when I relayed the fake message. She was so determined to ruin our happiness."

"So you waited for her in the records room and struck her in the head with one of those heavy milk jugs. Then all you had to do was drag her to where you could push the shelves on top of her to make it look like an accident."

"See, Pete? They know everything! She even knows about the note—I saw it in Mrs. Schultz's hand when you were standing outside the carriage house yesterday morning. I didn't even realize I'd lost it."

"Is that why you tried to kill me and Mrs. Schultz in the prop room last night?"

Mary Ann scoffed. "No, don't be silly. I just hoped

it would make a case for the other shelf being an accident. And if it hurt that old cougar Mrs. Schultz too, that would be a bonus."

Chief Womack began to have a coughing fit.

"We have to get him out of here!" Mary Ann pointed the gun at Baz who'd been standing behind Womack against the back wall with his hands in the air. "You! Help him up!"

Baz cautiously approached Womack and kneeled, trying to help the larger man to his feet. I couldn't stand Mary Ann jiggling the gun in Baz's direction—I rushed over to help him with Womack, briefly feeling Heath's hand slip off my shoulder as he belatedly tried to stop me. Baz and I positioned ourselves on either side of Womack, who put an arm around each of us, allowing us to steady him. He tried to speak to Mary Ann, but it only started another coughing fit.

"Don't try to talk," Mary Ann told him. "They'll get you out of here, and as soon as I get rid of them, I'll get you help."

"No, Mary Ann—" Womack struggled to say.

"Give me the gun!" It was Heath.

Baz and I turned our attention from Womack. Heath had brandished his own gun and was aiming it at Mary Ann.

Oh no.

Heath was still blinking rapidly, and I worried he couldn't see well.

Mary Ann tensed even more and didn't stand down. She kept the gun on us. "I might still be able to get one off. I've got nothing to lose. Are you willing to risk it?" she asked Heath.

"By the way you're holding that gun, I think I am," Hcath said.

Baz and I looked across Womack's chest at each other. What the heck was Heath doing? Mary Ann also seemed confused—her eyes darted between us and Heath.

"It's a fair bet, you'll end up shooting Pete," Heath continued.

"What are you talking about? I'd never shoot Pete," she said.

"It's not as simple as pointing and pulling the trigger," Heath continued in a conversational tone. "Do you know the tiniest difference in the way you hold a gun will cause your grip to pull it in a direction you're not aiming for? If you aim at Baz or Willa, you could easily shoot Pete by accident."

Mary Ann swallowed hard. "Then I'll go for you." She swung the gun toward Heath just as Shep sprang from the doorway from behind Mary Ann, immobilizing her and deftly wresting the gun from her. Another Yarrow Glen officer was right behind him, but Shep had it handled, handcuffing Mary Ann before I could barely register what had happened. It was only after I saw Heath stow his gun in the holster under his jacket that I let out a relieved breath. My arm, which was wrapped around Chief Womack, found Baz's and I squeezed it. It was over.

CHAPTER 35

Shep asked if we were all right, and Heath nodded for him to go. Shep led a sobbing Mary Ann out of the house as Heath instructed the other officer to help Chief Womack to an ambulance. He immediately relieved us of Womack's bulk and helped him through the front door.

"Are you two okay?" Heath asked me and Baz.

"Let's get out of here," Baz answered.

I nodded, and the three of us finally walked out the front door and down the steps. Sirens sounded in the distance, becoming louder with each whir. Baz bent over, hands on his thighs. I dropped onto the grass and Heath sat next to me. I filled my lungs with fresh air, hoping it would help expel the fear of what had just occurred.

Red and blue lights lit up the night sky, the sirens of emergency vehicles becoming deafening until fire-trucks and police cars pulled up to the house and were silenced. Firefighters raced into the house to make sure the fire was out. Paramedics rushed over with oxygen for Chief Womack. Police escorted Mary Ann to one of their vehicles.

Shep was back. "Are you guys okay?"

"Great job back there, Shep," Heath said.

"Thanks for saving us," I added, which felt wholly inadequate.

Baz straightened and gave Shep a proper handshake. "Thanks, man," he said, his voice still a little shaky.

A paramedic came over to escort us to an ambulance, but we told Baz to go first.

"You two ought to get checked out too," Shep said, offering his hand to help us up after Baz had gone. "Do you want me to call them over?"

We didn't, so we stood and started over on our own with Shep accompanying us.

"I knew you'd win the duel, even half-blinded, but I'm glad it didn't come to that," I said to Heath on our way to one of the emergency vehicles.

"Especially because I used all my bullets to rip open that dairy door when I was locked in the records room," he replied.

"It was an empty gun? Mary Ann might've shot you!" Goose bumps trickled down the back of my neck at the thought.

"We were running out of options, and she was getting more agitated," Heath said.

"And you say *I* do dangerous things? Get him some oxygen, Shep, *then* I'll kill him."

Heath chuckled. "It was a calculated risk. She didn't look like she knew how to handle a gun. I was counting on the safety still being on."

"He's right. It *was* on," Shep said.

Shep left us with a paramedic at one of the emergency vehicles. She gave us oxygen masks and did a quick pulse check. We checked out fine and were left alone. We sat side by side on the bed of the vehicle with our masks on, not speaking. From out of the red-tinted shadows, Womack appeared by our side. Heath and I removed our oxygen masks.

"Are you okay?" I asked, surprised to see him, especially upright.

"I feel fine now." A slight cough escaped, which belied his words. "I told them I'd go to the hospital in a minute. I feel I need to apologize to both of you first and explain some things."

Heath began to dismiss the necessity, but Chief Womack stopped him.

"Please, let me get this out. I have to explain about my wife, Sophie." He coughed out another deep breath, then continued. "She was in a bad way. We'd been trying for years to get pregnant through different means. She had several miscarriages by the time the kidnapping happened." He looked down and shook his head. "I knew she was depressed. I should've recognized how bad off she was."

"What happened that day?" I asked. Maybe it was insensitive, given that he was obviously feeling guilty about it, but since my life had been on the line, I allowed my curiosity to lead.

"Sophie was supposed to have lunch with Lynette. When she got there, she saw Tabitha in the backyard by herself. I don't know what made her decide to do it. It had to have been an impulse. She took the baby. She wasn't in her right mind—she brought her home and played with her all afternoon, as if Tabitha were our own child. I was the lead investigator, so I was running operations at the site in the woods behind Lynette's house. Normally, I'd call to check on my wife throughout the day—I knew how fragile she'd been lately. At the end of the day, I asked Nadine to look in on her. She found her at home with Tabitha." Chief Womack paused, closing his eyes for a moment, perhaps to shut out the memory. "It had to be all the hormones. Sophie had to have had some kind of psychotic break. I wanted to protect my wife from prison, so before I could think clearly, I made up the story about the anonymous phone call and got Tabitha back to Lynette as soon as I could. I tried to do what I thought was the right thing for everybody."

I felt bad for Chief Womack's wife, but I still wasn't moved enough by his plight to justify him not telling the authorities. As a police sergeant, he had a duty to uphold the law.

"Nadine wanted me to get Sophie some help, and I knew Sophie needed to leave before she said anything to anyone. Nadine and I made the decision together to send her to a hospital close to her parents." Again, Womack slowly shook his head, his eyes scanning the sky. "All these choices seemed the only ones to make at the time. In hindsight, I know they were wrong. Nadine kept the secret for Sophie's sake. But after all these years, the guilt was eating her up, especially after spending time with Lynette and Tabitha for rehearsals and seeing Lynette still so affected by what had happened."

That's why Nadine favored Tabitha.

"That big announcement Nadine was going to make?" Chief Womack continued. "She was going to announce her retirement from the pageant. After this year's festival was through, she was going to confess to Lynette what had really happened. She hoped it would give Lynette some peace of mind, but she didn't want her involvement in covering up the kidnapping to affect the pageant. That note must've been her wanting to talk to me about it again, because I told her I didn't want her to implicate herself. She had nothing to do with this, except to keep our secret. I told her when Dairy Days was over, I would confess and leave her name out of it."

Heath rubbed his jaw in a gesture I recognized—he wanted to say something but thought better of it.

"I appreciate you explaining," I said.

Chief Womack nodded. "I'm glad everything worked out tonight." By a slight turn of his head, I could tell he sensed the two officers standing nearby waiting for him. He seemed resigned, as he turned and walked toward them. They disappeared into the night.

Heath and I were silent. We looked at each other with the shared unspoken emotion of a solved case feeling less than triumphant. A life had still been sacrificed; other lives ruined.

"What were you doing here anyway?" he finally asked me.

"Saving you," I answered.

He smiled, one of those full-on smiles that slayed me. Then he pulled me in and kissed me.

EPILOGUE

Curds & Whey was closed on Mondays and, after informing Mrs. Schultz and Archie about our harrowing evening, none of us had any desire to attend the final day of the Dairy Days festival. I invited them to a Team Cheese fondue party in the kitchenette instead, so Baz and I could finish filling them in on the details and wrap up the case. After what Baz and I had been through and the disappointment for Mrs. Schultz and Archie of the pageant being canceled, we needed all the cheesy goodness we could get. The T-shirt I wore was even more apt than usual: "No matter the question, cheese is the answer."

* * *

Mother Nature must've been waiting for the unofficial post–Labor Day arrival of autumn like the rest of us, because Monday dawned cool and crisp. I could practically smell cinnamon spice in the air. I looked forward to decorating the shop with pumpkins and creating fall-inspired sampling platters for customers, which also made me put aside my worries about our forthcoming Cheeseboard Café and renew my excitement about it. But for now, I'd gather some cheeses for today's fondue.

"Your birthday's coming up, Guernsey. Don't you think this calls for a fall fondue?" I said to my bovine scarecrow, our store's homemade mascot. In my head, she agreed.

The pumpkin I'd bought from Lou's Market had recently come out of the oven and was now pureed in my food processor along with lots of roasted garlic. As I added the freshly shredded Gruyère and sharp cheddar to the simmering and seasoned chicken stock, I heard Baz say hello from the doorway. He came to the kitchenette and set his tall cup of cold peachy-orange pumpkin-spiced drink on the counter, the top third filled with whipped cream.

"You're in fall vibe mode too, huh?" I said, concentrating on stirring the cheese as it slowly melted in the pot.

"First cool day and I get a hankering," he replied.

I took my eyes off the pot of cheese and looked at Baz, noticing a change. "You cut your hair!"

"Yeah. There's no stopping thirty from coming," he said resolutely, looking again like the old Baz I knew and loved.

"It's not so bad, I promise. It's a good excuse for a party," I suggested.

"That could soften the blow." Baz nodded, looking more cheerful.

Archie came in, still in his shorts. It had to be downright cold, which it rarely was, before he'd wear anything else. He continued to the rear of the shop where Baz and I were, texting on his phone, and was about to collide straight into the kitchenette's marble island.

"Archie, watch out!" I called.

He looked up and stopped before slamming into it. "Sorry." He went back to texting, and walked over to the farm table, straddling its bench.

I recognized that smile on his face.

"Someone important?" I asked, taking a guess at who was on the other end of that text.

He shrugged one shoulder. "Just June," he said oh, so casually, but didn't look up from the phone.

I smiled.

Beatrice gave a quick knock on the shop door before entering with a "hello." Since she was unknowingly integral to solving the case, I'd invited her as well. She was dressed for fall in flared jeans and a crocheted multicolored vest over a deep orange turtleneck. Today, her silver hair was in double braids that brushed her shoulders.

Mrs. Schultz followed, dressed in vibrant autumn colors and with a chipper mood to match. She gave me a big hug and had another for Baz. "I'm so glad you two are all right," she said.

"All's good, Mrs. Schultz," Baz said.

With the cheese melted and everyone having arrived, I added the pumpkin puree into the cheese mixture and carefully combined the two until a thick, cheesy sauce formed. I transferred it to a fondue pot and placed it over the burner I'd asked Baz to light in the middle of the farm table as everyone gathered around it. Cubed pretzel bagels, apple chunks, and an array of veggies I knew Baz wouldn't touch were on the table for dipping.

As I joined the others, it occurred to me that the only thing more satisfying than cheese was eating it with a group of trusted friends. Although I'd already chosen the bistro tables for our new Cheeseboard Café, I'd have to find a way to keep the farm table. It was too precious to give up, as were the people gathered around it.

We dug into the fall fondue—a great kickoff to the season—and Baz and I gave everyone the details of what had happened the night before. The others sat listening, rapt, hardly able to believe Nadine's own cousin, Mary Ann, was the culprit.

"I worked side by side with Mary Ann on every pageant I've been a part of. She's sat at my kitchen table," Beatrice said in disbelief.

"It's so awful to think what she tried to do to Detective Heath too. How did she pull it off?" Mrs. Schultz asked.

I'd called Heath this morning to invite him to the fondue party, but he already had another invitation—Chief Womack had asked to meet with him today. Heath promised to come by afterward. I told the others what he'd shared with me.

"After she overheard Heath asking questions about Lynette and Tabitha, she put her plan in motion. She waited for Heath when he left the carriage house and told him she'd found proof at the crime scene that Womack had killed Nadine. After having just listened to my text message, Heath thought it seemed plausible that it could be the chief, so he followed her to the museum. She already had set it all up—Nadine ran the museum, so Mary Ann knew where the keys were to the doors and how to disable the smoke alarm. She told Heath what he needed to see was in the far side of the room where Nadine had been killed. In the meantime, Mary Ann stayed by the door and smashed those old gas lanterns that had been in the kitchen and used the extra accelerant she'd found there to cause a fire right by the doorway so he couldn't get out. Heath found out the details of it this morning. The fire broke out instantly, trapping Heath inside. She locked the door from the other side for extra assurance and left him to . . ." I didn't say the final horrible word. I felt my throat constrict as I pictured the scene. It was my fault he was there asking Chief Womack about Tabitha's kidnapping, and why he believed Mary Ann.

"How did Womack know Heath was trapped?" Baz asked, not having heard yet what Heath had found out.

"According to Heath, he didn't know. He was leaving the station and saw Heath's car still in the parking lot. He figured after the questions Heath had just been asking him, that he must be snooping around, so he went to the museum to see. That's when he smelled the smoke. He saw Mary Ann at the back door, but he didn't know she was responsible. He told her to go get help, and that was when he got a fire extinguisher and used it to break down the door and start putting out the flames."

"That was very brave of Detective Heath to return to save Chief Womack," Mrs. Schultz said.

It didn't surprise me that he had returned just in case someone else needed help.

Baz picked up the story from there and told them the end of our harrowing tale and how Mary Ann confessed to killing Nadine to keep Chief Womack's secret.

"I can't believe Pete Womack was involved in Tabitha's kidnapping!" Beatrice looked like she needed something stronger than the water we'd provided her. "I would've never guessed that he sent his wife away either."

I explained further. "Sophie's formal address was at her parents' home, which Heath discovered the first time he looked into her whereabouts. But when he dug a little deeper after talking to me last night, he found out she spent the first two years living in a mental health hospital, then moved to her parents' house as an outpatient. That's why Chief Womack couldn't bring himself to divorce her."

"You said Mary Ann was in love with him. Was he in love with her too?" Mrs. Schultz asked.

"No. According to him, he had no idea she felt that way. They'd worked closely together for a couple months a year during pageant season, but for him, that was the extent of it," I replied.

"He did a good job of pretending to go along with it to try to keep her calm," Baz said.

"So it was Mary Ann—who had nothing to do with the kidnapping cover-up—who wanted to keep the secret most of all?" Archie said, disbelief in his voice.

"Ironically, yes," I said.

Baz and I went on to tell them the rest, including Mary Ann's attempt to hurt me and Mrs. Schultz in the prop room.

"A cougar? I never!" Mrs. Schultz said after hearing Mary Ann's description of her.

"Don't let anyone tame your roar, Mrs. Schultz," Baz said with a wink.

"Basil . . ." Mrs. Schultz warned with a glint of humor in her eye.

Baz made sure to look contrite, but I knew he wasn't. Luckily for him, our fondue was almost gone.

A knock on the front door got me up from the table. I was happy to see through the door's window that it was Heath. I barely kept myself from swooning when he showed up wearing a leather jacket, as if he'd read my mind yesterday when I mentally compared him to a heartthrob of a different era. I wanted to kiss him again, but we'd save that for when we didn't have an audience.

"Sorry I'm late," he said, coming through the door when I got there.

"Not so late. Everyone's still hanging—" As I turned to show him the group at the table, I saw that my friends had suddenly risen and were parading to the front door.

Mrs. Schultz was the first one out the door. "Hi, Detective Heath. Bye, Willa!"

"Thanks for the fondue," Beatrice said as she followed Mrs. Schultz out.

"See ya," Archie said.

"Was it something I said?" Heath asked.

I had a feeling I might've known what was going on—Baz had spied what happened between me and Heath last night. "Not something *you* said, more like something *he* said." I blocked Baz's path. He wouldn't meet my eyes. I knew he must've at least alluded to the others about seeing Heath and me kiss last night, which was why they were so quick to leave us alone.

"I plead the Fifth," Baz replied, walking around me to get out the door.

"Hold up for a sec, Baz. I need to talk to both of you," Heath said.

Baz looked like the school principal had just stopped him in the hallway—he'd never been quite comfortable with Heath.

We all stepped back inside the shop, and I closed the door behind us.

"I just came from seeing Chief Womack. Or rather, Pete Womack. He's no longer the chief of police."

"No surprise there," Baz said.

"Why did he want to see you? It felt like he told us everything last night," I said.

"He wanted to apologize to me again. He felt responsible for my predicament with Mary Ann," Heath explained.

"She was the one who started the fire and locked you in the room, not him," I said, perhaps trying to allay some of my own guilt, as well.

"He believes that his poor decision concerning Tabitha's kidnapping was what set everything in motion. He feels horrible about Nadine, and he wanted me to pass along his apologies to the two of you too."

"What's going to happen to him now?" I asked.

"Lynette's not pressing charges."

"Really? Even with everything she's gone through?"

"Lynette was also very close with Sophie. She feels like hurting Sophie and Womack won't make her feel better. Now that she knows it wasn't some stranger who took her daughter, maybe her healing can progress more than it has all these years."

"I sure hope so," I said, again feeling terrible for Lynette.

"You helped to solve the case, and now Lockwood's gonna be looking for a new chief of police. Are you putting your name in for the position?" Baz asked Heath, half kidding.

Heath chuckled. "Working for Mayor Sonny? My boss isn't a bed of roses, but compared to Mayor Sonny, I think I have it pretty good right where I am." He looked at me and said, "I don't plan on going anywhere."

My heart hummed until Baz broke the spell. "All righty then. I'm gonna go. Glad everything's sewn up. See ya, Wil."

"Talk to you later, Baz," I returned.

He left and closed the door behind him, leaving me and Heath alone. It was suddenly very quiet in the shop.

I started toward the kitchenette. "There was some fondue left, the last I looked." I leaned over the table and looked in the fondue pot. They'd snuffed out the flame, and the thin layer of cheese that was left on the bottom had congealed. "Maybe not." I took the pot and stuck it in the sink. They'd stacked their small plates on the counter for me.

"I'm not hungry anyway. You wash, I'll dry?" Heath offered.

I smiled and handed him a dish towel. I soaped the plates and scrubbed while he stood beside me.

"It feels pretty good to close our first case together," I said, rinsing a plate and handing it off for him to dry.

"Our *first* case? First and last," he said emphatically.

I knew it was too good to be true and casual Heath wouldn't last. "Okay, but I have to be honest, I'm going to miss working together."

"Maybe we could do something else together. Like go on a date?" His gaze left the dish in his hands to focus on me.

My humming heart returned. "I'd like that. When?"

"How about right now?" He turned off the water and handed me the dish towel.

I dried my hands. "Sure. What do you have in mind?"

"Oh, I don't know. I was thinking of going someplace cramped and smelling of cow manure . . . just for old times' sake," he joked.

We laughed together and I let him lead me out of the shop, feeling the comfort of his hand on the small of my back.

RECIPES

Pimento Cheese Sandwich

When I needed to pack my lunch for the Dairy Days festival, I chose this classic Southern sandwich and kicked it up a notch. It was easy and oh, so satisfying.

Start-to-Finish Time: 10 minutes

Makes: 12 sandwiches

Ingredients
- 6 oz. whipped cream cheese
- ½ cup mayonnaise
- 1 teaspoon cayenne pepper
- 3 tablespoons chopped pimentos
- 1 cup cheddar cheese, shredded
- 1 cup Colby Jack cheese, shredded
- white bread
- Optional: garlic powder, black pepper, diced dill pickles

Instructions
1. Mix cream cheese with mayonnaise.
2. Add cayenne pepper and any optional ingredients.
3. Add chopped pimentos.
4. Mix in shredded cheeses.
5. Spread on bread. Enjoy!

If you're not serving a crowd, keep the spread in a container in the fridge. You can have pimento cheese sandwiches for weeks!

Extra-Cheesy Alfredo

Nothing's more comforting after a stressful day than this extra-cheesy dish. It's a perfect blend of smoky and salty flavors, and the hearty meal Team Cheese needed to get our sleuthing gears in motion.

Start-to-Finish Time: 15 minutes

Serves: 6

Ingredients
- pasta of your choice. (Linguine is the classic choice. I like fusilli.)
- 1 quart heavy cream
- ½ cup butter
- 4 cloves garlic, minced
- 2½ cups Parmigiano-Reggiano cheese (or simply Parmesan), shredded
- ½ cup smoked mozzarella, shredded
- ¼ cup Asiago cheese, shredded
- ¼ cup sharp white cheddar cheese, shredded
- 2 tablespoons cream cheese, cut into bits
- black pepper

Instructions
1. In a large pot, bring water to a boil for the pasta. Cook as directed.
2. In another pot, slowly heat the heavy cream and butter on LOW. Continuously stir just until the butter melts. (You can use a double boiler if you prefer.)
3. Add the garlic and the shredded cheeses, plus the diced cream cheese.
4. Stir with a whisk until the sauce is smooth.

5. Remove from heat and season to taste with black pepper.
6. Add the cooked and drained pasta to the Alfredo sauce and fold in.
7. Serve warm. Enjoy!

Fall Fondue

Warm and cheesy with seasonal flavors of pumpkin and nutmeg, this fondue is the perfect meal to serve to friends or family on a chilly autumn day.

Start-to-Finish Time: Appr. 1 hour
Serves: 6–8

Ingredients
- 1 head garlic
- 1 medium sugar pumpkin or acorn squash OR 1 15-oz can pumpkin puree
- 2 cups chicken stock
- 2 teaspoons each cumin, sweet smoked paprika, and dry mustard
- ¼ teaspoon freshly grated nutmeg
- 3 tablespoons cornstarch
- ¼ cup apple cider or apple brandy
- 3 cups cheddar cheese, shredded
- 1 cup Gruyère cheese, shredded
- olive oil
- Dippers of your choice: pretzel rods, pretzel bagels, rye bread, roasted vegetables, apples, etc.

Instructions
1. Chop head off of garlic, drizzle olive oil on it, and wrap it in foil. Roast in 400° F oven for about 40 to 50 minutes, until garlic comes out squishy.
2. **If using fresh pumpkin or squash**, peel and chop, then place on foil-covered baking sheet. Drizzle with olive oil. Season with salt and pepper.
3. Roast for 35 minutes until tender and golden. Let it cool a bit.

4. Puree cooled, roasted pumpkin and garlic in food processor until smooth.
5. **If using canned pumpkin puree**, skip steps 2 through 5. Just mash the garlic and mix thoroughly with the pumpkin puree.
6. In a large pot, bring chicken stock to a simmer over medium-high heat.
7. Add cumin, paprika, mustard, and nutmeg.
8. Mix cornstarch with apple cider/apple brandy in a small bowl until combined (should be almost the texture of paste).
9. In a slow and steady stream, whisk the cornstarch into the stock. Cook to thicken slightly, about 2–3 minutes.
10. Add the garlic and pumpkin puree to the stock and whisk until combined.
11. Gradually add cheeses to the pot while stirring continuously with a wooden spoon.
12. Cook until cheese is melted and smooth, about 5–8 minutes.
13. Transfer to fondue pot. Enjoy with dippers!